FIGURE
SPEECH

HALLE SHIFTERS BOOK 4

BY
DANA MARIE BELL

DM
B

Dana Marie Bell Books
www.danamariebell.com

Dana Marie Bell
PO Box 39
Bear, DE 19701

Figure of Speech
Copyright © 2015 by Dana Marie Bell
ISBN: 978-1984918048
Edited by Tera Kleinfelter
Cover by Kanaxa

First Edition electronic publication by Samhain Publishing, Ltd.: March 2015
Second Edition electronic publication by Dana Marie Bell: March 2017

ABOUT THE AUTHOR

Dana Marie Bell lives with her husband Dusty, their two maniacal children, an evil ice-cream stealing cat and a dog who thinks barking should become the next Olympic event. You can learn more about Dana and her addiction to series at www.danamariebell.com.

DEDICATION

To Mom, I did tell you that someday I'd have twins and name them Apollo and Artemis. Well, here you go!

To Dad, who is probably damn grateful none of his kids had twins, but loves all his grandkids equally, even if none of them have cool names like Thor or Fenris.

To Dusty, who gave our kids normal names with unique meanings because, and I quote, "No child of mine shall experience the school-time butt-hurt that comes with a name like Aloysius."

And to my readers who have followed me since *The Wallflower*. What did you expect Bunny and Tabby to name their child?

CHAPTER ONE

"Want some Red Butt?" Chloe held up the energy drink, wincing at the words coming out of her traitor mouth. When it came to speech impediments Chloe had gotten one hell of a winner.

Her cousin Alex blinked rapidly before smiling. "Um. No thanks, sweetie."

She was getting used to the odd looks she got every time she spoke, but that didn't mean she liked it. "Man, I hate this." She couldn't quite keep the sorrow from her voice no matter how much she wished she could hide it from her friends and family.

Alex shrugged. "Yeah, but I knew what you meant." He ruffled her hair. "Don't sweat it, kiddo."

Chloe sighed, but she tried to listen to her cousin. Her condition sucked rocks, but she was already doing everything she could to help herself get better. Without the support of her family and friends she wasn't certain if she'd be as well as she was now. She'd probably be curled up in a ball somewhere, babbling nonsense and terrified that her assailants would come after her again.

Chloe had been attacked a year ago, beaten savagely and left for dead. She'd been in a coma for weeks before Julian healed her. But that healing had come at a cost. Super Bear, as his mate Cyn called him, had brought her back from the brink of death but had been unable to heal all of her wounds. The head trauma alone had been horrific; the brain damage that had been inflicted as a result was permanent.

Conduction aphasia with phonological paraphasia. Such pretty words for such a sucky disorder.

Basically, she could read and understand words just fine. It was *saying* them that was the problem. She would replace a word with one that sounded similar, and the more upset she got, the worse her paraphasia became. Sometimes it would become so bad her speech was completely garbled or, worst of all, she couldn't speak at all, her mind a jumble as it sought to spit out something that just wasn't coming to her. Her speech had gotten better with therapy, but already her therapist was beginning to make noises that she was as good as she was going to get.

For a while she hadn't even been able to tell that she'd said something wrong. It wasn't until therapy that her brain began to make the connection between the odd looks on other people's faces and her speech. Now she could tell before the odd looks that she'd said the wrong word, but in her mind it felt, and sounded, correct right up until it came out.

But that wasn't the only thing the beating had left her with. Oh, no. It got *better.*

Her left hand no longer worked correctly. She couldn't make a fist at all, and her hand had no grip strength, causing her to drop things often. Her left-handed fine motor skills no longer existed. Peeling a potato had become an exercise in frustration.

Performing surgery on small animals was no longer possible.

All of her visions of the future had been dashed. Chloe would never become a veterinarian. That had to be the hardest thing of all to deal with. She'd worked so hard, moved all the way across the country to a shifter-friendly college, only to have her future ripped away from her in one night of unimaginable horror. Her lifelong dream had been to work with animals, to heal them and help them any way she could. Thanks to the beating, that dream was now forever out of reach.

Ryan hugged her from behind, the big-brother kind of hug that made her ribs creak. "It's going to be okay, little vixen. No matter what else happens, you'll always have us."

"I know." She patted her brother's arm, more grateful than she could say. She had the best friends and family in the world. When she'd been hurt they'd come running, leaving behind work and home to give Chloe whatever it was she needed. Now they were all moving to Halle, Pennsylvania, uprooting the business and their lives to keep the family together.

Julian leaned forward, staring into her eyes. His deep brown ones turned gray, and a silver streak appeared in his long black hair. "You're hurting."

She grimaced. She should have known better than to try and hide her pain in a room full of Bears. "My hand is cramping." And her right hand had begun tingling recently, a new development that scared her spitless.

"Your head hurts too." Julian swiped his fingers across her brow, easing the headache that had been torturing her all day.

Ryan grabbed her left hand and began massaging it, the pain easing as he used his healing ability to relax her muscles.

Chloe whimpered happily as the pain dissipated. "Have you guys considered becoming massage therapists?"

Julian chuckled. "I don't think Cyn would take well to me rubbing other people."

Alex winced. "Yeah, until Tabby drops the cub she's going to be pretty cranky. Let's not give her something to beat me over."

"How's Glory doing?" She was worried about her future sister-in-law's panic attacks, but Ryan's solution had been ingenious. He'd packed up his laptop and started working from her business. Doing so enabled him to be there whenever one of Glory's attacks happened.

Ryan let go of Chloe's hand. "Working from Cynful has been great. Glory's panic attacks aren't nearly as bad."

Chloe smiled, genuinely happy for her brother. "Good, I'm glad. She's all right that you came to visit me?" The guys had shown up on her doorstep with burgers and grins, but they couldn't hide their concern. Somehow they'd known she was depressed and in pain, and had ridden to her rescue.

"She's fine." The look that came over Ryan's face was priceless. The sheer joy when Glory's name was mentioned, the way he just lit up when he thought about his mate, made Chloe so happy for him. He deserved the happiness he'd found, and so did Glory. "She had some appointments this afternoon, so she's busy, plus she knows if she calls I'll come running."

And Chloe didn't begrudge Glory that one little bit. She'd seen one of Glory's panic attacks and knew how rough they could be. Glory sometimes needed Ryan just to breathe. Literally. The panic attacks made her hyperventilate. She'd passed out twice that Chloe knew of, all due to her inability to breathe without her mate.

"Speaking of running, heard anything from Jim?" Alex's smile was sweet, but it didn't fool Chloe for one little minute. Out of all of them, Alex was the one most likely to begin ripping arms off if he felt Chloe was being mistreated. "Rumor has it he's been hiding from everyone, even Max and Emma."

Oh, that couldn't be good. Chloe tried to beat back the sudden panic that assaulted her. "He's not taking well to becoming a shifter?" Jim had been attacked by a rogue Wolf, bitten and changed against his will. He hadn't even been aware that shifters existed before then, and not everyone who was changed could handle it, especially when it happened in such a traumatic fashion. If Jim turned out to be one of those few who couldn't deal with it he'd be…dealt with.

Chloe shuddered. She couldn't bear the thought of something happening to Jim.

"I don't know. He's gone again." Alex winced when Chloe accidentally let loose a distressed yip. "I don't know what's going on, all right? I was hoping he'd contacted you."

Ryan patted her hand. "Now that he's one of us he should be feeling the mating pull. The mate dreams should be hitting him hard."

"Yeah, he should succumb to your charms soon." Julian winked. "We just have to lock the two of you in a closet together and let nature take its course."

Oh yeah. That would go over real well. "In the dictionary under 'stubborn' is Jim's stricture."

Again, that rapid blinking as the guys processed what she'd said.

Chloe propped her head in her hands. "This sucks monkey balls."

Ryan ruffled her hair. "Anyone who knows you accepts that this is a part of you, kiddo."

"Yeah, don't let it get you down." Julian hugged her. "Trust me, it could have been a lot worse."

"You mean I could be dead?" Chloe groaned. Man, she sounded like a Sad Sue, and she really wasn't. At least, not most of the time. "Sorry, it's just…"

"We understand. You're missing your mate." Ryan's tone was sympathetic. While Glory had denied their mating for months, at least Ryan had been able to see her every day. Chloe didn't have that luxury. Jim was gone with the wind, but she'd think about that tomorrow. For now, she had to bring her spirits back up, and talking about her absent mate was no way to do that.

She'd get her Wolf if she had to tranquilize his ass and carry him off to some remote location where he wouldn't be found for weeks. She'd tie him to a bed and have her wicked way with him…

And get arrested for felony kidnapping. Let's face it, Chloe, you don't have the best luck with men.

Ugh. Chloe pounded her head on the table.

"Don't let it get you down." Alex's big hand stopped her from giving her forehead a huge-ass bruise. "We'll figure out a way to get you mated off."

She lifted her head and stared at him. "You're going to offer Jim some goats and a sheaf of wheat?"

"I was thinking you're worth at least a cow or two, but it's negotiable."

Chloe giggled. "Asshole."

The boys dog-piled on her, careful not to hurt her, and tickled her until she cried uncle.

Once the big lugs got off of her she sat up and pushed her hair off her forehead. Breathless and happy, she gasped, "I hate you all."

Alex winked. "Anyone know where I can get some cows?"

***

James Woods sighed as he hung up the phone. God, this sucked big time, but what else was he going to do? There was no one else who could deal with the issues he faced, no one who cared enough to bother with the fucking paperwork, the long hours, the flights back and forth, or the horrendous expense, both financially and physically. He was exhausted, run ragged, and the little sleep he got at night was littered with dreams of a damaged redhead far too young and vulnerable for him. She did *not* need his shit piled on top of her own. When things had been taken care of, when they finally knew what they were dealing with, *then* he'd give in to the mating pull.

He was *not* making her deal with his bullshit.

He.

Was.

Not.

He leaned back in his chair and rubbed his hand over his forehead as the creature inside him howled with longing. The headache that had become his constant companion wouldn't go away. The Wolf whimpered, wanting out in the worst possible way.

The Wolf wanted its mate, wanted her touch, her comfort, and it couldn't have it.

"Not now," Jim muttered, hoping to soothe it.

It grumbled, but quieted down. It knew the truth of what Jim was going through, and the support and love it gave him had made everything more bearable. When he felt at his most alone and he just couldn't bear it any longer, the Wolf was there, reminding him that he would never be alone again.

His life was completely fucked up, but the Wolf was one of the bright spots.

A nurse in blue scrubs stuck her head out the door. "Dr. Woods, Mr. Strickland?"

Jim stood, putting down the magazine he'd been halfheartedly leafing through. "Yes?"

The nurse smiled. "Dr. Abbot will see you now."

Jim nodded and turned to Spencer. "Ready?"

Spencer blew out a breath. "As I'll ever be." The cheeky grin and blond hair reminded Jim of his father, but the golden brown eyes came straight from Spencer's mother. Jim pretended he didn't see how that grin shook, or the way Spencer clutched at the wheels of his chair. "I mean, it's not like it's life or death, right?"

"Right." Jim rolled his eyes, smiling as his little brother laughed.

Jim had nothing to laugh about. They would finally find out, after numerous tests and multiple diagnoses that turned out to be wrong, exactly what was going on with his half brother.

The nurse held the door open as Spencer wheeled himself past with a jaunty wave. His brother couldn't walk any longer, but he made the most out of his situation. Spencer rarely let himself get down, facing his difficulties with a smile.

Jim wasn't quite so optimistic.

The last diagnosis Spencer had gotten was ALS, also known as Lou Gehrig's disease. It was a debilitating and, in most cases, ultimately fatal neurological disorder that affected voluntary muscle movements like speaking, walking and swallowing. ALS eventually affected the ability to breathe, causing respiratory failure and death.

There was no known cure.

If it was confirmed by Dr. Abbot that Spencer had ALS, his prognosis was not good. Most patients died within five years of onset, and Spencer had been ill for three of them. Dr. Abbot had finally agreed to see them after numerous phone calls from Jim and Spencer both.

Spencer felt he did *not* have ALS. After all, he could still speak and function normally other than the tingling and weakness in his body. It was beginning to spread to his hands now, and he'd already lost use of his legs. If it spread to his upper extremities as well he would be utterly dependent on others for even the simplest things.

Jim was determined to be that someone. He wasn't there when his brother was growing up, but he was here now, dammit. And unlike his father, Jim planned to do the right thing.

"Time to get weighed, Mr. Strickland."

"Oh, joy." Spencer blinked up at him. "Help me?"

"Of course." One of the things Jim liked best about his new shifter status was his increase in strength. He couldn't bench press a Buick or anything, but he could easily lift his brother into his arms.

Spencer had lost five pounds since the last time they'd gotten weighed together. "You need to eat more."

"Can I has McDonald's and a lollipop when we're done here, Daddy?" Spencer gave him the biggest puppy-dog eyes Jim had ever seen outside of anime. "I promise to be good."

The man was a pain in the ass. Jim put the brat back in his chair. "Get your butt in the exam room, smarty-pants."

Spencer wheeled after the nurse, Jim right behind him. In the exam room, Spencer amused himself by popping wheelies and giving Jim a minor heart attack every five seconds.

The door popped open, and a middle-aged man with a stethoscope stepped into the room. "Mr. Strickland?"

Spencer held up his hand after landing on all four wheels. "That would be me."

"It's nice to meet you, Mr. Strickland. I'm Dr. Abbot."

"Nice to meet you too, or at least I hope it will be." Spencer pointed toward Jim. "This is my brother, James Woods."

Dr. Abbott nodded to him, but kept his attention primarily on Spencer. "We have the results of your tests, Mr. Strickland."

"Okay." Spencer nodded jerkily. "Lay it on me, Doc."

The doctor smiled and settled on the stool next to the built-in desk. "The good news is you do not have ALS."

"Yes!" Spencer pumped his fist into the air, high-fiving Jim when Jim held out his hand. "We are *so* getting Big Macs!"

Jim laughed. His brother was a nutter. The man was twenty-four and acted fourteen.

Dr. Abbott smiled. "That's the *good* news."

Jim didn't like the way the doctor had emphasized *good*. "So, what's the bad?"

Dr. Abbott turned to his computer screen, the smile leaving his face. "Your brother has a rare autoimmune disorder called chronic inflammatory demyelinating polyneuropathy, or CIDP."

Spencer looked stunned. "Can you say that in English?"

Dr. Abbott spun to look at them once more and picked up a picture labeled *Typical Neuron Structure*. To the untrained eye it might look like a weird alien flower, but to Jim, a veterinarian, he was all too familiar with it. "Basically, CIDP is a disorder that causes the myelin sheath surrounding the peripheral nerves to be destroyed. This causes weakness in the limbs and, if not correctly diagnosed, wheelchair dependency."

"Right. Okay." Spencer patted the arms of his chair nervously. "What's a myelin sheath?"

"The fatty tissue that surrounds the nerve and protects it. It assists in transmitting the electrical impulses from nerve end to nerve end. Without it, the signal is degraded. In the case of CIDP, this means you think you've lost strength in your legs, when in actuality it's the nerve signal that's not quite reaching where it needs to go rather than true muscle weakness."

"What causes it?" Spencer tilted his head, his expression confused.

"We're not entirely sure. It's a disorder closely related to Guillain-Barré syndrome, but that *is* treatable and will usually clear up with no side effects. What we believe is that, unlike GBS, it is an autoimmune disorder that is *not* set off by a preceding illness."

Jim asked the only question that mattered to him. "Is it fatal?"

"No."

Spencer glanced at Jim and grimaced. "Is there a cure?"

Dr. Abbott slowly shook his head. "I'm afraid not, Mr. Strickland."

Spencer blew out a breath and leaned back in his chair.

"But we can slow, even stop, the progression of the disorder through the use of corticosteroids, intravenous immunoglobulin treatments and plasmapheresis. And with physical therapy you may even regain some use of your legs."

Spencer looked up at Jim. "Plasmawhat?"

Jim translated. "Okay. Think of it this way. Your immune system is the Empire. It's decided that your nerves are the Rebel Alliance, and it wants to stomp them into submission. In reality, your nerves are loyal followers of the Emperor, so they can't understand why they're being pounded into the ground. Their shields are failing, and they have nowhere to turn."

"Enter Han Solo?" Spencer was grinning.

"Sort of." Jim ignored the doctor's quiet laughter and continued his explanation. "That would be the treatment options. The prednisone would be the X-wing fighters, swooping in to battle but might not wind up sticking around. The immunoglobulin treatments are the Mon Calamari Star Cruisers, the heavy guns, and the plasmapheresis would be the, um…" How would you use *Star Wars* to describe a process where your blood was removed, the plasma filtered out, and new plasma introduced?

"If you say midi-chlorians I'll be forced to beat the stupid out of you." Spencer rolled his eyes. "Fine. I'm going to be poked and prodded on a regular basis. Got it."

"We'll be starting treatment soon, unless…" Dr. Abbott frowned. "I see here you're going to be moving, Mr. Strickland?"

Jim turned to stare at his brother, joy racing through him. Had Spencer finally decided?

"Yup. I want to be closer to my family. That would be him." Spencer hitched his thumb toward Jim.

Dr. Abbott closed the file. "In that case, I'll refer you to an associate of mine closer to Halle, Pennsylvania. I can assure you she's good, and I'll make sure she's familiar with your case."

"Thank you, Doctor." Spencer held out his hand. "It's nice to finally get a real diagnosis."

"It's in your head, it's fibromyalgia, it's GBS, it's MS—believe me, I've heard it all." Dr. Abbott took

Spencer's hand and shook it firmly. "I'm glad I was able to help."

The doctor left, and Jim looked at Spencer. "So. Moving to Halle, huh? Are you sure? When we started this you didn't want anyone to know you were sick." Spencer had once been a vibrant, athletic man. His disease had hit him hard, but it hadn't dimmed his spirit. Still, he hadn't wanted his problems to affect Jim's life and had asked him to remain quiet about the fact that Jim had a bastard half brother.

Jim hated that. He wanted to tell the world about his brother, how strong and brave he was, but Spencer had been adamant. Rather than stress his brother any further, Jim had reluctantly agreed.

"I got over it." Spencer winked. "Must have been the midi-chlorians."

"Does this mean I can finally introduce you to everyone?"

"Aw, man." Spencer looked away for a moment, a blush on his cheeks. "You know the only reason I said no was because I never wanted to be a burden on you."

"You aren't. How many times do I have to tell you that?" He might have only known Spencer for a little over a year, but they'd formed a strong, unbreakable bond. He couldn't imagine his life without his brother in it now.

"Then take me home." Spencer blinked innocently up at Jim. "Can we have a kitty?"

Jim's Wolf howled. It wanted a vixen, not a kitty. "Um. No."

"Please?"

"How about that Big Mac?"

"Oh, even better." Spencer wheeled toward the exam room door. "And a McFlurry. And when we get home, you can have a McChloe."

Jim blinked, not sure he'd heard that one correctly. "Excuse me?"

"You need to bring her home too."

"Maybe." Jim shrugged. He couldn't think about Chloe right now. Just the thought of the little redhead had him longing to be in Halle once more. He reached for the door, eager to get on the road as soon as possible.

"C'mon. Tell me woof-woof doesn't want to play chase."

Jim bit back his laugh as his brother wheeled down the hall. "Woof-woof?" Jim had returned from a late-night run and changed, not realizing Spencer was in the room. Spencer's reaction had been wide eyes and a slew of questions Jim still wasn't sure he knew all the answers to.

"She can be the Fox to your hound."

Spencer was one in a million.

They got the information from the front desk that they needed to transfer Spencer to the doctor who worked out of Halle General. When they reached the car, Spencer grinned over his shoulder at Jim. "I call shotgun!"

Jim shook his head, awed he had such a strong, vibrant sibling. "Weirdo."

CHAPTER TWO

Chloe still wasn't sure how she'd gotten roped into bringing lunch to Emma, Becky and Sheri, but here she was, trudging through the stifling heat with a bag of sandwiches from Frank's Diner. Emma had just returned to work from maternity leave, but since Emma co-owned Wallflowers with her business partner and BFF Becky, she was able to bring the baby with her. Chloe had stopped in to see the newest member of the kitty family and had been commandeered into snagging their takeout.

At least she got free food out of it. They'd called and added a sandwich for Chloe so she could join them for lunch.

Chloe finally made it to the door of Wallflowers, for once glad her long red hair had been chopped off during all those surgeries. The back of her neck felt cool for a change, but she still missed the way her hair felt as it flowed down her back. Maybe she'd let the girls at Cynful put some colors into it, some blues and purples to contrast with the bright copper.

"Chloe?"

She blinked, her Fox yowling in desire at the sound of that deep, masculine voice. "Jim." She turned, smiling weakly. He'd been gone for a week this time.

Not that she'd been stalking him or anything.

Erm.

Maybe a little.

"How are you?" The way he gazed at her, his hazel eyes glittering, his smile warm, had her wondering what the hell he was up to. Jim *never* looked at her like she was a yummy treat he was dying to lick.

"I'm fine. How are you?" She wasn't going to throw herself at him. She had that much self-respect.

"Better." He glanced behind him and grimaced. "Listen, I don't have time to talk, but—"

"Bye." Chloe opened the door to Wallflowers, leaving Jim standing there, his mouth hanging open. Sort of like he'd left *her* hanging for so long.

Score one for the Fox.

Chloe rattled the bag. "Food!" She set the bag on the table and hastily backed away.

But unlike Cynful, where a hungry group of hyenas would descend on the bag like a ravaging horde of Vikings confronted by naked, nubile women after a year at sea, the ladies at Wallflowers simply walked out of the back room like, well, normal people.

Of course, they were the farthest from normal she'd ever met in her life. And that was saying something, considering her family.

"Thank you, Chloe." Emma Cannon, the Curana of the Halle Puma Pride and new mother, settled down on the sofa next to a blue-checkered car seat. She transferred the sleeping babe from her arms to the car seat. "God, I'm starving. I could eat a rhino."

"No you wouldn't." Sheri grimaced. "They're an endangered species."

"Besides, they're way too chewy." Becky glanced around when everyone went silent. "What?"

Emma shook her head. "I swear, Becks, you never cease to amaze me."

"It was a joke." Becky rolled her eyes.

"Uh-huh." Emma's expression turned sly. "Sort of like the time you bought Simon a corset and stockings?"

Chloe blinked, trying to picture the very masculine glass artist dressed as someone from *The Rocky Horror Picture Show*. She started laughing as she pictured fem-Simon singing "Sweet Transvestite".

"I never understood why he didn't find that funny." Becky sat next to Emma, cooing down at the blue-wrapped bundle of baby shifter before turning to the bag. "Did you want something to drink, Chloe? You can go in the back and get anything you want."

"Thanks." Chloe shifted past Sheri, who'd sat in one of the chairs across from the cream Victorian sofa, her seeing-eye dog waiting patiently next to her. Jerry was a Golden Retriever and had been with Sheri for years. "Can I bag anything for anyone else?"

"Pepsi, please. I needs caffeine, my Precious." Emma gave her puppy dog eyes, no mean feat for the queen of the kitties.

"Would you bring me some water?" Becky pulled an apple out of the bag and sighed. "I still can't eat these. Too many bad memories of eyeballs and evil bitches."

"Huh?" Chloe had no idea what Becky was talking about.

Emma and Becky exchanged a quick glance before Emma replied, "Someone drugged Becky. She wound up having hallucinations and landed in the hospital. That person…is no longer a member of the Pride."

"I'll take it." Sheri held out her pale hand. "And could you bring me some water as well, Chloe?"

"No problem." Chloe, who'd been a waitress before the attack, could easily remember the drinks they'd asked for. It was carrying them that was the problem, but she solved that by putting them in a plastic bag she found in the back and carrying it with her good hand.

When she returned from the back room, she could see Jim outside, speaking to a man in a wheelchair and gesturing toward the entrance of Wallflowers. "Huh. Wonder what that's about."

"What what?" Emma looked up from her sandwich toward the plate glass window of her shop. "Hey, Jimmy's back!"

"Yeah." Chloe was determined to ignore her wayward mate, instead focusing on the new addition to the Pride. She might not be a Puma, but she lived in Halle, and the Pride had accepted her as one of their own. As far as she was concerned, she was an honorary Puma. "How's Felix?"

"Demonic," Emma grumbled, biting viciously into her sandwich.

Becky cupped her hand over her mouth, laughing silently.

Sheri shook her head. "I still can't believe you named him Felix."

Emma shrugged. "Garfield was too obvious." The fact that she said it like it made perfect sense was all Emma. "And Heathcliff was too tragic."

"I think you should have gone with Nermal. I mean, look at him." Becky smiled down at her godson with a besotted expression.

Emma just stared at her. "He looks like Winston Churchill and Lady Gaga had a drunken one-night stand."

Chloe almost sprayed capicola and salami all over the table. "Emma!"

"What?"

The bell over the door jangled, announcing they had a customer. Chloe turned to find Jim and the wheelchair man coming into the store. Jim held the door open for the man, who quietly thanked him. "Geez. You didn't say it was like estrogen central in here, Jimbo."

Jim rolled his eyes, but Chloe could see the nervousness in his expression. "They're going to love you, bro."

Emma started. "Um." Her brows rose as she stared at Spencer. "Bro?"

Jim nodded, smiling shyly. It was oddly endearing. "Yes. This is Spencer, my half brother."

"Yo." Spencer waved. He then hitched his thumb toward Jim. "This is my brother from another mother."

Jim totally face-palmed at his brother's irreverent words.

"Wait a sec." Emma held up her hand. "You're serious?"

Jim nodded, lifting his head from his palms. "Dad had an affair with a woman in Chicago about twenty-five years ago. Twenty-four years ago this weirdo was spawned."

"We didn't find out about each other until about a year ago. Seems Daddy wanted nothing to do with me when Mom died. Lucky for me, this big galoot found out about me and came for a visit."

The sour expression on Spencer's face was not echoed by Jim, who patted his brother's shoulder. "I'm glad I did, or I would never have met you." Jim's gaze darted toward Chloe. "We need to talk."

"Hallelujah," Emma muttered.

"About damn time." Becky glared at Jim.

"Hmph." Sheri crossed her arms over her chest and sniffed.

Chloe ignored them all. She continued to eat her sandwich, studiously avoiding making eye contact with either Jim or his brother.

Jim sighed. "There's a lot more going on than you know."

"You said that fast time." Chloe caught a glimpse of the confusion on Spencer's face. Jim must not have told him about her paraphasia.

Jim sighed. "And we were attacked, remember? I never got to tell you what you…no, what *I* needed to."

Chloe refused to feel sorry for the son of a bitch. Being changed against your will, being bitten by a shifter who wasn't your mate, was an extremely painful way to be turned. But if he'd just accepted their mating none of that would have happened to him. He would have been a Fox instead of a Wolf, mated to her before the attack.

"Chloe? Are you ever going to speak to me again?" His tone was soft and disappointed.

As if he had the right to be anything but on his knees, begging for forgiveness. She sniffed. "I'm tinkling about it."

Spencer held up his hand. "Can I explain?"

Before Jim could reply his phone rang. Unable to stop herself, she glanced at his expression long enough to see him wince. "You'll have to."

"Uh-oh. I know that tone, bro. Is that who I think it is?" Spencer frowned, holding his hand toward Jim.

"Yeah. I'll be right outside if you need me."

Spencer watched his brother leave the shop, then turned with a determined look and wheeled himself until he was next to Chloe. "Let me tell you about the birds, the bees, and a little thing called CIDP…"

***

Jim held the phone to his ear and listened to his mother rant and rave. Inside Wallflowers he could see Chloe leaning toward Spencer, listening intently to his words. The horror and sympathy that flashed across the faces of all three women made up at least a little for the raving lunatic his mother had become.

"I cannot believe you brought your father's bastard home with you, James." Wanda Woods was practically snarling in fury. "That son of a bitch has done nothing but hurt this family."

"Spencer hasn't done a thing wrong, Mom." Jim watched Chloe as the familiar argument rolled over him. "That was all Dad."

"He exists. That's enough for me."

Jim sighed. "Blame Dad, not Spencer." Spencer was the only bright spot in his fucked-up family.

"What did I tell you? Leave that skanky ho's brat alone! Why couldn't you just leave him in Chicago?" As usual, his mother wasn't listening to him. Ever since she'd discovered that not only had his father cheated on her, but had a child with the other woman, she'd lost her damn mind. The ongoing divorce proceedings were vicious on both sides as each one of his parents tried to get the upper hand over the other.

He might have felt more sympathy for his mother if he hadn't been on the receiving end of her rages. This wasn't the first time she'd called him to bitch him out over something he had little control over. "It's not my fault Dad cheated, and it's not Spencer's fault either."

"But it's your fault for shoving it in my face!"

"I can't ignore him, Mom." He doubted he'd be able to get through to her, but he tried. God knew, he tried. "He's my brother."

"And I'm your mother." The chill that came into her voice made him sigh. "By bringing him to Halle you've told everyone you side with your father."

"I'm not siding with anyone, and you know it." His parents' divorce was going to be the death of him. "I love you both equally."

"If you did you would have left Spencer where you found him. Not even Arthur wants him in Halle."

That, at least, was true. Jim's dad wanted less to do with Spencer than his mother did. The man couldn't even be bothered to call Jim to bitch about it. The silence from Arthur Woods was as hurtful as the shrill diatribes Wanda shot his way.

The family he'd known and loved was gone, burned away in betrayal and rage, and Jim was left to deal with the shattered lives left behind. An only child, he'd been forced to listen to both of his parents disparage the other as their marriage disintegrated. He'd had to act as not only their therapist but their mediator as each dumped their accusations and misery on his shoulders.

When Jim found out about Spencer it had only gotten worse. If he hadn't listened to his father's drunken rants about Spence he might never have found his half brother, never have known the strong spirit of the man who'd grown up without a father in his life. While Jim bitterly mourned the loss of his parents, he couldn't help but be grateful for finding Spencer when he had. Spencer was the only one who seemed to give a shit about what Jim was going through. Even his friends told him to suck it up, that he was an adult. Just because Jim was an adult didn't mean he didn't need his parents, didn't wish things hadn't become what they were.

But nothing could bring back the bright, loving parents he'd thought he once had. Maybe once the divorce was finalized they'd realize what they'd done to him, but Jim wasn't about to hold his breath. No child should have to go through what Jim was, no matter what their age.

So he fought the only battle he could, knowing he wouldn't win no matter which way he went. "Spencer is my family, Mother, and that's the end of it."

He should have been surprised when she hung up on him, but sadly it was an all-too-common occurrence these days. Both of them expected him to pick sides. When he tried to be fair, to treat each of them equally, he got crap like this in return.

Some days he wished he could bring himself to ignore the ringing phone, or stop wishing that it was his father instead of his mother. Just once, he wished they'd tell him that everything would be all right rather than leaving him to deal with all of this shit on his own.

At least Spencer seemed to be getting through to Chloe. His brother was holding Chloe's hand, and she was nodding sympathetically.

Perhaps, just perhaps, instead of trying to cling to the old, he needed to get started on the new. It was time to make his own damn family, and to hell with his parents. Let them deal with their own shit-storm. He was going to concentrate on Chloe and Spencer and the rest of the people he loved. They'd be the family he'd been missing for so long.

Jim stepped into Wallflowers, fully expecting to be greeted with smiles. What he got was—

"Oof." Jim laughed as Emma practically jumped him. "Hey, pretty girl."

A pissed-off yip came from the couch.

"You are such a good boy, Jimbo." Emma pinched his cheeks. "Yes you are. Oh, yes you are."

Jim laughed and shoved her off of him. "Knock it off."

Becky shook her head at them while Sheri simply smiled serenely, well used to Emma's madness by now.

Their reactions weren't the ones that interested him, though. It was Chloe, who still sat holding on to Spencer, whose opinion truly mattered. "Chloe?"

"Tell me." She stared at him, her eyes reddish-brown, her tone clipped.

He maneuvered past Emma, kneeling next to Chloe's chair until they were eye-to-eye. Her Fox was close to the surface, driving his Wolf to respond. His vision blurred, Chloe's brilliant red hair becoming a muted yellowish-brown. He'd known that canines were unable to see reds or greens, but until his eyes first changed he hadn't realized how it could impact his world.

He loved Chloe's red hair.

"Spencer filled you in on what's wrong with him?"

She nodded. "And I'm sorry about that, but I'm not sure what this has to do with you and me."

He ran his fingers nervously through his hair. Here was the rough part, the part where he worried she wouldn't be able to forgive him. "We thought he was dying."

"And?" Her eyes went wide. "Oh. This happened right around the time—"

"When you were in the hospital, yes." Even worse, at the time he'd still believed her not only too young for him, but pining for another man. That was a discussion for another day, though. "I'd just found him, and we thought he was dying. Everything I heard was that you were here, you were unconscious but stable, and the best of the best was working on you."

"While I had no one." Spencer's tone was soft, but even now he didn't sound sorry for himself. Spencer was far too comfortable in his skin to ever display sorrow over his situation. "Jim stepped in when no one else wanted anything to do with me, including my sperm donor."

Jim smiled wryly. "I hate to say it but I'm beginning to think of him that way too."

The brothers shared a sympathetic glance before Jim gave his attention once more to Chloe. "So. Once my parents figured out I was helping Spencer, they both freaked and demanded I stay away from him."

"Yeah, the sperm donor even went so far as to call and threaten me. Said he'd cut Jim off if I didn't drive him away."

Jim glared at Spencer. "You didn't tell me that."

Spencer shrugged. "It didn't matter." That cheeky, lovable grin crossed his face. "Besides, you would have ignored me if I'd tried."

"True."

"Worse, it happened." Spencer tightened his grip on Chloe's hand when she tried to pull away. "His father stopped speaking to him months ago, and his mother? She's kind of…well…"

Jim shrugged fatalistically. "Rage-tastic?"

"Status Dramaticus?"

He frowned as he tried to come up with another one. It was a game they played, both of them enjoying the play on words. "E-vil-gelical?

Spencer tapped his finger on his chin. "She likes to go mid-*evil* on your ass."

Jim rolled his eyes at that one. "That was bad."

"I try."

"Next time she calls you'll just have to grim and bear it." Chloe blinked innocently. Whether the misspoken word was meant or not, Jim chose to believe it was. She was playing their game.

Spencer sighed happily. "I like her. Can we keep her?"

"Do I get a say in it?" Chloe tried to pull free once more, but Spencer was like a dog with a bone when he wanted something, and he wanted Chloe for Jim.

His poor mate didn't stand a chance.

"Nope." Jim stood, holding out his hand. "So, take a walk with me?"

"Wait. Hold up there." Spencer let go of Chloe. "You're leaving me in estrogen central?"

"Why do guys keep calling it that?" Emma tilted her head, her ponytail brushing her shoulder.

"I don't get it," Becky added.

Sheri chuckled. "I do, but I'm not telling."

Jim ignored the playful banter between the three women and pulled Chloe to her feet. Like Emma Cannon didn't know *exactly* what men thought when they entered Wallflowers for the first time. "Come on. I promise you won't regret it."

Chloe glared at him but took his hand. "I mill haven't decided if I forbid you yet."

"I know. But are you willing to give me the chance to earn your forgiveness?" He didn't know what he'd do if she said no. Probably become some sort of creepy stalker she'd need a restraining order and some wolfsbane pepper spray to get rid of.

She nodded slowly, her expression almost reluctant. "I can try."

"Good." He lifted her hand to his lips, kissing her knuckles.

The color that flooded her cheeks made him grin. He loved that she blushed so easily. He had so much to learn about his mate, so much that he'd let slide by him. Now that Spencer was home, he could concentrate on fixing the mistakes he'd made with Chloe, starting now.

And if she wouldn't let him, well…

Wolves were very good at stalking their prey.

CHAPTER THREE

Chloe couldn't believe it. She was walking down the street with her mate, her hand held tightly in his. The quick little glances he kept sending her, as if he expected her to run if he loosened his grip, were oddly reassuring. He was making it clear he wanted her right where she was.

Chloe blew out a breath and tried to steady herself. She was so nervous she was afraid she might not be able to speak, and her left hand kept twitching uncontrollably.

"How's the speech therapy going?"

Chloe startled. They'd been walking in silence for so long she'd sort of expected it to continue that way. "I'm trying to burn to slow my beach down, but it's harder than it creams." She sighed wearily, wondering how Jim would take her garbled speech.

"Take your time. I won't rush you." Another quick glance. "Your speech is barely slurred."

"It was glad in the beginning, but it's gotten a slot better."

Jim stopped and turned toward her, forcing her to halt as well. "I want you to do what your therapist said, and slow down a bit. All right? I'm listening, and I know what you're trying to say."

Chloe once again tried to relax. Jim smiled sympathetically, but that didn't help at all. "I…" She frowned, the words lost for a second. Sometimes it was almost worse when she tried to concentrate. It was as if she could feel the words slipping and sliding through her mind, hiding from her. "I'm. Still. Hungry."

Jim laughed. "You didn't get to finish your sandwich, did you?" He began walking again. "Let's hit Frank's, and we can talk some more."

"Yay." Chloe grimaced. Her family might put up with her weirdness, but she doubted Jim would for long.

"You don't want to talk to me?"

She blew out a frustrated breath, the words sliding away again. "No." She shook her head. "Yes."

Jim lifted her hand to his lips, kissing her knuckles. While her Fox was doing the Snoopy dance, her head was telling her that at some point he'd pull away again. A one-eighty like this couldn't last, could it?

They entered Frank's Diner. Jim put his arm around her shoulders and began maneuvering them through the lunchtime crowd.

"My valance is fine."

Jim blinked, but it didn't take him very long to figure out what she was trying to say. "Oh. Balance? I know."

"Then why are you holding me?"

He grinned sheepishly. "Because I want to."

Before she could respond they were at a booth. She slid into the seat, and Jim took the one across from her. "So." She picked up one of the rolled napkin and silverware thingies and began to unravel it, picking the napkin apart into tiny little pieces. "Spencer."

He nodded. "My father had an affair with a woman living in Chicago. When she became pregnant, he abandoned her. She was a single mom with no support from him or the rest of her family, and she was too proud to go after a married father for child support. She raised Spencer on her own and did a damn fine job of it."

"That stucks." Chloe didn't know what she would do if she lost her family.

"Yeah, it does. When she died, Spencer reached out to my father, who told him to basically go to hell. When I found out about it, I decided to meet him."

"Why?" Chloe would have done the same thing, but she wanted to hear his reasons from his own lips.

"Why did I want to meet him, or why did my dad *not* want to?"

"You," Chloe replied softly.

"Because he's family." Jim shrugged. "My mother found out about Spencer and flipped out, throwing my father out of the house. He tried for a month or so to get her to take him back, but she turned vicious, and he decided it wasn't worth it."

"And you were dealing with Spencer?" Chloe was careful to speak slowly, sounding out each word to herself before speaking.

"Yes. We thought he had Lou Gehrig's disease. Most people who have it die within three to five years due to respiratory failure. Spencer has been sick for three, so…"

The pain in Jim's tone couldn't be faked. "You taught he was dying."

"I did. When the latest doctor told us it wasn't ALS but chronic inflammatory demyelinating polyneuropathy, we were ecstatic."

Chloe frowned. She'd never heard of… "What is that?"

"It's the chronic form of Guillain-Barré syndrome, sort of. Spencer might never walk again, but we've caught the disease before he lost any other motor functions."

"Ouch." Chloe winced in sympathy. "He didn't tell me that part."

"The good news is that, unlike ALS, it's not fatal. He'll live a long, happy life with the right therapies. And he has me now, so he has family again."

"I'm glad for him." Chloe jumped when Jim covered her hands, stopping the destruction of the poor paper napkin. "What?"

"Why didn't you tell me?" His gaze remained kind, but his tone was firm.

"Tell you butt?" Man, her brain *really* seemed to like that word lately.

"That I was your mate."

"Shh." She looked around, grateful that the other diners seemed to be immersed in their own conversations. "You can't talk about that in public."

"All right. Calm down." He patted her hands and let go, sitting back in his seat. "You want a burger or something else?"

She blinked. "There's something else?"

He laughed. "Yeah, the burgers here are the best." When the waitress, someone Chloe had never met before, walked over to their table Jim ordered for both of them. How the man knew she liked to get the extra-thick chocolate shake along with a glass of water, she had no idea, but that's exactly what he asked for.

"Thank. You." Chloe smiled.

"You have conductive aphasia, right?" When she nodded, he continued. "I want you to relax. The tenser you are, the harder it is to speak using the correct words."

"I can read and write them dine, but…" She paused, trying to spit out the word on the tip of her tongue. She couldn't quite get it to come out, but Jim waited patiently, and eventually she was able to speak. "Talking is card sometimes, and I switch words."

"Paraphasia." He nodded. "I looked some of this stuff up when I realized what was going on. Took me some time, but I figured it out."

He seemed so proud of himself for that.

"Why would you? As far as I drew you wanted nothing to do with me."

He actually flushed. "Because you're important to me, more than I wanted you to know. I tried to stay away, to keep you out of my mind, but I just couldn't."

Ouch. That hurt, but at least he was being honest with her.

"Any weakness on your left side other than your hand?"

"Go. I primp sometimes in bad weather or when I'm fired, but otherwise everything else seems fine. I've got some tingling in my right bland that I need to have checked out soon, though." Chloe's left hand was still trembling, the spastic movement outside her control. "And the aphasia is mild."

"Do they say whether or not you'll recover any further with more speech therapy?"

She shrugged. "Pretty sure it's as good as it's going to set."

"What about for your hand?"

She held it up. "Same thing." While she'd lost some control over her motor functions, at least she could still use it to a small extent. She could hold a burger if she was careful.

Speaking of which, a plate of hot, greasy goodness was placed in front of her along with a thick, creamy shake. Another plate was placed in front of Jim, who nodded his thanks to the waitress. "Can we have two brownie sundaes for dessert?"

Chloe blinked. How in the world had he discovered her favorite dessert?

When the waitress left, Jim winked at her. "I have a weakness for chocolate and ice cream."

She bit her lip. Sure he did. She'd seen what he ate for lunch on a regular basis. Salads with grilled chicken and light dressing, diet soda or water, and if he was *really* hungry he had an apple or orange for dessert. She'd worked for, and lusted after, him for quite a while. "Liar."

"Nope. I just hide my addictions well." He took a huge bite out of his burger, moaning in appreciation. "Besides, all those salads allow me to eat like this for dinner."

Chloe took a much smaller bite of her own burger, savoring the taste of well-cooked meat, melty cheese and ketchup. "S'good."

"Mm-hm." He wiped his lips with his napkin. Frank's burgers were not neat food. "So. What do I need to do to get you to forgive me?"

She suddenly had a hard time swallowing. Shrugging, she took a sip of water, hoping it would loosen her tight throat.

"Are the dreams as bad for you as they've been for me?"

She whimpered before she could stop herself.

He laughed softly. "I'll take that as a yes." The laughter slowly faded, a deepening hunger taking its place. "You're stronger than I gave you credit for." He grimaced. "Stronger than I am, that's for sure."

She nodded. She sure as hell was.

"Will you at least give me a chance to make it up to you?" He held up his hand before she could respond. "I know I don't deserve it, but I'd like to try."

She thought about that while she took another bite of burger. While she was pissed that he hadn't come to her when he'd first discovered Spencer, in a way she could understand it. He hadn't felt the same way she did. He hadn't felt the pull or had to deal with the mate dreams tormenting him night after night.

Even when he'd been turned he'd done what was needed for his family first, and that was something a member of the Bunsun-Williams clan could fully understand. "Yes."

The relief on his face was worth the courage it had taken to say that one little word. "Thank you."

That didn't mean she wasn't going to make him work for it, at least a little. "Don't fake me regret it."

His hazel eyes turned brown. "I promise."

She planned on holding him to that.

***

Jim waited patiently in line at the grocery store, praying he wouldn't have to be there much longer. He had a meal to make and a brother to eat with, not to mention a phone call he was very much looking forward to. Chloe had been more than generous when she'd given him permission to try and make things right between them, and he had every intention of taking her up on that offer.

Honestly, if he were her, he would have kicked his ass to the curb. Instead, she'd offered to take things slowly, give them time to learn one another before he finally claimed her.

His Wolf wasn't too thrilled with that, but as much as it pouted and grumbled, Jim knew it was the right way to go. He'd hurt Chloe badly, and he needed to make sure she knew that he valued her just as much as he did Spencer. If he rushed things he might never gain her full trust.

"Ahem."

Jim rolled his eyes. *Oh, joy.* He recognized that voice. In fact, he'd been expecting this for a while now. "Hello, Ryan." A tap on his shoulder had him turning. "And Alex."

Ryan Williams and Alexander "Bunny" Bunsun stood behind him in line, wearing identical scowls. Ryan was the first to speak. "I hear you're dating my sister."

A snicker from the front of the line and an *oh shit, dude's dead* had Alex smirking. "You have no idea how badly I've wanted to kick your ass."

It was no secret that Alex was very protective of his female cousins, Chloe and Heather especially. "Chloe told you not to?"

Alex growled, while Ryan simply glared.

"Did she explain what's been going on?" Jim pushed his cart forward as the line moved, hoping the two weren't planning on putting on a bloody showdown in the middle of the Super Foods.

"Something about a bastard, but I figured she was talking about you." Ryan's smirk was annoying. Jim had the urge to wipe it from his face, but the Grizzly could probably mutilate him with his pinky finger. While Jim could take on a human, a Grizzly Bear was a whole other matter.

Besides, even if there was a chance he could win he wouldn't hurt Chloe's brother. She might be willing to forgive him for a lot of things, but he doubted even she would forgive Jim for making Ryan bleed.

"She was talking about my half brother." Jim started emptying his cart onto the conveyor belt as the person ahead of him moved forward. "My dad cheated on my mom and wound up having a son out of wedlock. Spencer is living with me now." He wasn't going to go into details with these two until their attitudes changed. He understood how they felt, but while Chloe was Ryan's sister and Alex's cousin, Spencer was his brother.

"And you think that makes what you did to Chloe okay?" Alex flexed his hands, almost making fists.

"You want to tell me what Chloe said, or do you just want to threaten me?" Jim wasn't about to allow these two to intimidate him. They might maul him, but he'd get a few good licks in himself. Besides, he was pretty sure that if they damaged him Chloe would be on their asses like a burning rash. "Because I'm not telling you jack shit unless you back off." While he wouldn't get himself in trouble with Chloe by starting a fight, he sure as hell was willing to defend himself if need be.

The two exchanged an angry glance while Jim finished unloading his groceries. They spoke quietly while the cashier rang him up, then followed him out of the supermarket to his car.

"Fine. Chloe said Spencer was in a wheelchair, that he had something wrong with his nerves."

Jim quickly explained CIDP. "He's got a rare inflammatory disorder that's eating away at the myelin sheath surrounding the nerves that deliver the signals to his arms and legs. Because he went so long without a correct diagnosis, he's wheelchair bound. It's still better than when we thought he had Lou Gehrig's disease or MS, though. CIDP isn't fatal."

The two men looked shocked.

"Worse, the sperm donor wants nothing to do with him, so I'm the only family Spencer has left." Jim finished loading the groceries into his car and slammed the trunk shut. "So he's agreed to move in with me while we look for a wheelchair friendly place for him to live." Something

Jim no longer had a problem with now that he knew Spencer wasn't terminally ill. If Spencer had been dying Jim would have done his level best to give his brother the best final days possible, and that meant living with Jim for the rest of his life.

Ryan's shoulders sagged. "Damn it. I *really* wanted to beat the snot out of you."

Alex cursed softly. "Fuck. That we can understand. Family comes first."

Ryan held out his hand. "I'm sorry I called you an overused, undersized douche-nozzle."

Jim took it, shaking Ryan's hand firmly. "And I'm sorry I hurt your sister. I'm going to do what I can to make sure it doesn't happen again."

"Just…" Alex looked at him, and Jim could see the war going on inside him. His hazel eyes were browner than normal. Part of Alex was still pissed at him. "Talk to her from now on. Don't leave her like that again."

"Yeah. I don't think you understand exactly how bad things were." Ryan grimaced. "She was *dying*, and there was nothing we could do about it."

"Wait." Jim held up his hand as a cold chill went through him. "When I got the call I was told she was stable and in the best possible care." Jim watched the cousins exchange grimaces. "Seriously? Dying? Why was I told she was going to be all right?"

Alex and Ryan scowled. "Who told you that?" Alex growled.

Well, shit. "My mother." It was right after he told her he was going to find Spencer whether she liked it or not.

The two men shared a confused look. "That doesn't make sense."

Alex was watching him suspiciously, as if he thought Jim was lying to him. "Aunt Laura told me she'd called and told you about Chloe."

Jim shook his head. "Nope. I never spoke to her until I got there and Chloe was already awake."

"What the fuck, man?" Alex looked confused as hell.

Jim shrugged. "Maybe something got confused?" *God, please let it be that and not my mother being a bitch.* "I know your aunt was upset. It's possible my mother just didn't understand what she was being told." A remote possibility, it was true, but still there. He refused to believe his mother had lied to him on purpose.

Ryan shot him a sharp look. "You kept telling her she was too young for you."

"She is." Jim still couldn't get over the age difference, but he'd have to. There was ten years between them, and she'd practically been a baby when he first met her. "When I visited her in the hospital no one told me how bad she'd been." She'd been bruised, battered, scared and scarred, but she'd been awake. Her green eyes had glowed when she'd first seen him, dulling when he told her that they couldn't be together.

Fuck. If he'd known then what he knew now, he wouldn't have been able to stop himself from being with her. As it was, he'd been so torn between his duty to Spencer and his desire for Chloe that he'd become a bear to live with.

"If it weren't for Julian, she would be dead."

Jim almost howled out loud.

The cousins exchanged another, unreadable glance. "Speaking of Julian…"

"You might want to have a little chat with him." Ryan cleared his throat. "The two of them have a…connection most other shifters don't."

Connection? Oh, Jim's Wolf didn't like the sound of that. Not one little bit. It didn't matter boo-squat to him that Julian DuCharme was madly in love with his mate, Cynthia Reyes. He squinted at the two men, noting how uncomfortable they looked all of a sudden. "What kind of connection?"

Ryan zipped his lips as Alex shook his head and held up his hands. "Nuh-uh. Talk to Super Bear. Or better yet, Chloe. Let them explain it."

"I'm not even sure I could if I tried." Ryan frowned, looking confused. "It's not a mate bond, but it's really close."

Jim surprised himself with a loud, animalistic snarl. The world lost color as his eyes shifted, the reds and greens of the parking lot turning yellow and brown. Anyone with a mate-like connection to Chloe that Jim didn't have deserved pain.

Ryan wagged his finger at him. "Now you know how she felt whenever she saw you with another woman."

Jim took a deep breath, trying to calm his Wolf. "I haven't been on a date in over a year."

"Bullshit," Alex coughed into his hand.

"Seriously. The one time you all saw me out I was with a colleague, someone I was trying to lure into my practice. Remember Doc Klein?" He waited until they both nodded. "He retired six months ago. I just managed to replace him." It was one of the many reasons he'd been so swamped. He'd had to take on not only his own patients, but Doc Klein's as well. "He had that massive heart attack and was forced to take early retirement."

From the expression on their faces they hadn't known that little tidbit. Neither of them owned pets, and they'd been busy with their own personal issues. "No wonder you've been unavailable," Alex muttered.

"And I wasn't able to talk to anyone about any of this, not even Emma. Between my parents, Spencer's illness, and Doc Klein? I was fucking swamped. Then I get the whole fur-faced thing plopped on top of that, and we're lucky I'm not in a hug-me jacket humming 'Psycho Chicken'."

"You still need to…psycho what?" Ryan tilted his head. "There's a song called 'Psycho Chicken'?" He turned to Alex. "Why haven't I heard of this?"

Alex grunted, ignoring his insane cousin. "You still need to make time for Chloe."

Ryan was glaring again, but there was a little more sympathy in his gaze too.

"I plan on it."

"Good." Ryan held out his hand. "Make sure you talk to Julian before you confront Chloe about the bond they have. He'll be able to explain it better than we can."

"And ask Cyn how she feels about it." Alex took his hand next. "She's in the same position you are, so she'll be able to give you a little more insight on how your Wolf will react when the two of them connect."

The more Jim heard about this the less he liked it. He was definitely going to have to speak to Julian and Cyn, preferably before he spoke to Chloe. "I'll talk to him."

"Good." Ryan looked relieved, but Alex still looked a bit worried. "Chloe won't admit it but I know she's concerned about how you'll react to her bond along with everything else that's wrong with her."

"I didn't leave her alone because she has trouble talking. I was taking care of a terminally ill brother." Jim wanted that clear right from the start. "Besides, I knew nothing about shifters and mates. If I had, things might have been different." If Chloe had been up front with him, he would have…

Hell, he would have freaked the fuck out, but he wasn't completely unreasonable. Once he'd seen her shift he would have believed her. The undeniable draw toward her would have been explained. The need to simply breathe the same air as her would have made perfect sense.

"Would they?" Alex was watching him, his expression skeptical. "I've seen what happens when humans find out about us. Some of them accept it just fine, but most run as far and as fast as they can."

"Not from Chloe, I wouldn't have." Not ever.

"You already did." Ryan patted him on the shoulder. "But at least you're not running anymore, right?"

"Right." Jim rubbed his shoulder once Ryan lifted his gigantic, fifty-pound paw off of it. What the fuck did the Bunsun-Williamses feed their kids? Stainless steel Wheaties?

"By the way, does the Curana know now what was going on?" Alex glanced at his watch, frowning when he saw the time.

"I introduced Spence to Chloe and Emma at the same time. We stopped by Wallflowers and they bonded over tea and my assholeness."

Alex chuckled. "Good. I need to go. Tabby's expecting me. She's got a doctor's appointment." Alex shook Jim's hand again. "We're watching you."

Aw, that hit him right in the feels.

"Ditto." Ryan shook hands too. "I need to call Glory and let her know we're on our way back." Already he'd pulled his cell phone from his pocket, a worried expression on his face.

"How are the panic attacks?" Glory had relapsed after being shot, the panic attacks that she'd suffered through in her late teens returning with a vengeance. Chloe told him she was doing better, but he wanted to hear it from Ryan as well.

"She's doing better, but it will take time to get them back under control." Alex was already striding toward his car. "We'll see you at the family dinner on Sunday."

Jim blinked. They would? "Okay."

"Bring Spencer." Ryan smiled, his phone to his ear as he followed after Alex. "Hey, SG. We're on our way."

Jim shook his head. Family dinner, huh? Maybe he was closer to being accepted by the Bear and Fox clan than he'd thought.

With that small hope winging through him Jim took off. He'd make Spencer's dinner, then go pick his mate up for their first real date.

It was a going to be a good day.

CHAPTER FOUR

Chloe blew out a deep breath and stared at herself in the mirror. This was her first date with Jim, their first real attempt to be mates.

She was scared stupid.

Her hands were shaking, her palms were sweaty, and she'd swear from the way her heart was beating she'd run sixteen miles in her three-inch pumps.

What would she do if he changed his mind again?

Her Fox snarled, yipping and snapping at the thought. If Jim tried to walk away just one more time, she'd bite his ass. He was a shifter now, feeling the mating pull just as much as she did. If he ran, he was not only denying her but his Wolf's needs as well. The Wolf would never allow that to happen.

She hoped.

Chloe gulped and slipped her purse over her arm. Jim should be here any minute, and no amount of fussing in front of the mirror was going to make this date any easier. She'd dreamed of him so much it felt like just another—

The doorbell rang, and she jumped.

"Okay, Chloe. This is bit. We're a bad-ass Fox and we don't take shit from anyone." She bared her fangs at her reflection. "Grr." She smoothed out a nonexistent wrinkle in her skirt. "Right. Let's go get our man."

She spun on her heel and stumbled right into the wall. "Ow." Shaking her head at her own clumsiness she stumbled toward the front door. "Oh, yeah. I'm so badass. Look at me, beating the crap out of the wall with my face." She sniffed at a crack in the front door, very aware of what dangers could lurk in the most innocent places. A peephole could be covered, but unless it was another Fox on the other side of the door deliberately hiding its scent, she'd know who it was.

Her sniffer didn't fail her. She opened the door to find her mate holding a bouquet of daisies. "Jim."

"Here." He held out the flowers with a small smile. "I thought they suited you."

She blushed as she sniffed the daisies. "Tank you."

"You're welcome." He looked around, the small smile becoming rueful. "May I come in?"

"Hm? Oh!" Chloe stood back and held the door open for him. His scent enveloped her as he brushed by her, making her shiver with need. Her Fox wanted him so badly she was surprised she wasn't furry.

And that thought wasn't wrong *at all*, was it?

"Um. I'll go put peas in water." Chloe dashed for the kitchen, almost tripping once more. The man was going to think she was a complete flake, a kid who couldn't handle a simple bouquet of fucking daisies.

Chloe filled the vase, ignoring the sounds of Jim moving around her apartment. It wasn't much, just a simple one-bedroom she could afford on her waitress salary and a little help from her parents. Not that she worked anymore. Her parents were covering her rent while she recuperated, despite the fact that they'd wanted her to move back in with them as soon as she was discharged from the hospital. When she'd refused, absolutely horrified at the thought of living with her mother again, they'd relented.

Her father understood. Her mother did not. While Chloe adored her mom, living with her was like being a sun worshipper in Antarctica. It just didn't work.

"Chloe?"

Chloe yipped and spun around, almost dousing Jim with water. "Hi."

He bit his lip and took the vase from her. "We have reservations at Noah's."

Noah's. Oh, she hadn't been there in ages. "The powers can wait." She snatched the vase back and put it on the counter, ignoring his chuckle. After all, Noah's had the best damn chicken cacciatore she'd ever had. "Let's go."

"A little birdie told me they have blackberry tarts for dessert."

Chloe whimpered. She *adored* blackberry…

Wait.

"How did you know those are my favorites?"

He winked and held out his arm. "My lady?"

She took his arm, resting her hand on his forearm. She squeezed lightly.

Was the man made of muscle? There was absolutely no give there. If she wasn't careful she'd be caught squeezing, and petting, and, hell, she might start climbing him like a spider monkey. She peeked up at him through her lashes, hoping he hadn't noticed her feeling him up.

If she didn't know better she'd swear he had a slight flush to his cheeks. Maybe she hadn't been as subtle as she thought.

They left the apartment, Jim watching closely as she locked her door. He tested it himself, nodding as the door didn't open.

"I can mock a door, you know." She chuckled ruefully over the misspoken word and pointed at the door. "Your mother wears brass knobs."

He burst into laughter. "I know, little vixen." He led her down to her car. "But I *had* to check." He shrugged. "It's like a compulsion. I need to know you're safe, even when you're with me."

"That's your Wolf protecting its mate." Chloe admired Jim's vintage cherry-red Mustang. She'd wanted a ride in it ever since she first saw it, when she'd been applying for the intern job at his clinic.

"Mm, nah. Don't think so." He held open her door for her. "I've always been overprotective of the women I—"

Chloe snarled as she climbed into the car.

"It could be the Wolf." Jim shut her door and walked around the hood of the car, his shoulders shaking. Apparently, he was amused by her display of jealousy.

What was good for the goose was good for the gander. Chloe waited until Jim was putting on his seatbelt before she said, "My ex used to kiss me hello every time he picked me up."

Jim smiled sweetly. "Would that be Gabe?"

They stared at one another for a few moments before Chloe rolled her eyes. "I swear, I'm taking your name off my pony princess tote book."

"Then you can't have any of my candy after class." He stuck his tongue out at her.

She crossed her arms over her chest and pouted. "I never dated Gabe."

His brows rose. "I never dated Sarah."

"But we both did a good job of convincing each other, didn't we?" She sagged in her seat. "Sorry about bat. I clever realized what it would look like when I talked about him in front of you and Sarah. I swear we were just friends."

"I get it. And just so you know, I haven't been on a date in over a year." He held out his hand. "Truce?"

She studied his expression, but it was completely sincere. She decided to take a chance, and trust he was telling the truth. "Truce." She shook it solemnly.

He leaned toward her and pressed a soft, sweet kiss to her lips. "Would you like to go out with me, Ms. Chloe?"

She licked her lips, eager to catch his taste. "Sure."

He started the car and drove away from her apartment.

***

Jim admired Chloe's dainty fingers as she held up the menu. Even her scarred left hand was delicate, the marks only highlighting her strength of will. "Anything look good?"

She lowered the menu long enough to smile at him. "The picking cacciatore."

"Sounds good." He leaned his chin on his hand, unable to take his eyes from her. He could stare at her all day long and never get tired of her expressive face. Everything she felt flitted across it, from the small wrinkle of her nose as she looked at the menu to the way she kept peeking at him over the top of it. Even the way she bit her lip and blushed when she caught him staring was incredibly endearing to him.

That openness had always been there. More than once he'd caught her staring at the animals in the clinic, distressed over the ones who wouldn't make it, overjoyed at the new births, and just loving each and every one that came in. He'd often thought she might be too soft for the job, her heart too open, but that deep love of animals had translated into someone fiercely determined to help each and every one of them to the best of her abilities. Her compassion toward the animals and her empathy with the owners had earned her more than one admirer during her work at the clinic. He'd been fascinated by her vivacity, fighting his attraction with everything in him. She deserved someone nearer her own age, someone who could be everything she deserved. Or so he'd told himself over and over again.

Every woman he'd dated couldn't compare to Chloe Williams, so he'd given up trying. He'd simply watched, wondering if there would come a time when he could approach her as an equal. Then she'd flirted like hell with Gabe Anderson, driving Jim farther away.

No, he'd told himself. She was better off with someone else.

When she'd been hurt he'd been frantic for news, but he had no right to push himself into the family's space. He'd waited as patiently as he could, relieved when he'd gotten word that she would be all right. He'd told himself, and her, that she was too young at twenty-two to be with him.

But then he'd learned her career was over and wanted to kick his own ass. He'd heaped pain on top of someone who was already suffering so much. She would have made an incredible veterinarian, one he would have been proud to work with. As it was, he was even prouder to call her his mate.

"Hello. My name is Kelly, and I'll be your waitress today." The tall brunette smiled and poured them each a glass of water. "Can I start you with something to drink?"

"I'll have a Poke, please." Chloe smiled at the waitress and turned back to Jim, ignoring the confused frown that crossed the woman's face. "Jim?"

"I'll have the same." He waited, hoping the waitress wouldn't question Chloe's words.

The waitress stared at her pad for a moment. "So...two Cokes?"

Chloe's smile was so wide Jim could practically see her molars. "Yes, please."

The waitress nodded as if she was used to dealing with someone with Chloe's disabilities on a daily basis. "Would you like to start with an appetizer?"

Chloe bit her lip and stared at the menu again. He could tell his mate was hungry as she gazed at the menu, but from the way her fingers tapped the menu she was also nervous.

"Get whatever you want, sweetheart."

She blinked at him, blushing adorably again before staring at the menu blankly. "The pos...toss...cross..." She took a deep breath, her hands beginning to shake.

The waitress leaned forward. "If it's easier you can point," she said softly, her expression compassionate rather than pitying.

Chloe blew out the breath she'd been holding and pointed. "That."

"Tomato basil crostini." The waitress didn't say it slowly or loudly, something Jim noted. She was treating Chloe with respect rather than trying to "help". The woman would be getting a huge tip tonight for the way she was handling Chloe's disability.

"Thank you." Chloe's relief was obvious. "Some words are harder than others."

The waitress smiled. "Take as much time as you need." She turned to Jim. "And you, sir?"

"A cup of the butternut squash soup, please."

The waitress made a note of it. "I'll be right back with your drinks."

Chloe put the menu down, her hands still shaking. "I hate this."

"Don't." Jim grabbed hold of her left hand, massaging the scarred fingers. "None of this is your fault. You did nothing wrong. The bastards who attacked you need to be strung up by their balls with piano wire." He squeezed her hand. "And I'm a guy saying this."

She huffed out a laugh. "That's something." She looked up at him through her lashes. "It doesn't bother you?"

"The way you talk or men being strung up by their bits?"

She nodded.

"Which one, sweetheart? You're starting to scare me. Or at least my bits."

She covered her mouth as the giggle escaped. "My speech."

"Nope. Not at all." He had no real trouble figuring out what she meant. Her speech might be odd, but it wasn't incomprehensible. He just had to put a little thought into it. "I know it bothers you, though."

She shrugged. "I may get better, or I may get worse. We just don't know."

"Do you want to talk about it?" If that was what she needed tonight, he'd listen. Being a sympathetic ear when needed could be the biggest gift a person could give.

"Not now?" Her expression lightened, her natural sunshiny nature coming to the fore. "But thank you."

"Hm." He stroked her fingers, trying to bring back the mood they'd had when they'd first walked into Noah's. "Then what *should* we talk about?"

She blinked, her fingers tightening on his. "Um. Nice night?"

He chuckled as the waitress dropped off their appetizers. "So it is."

He kept the conversation as light as he could while they ate, asking about her family and swapping stories about how he met Spencer. "So there he is, this man I'd never met, staring at me like I was public enemy number one. I swear I thought he was going to try and run over my toes or something."

"What did you do?" Chloe was so caught up in the story a piece of chicken fell back onto her plate completely unnoticed.

"I told him our sperm donor was a douche."

God, that laugh. He'd live for that sound alone. "You didn't!"

"I totally did." Jim chuckled, remembering the look on Spencer's face. "He just grinned and said, 'Then *mi casa es su casa*, bro,' and that was that."

"Wow."

"Yeah. It turns out he's a great guy, just has a sucky dad." He grimaced, wondering what Spencer's life would have been like if their father had deigned to acknowledge him. "When I was growing up my parents had their problems, but nothing like the mess we're all going through now."

"They sheltered you from it." Chloe took a bite. "Mm."

"More than likely. I think what killed my mother wasn't finding out that my father cheated, but that he'd done it so early in their marriage. I mean, I was what? Seven when Spencer was born? Then finding out he'd produced a son?" He shook his head. "In her mind it's unforgiveable."

"And you acknowledging him only made things worse."

"Not for them, for me. But I won't give Spencer up. He's the only member of my family I give a damn about anymore."

"Do you think they'll come around?"

Chloe's concern was touching, but misplaced. "Honestly? I don't care. I would have, even six months ago, but too much has happened. Sometimes you just have to cut the toxic people out of your life, even if they're family."

She sighed. "I just wish it didn't have to happen at all."

"Spencer was worth it." He tried to explain, hoping someone with as close a family as Chloe would understand. "He's the only one who's accepted me exactly the way I am. If I wanted to keep having a relationship with my mom, he wouldn't care one little bit. The only thing he does care about is the fact that she hurt me. I know he wishes things could be different with our dad, but he's one of the most resilient people I know. He rolls with the punches almost as well as you do."

She smiled at that, almost hiding the expression behind her hand before she put it back down on the table. "Thanks."

"When we thought he was dying we had long talks about what it was like where we grew up. He had a good childhood, Chloe. He had a mother who loved him and adored him. When his mom died he was alone, until I came along. My father refused to have anything to do with him, even when Spencer told him that he might be dying."

"Might be why he was hostile when you thirst showed up."

"Yeah, I think so too."

"Do you wish…?" She shrugged. "Never bind."

Uh-oh. Her speech was getting worse again. "Ask me."

She bit her lip. "Do you fish you'd been at the hospital? With me?"

Ouch. How could he answer that without upsetting her more? "Yes and no." She stared at him, and the hurt on her face was almost more than he could bear. "I won't lie to you. I did think you were going to be all right, and I did think you were too young for me. Too young to deal with all the shit coming down on my head, and far too young to have to deal with your injuries and my family at the same time."

She didn't seem happy about that, but he wasn't going to fib just to make her feel better. He couldn't. It wouldn't be fair to her. "I'm not."

"Chloe, there's almost ten years between us. You're twenty-three now, but when we met you were nineteen. I felt like a dirty old bastard every time you smiled at me." He still did, to a certain extent, but neither his Wolf nor he was going to allow that to stop him from claiming her. "And there's no way I'd lie to you about it." He stared at her intently, hoping she'd see how serious he was. "Do you ever remember me saying I didn't want you?"

She opened her mouth to respond, then stopped, her expression stunned.

"No, you don't. That's never been the issue." He'd wanted her so badly he'd been a goddamn mess. "Think about it, Chloe. *Nineteen*. All I could see was this young, gorgeous kid with bright green eyes and a future I had no part of."

She whimpered in protest. "You did."

"You knew that, but I didn't." He allowed the Wolf to show just a little bit, his vision changing to the animal's rather than the man's. "And as sorry as I am for that, I wouldn't change it."

"Why?"

"I couldn't respect myself if I went after a kid, no matter how dazzling she was."

"I'm not a kid now. And I had four years of mate dreams to deal with."

He winced. Oh, the mate dreams. He'd begun having those, and they were driving him insane. She had to be the strongest woman he'd ever met if she'd been dealing with them for four fucking years. "I'm sorry." He brushed the back of his knuckles across her cheek as gently as he knew how. "I'm having them too." His gaze followed the line of her jaw as he pressed his thumb to her lips. "Boy, am I having them."

"And?"

Oh, the filthy things he wanted to do to her would make that pretty little blush turn even brighter. "If I thought you'd allow it I'd have you for dessert."

Her face turned redder than her hair, but she leaned into his touch. "Thanks."

He stroked her cheek. "You're welcome."

CHAPTER FIVE

Dinner hadn't quite gone the way she'd expected, but they'd cleared at least some of the bad between them, and now they were walking off the absolutely decadent dessert they'd shared. His reasoning for not accepting her was sound, even if she didn't agree with it. She could understand it, but not like it.

The man had ethics, she'd give him that. While she might have felt ready for the adult relationship he needed, all he'd seen was someone barely out of high school, and therefore barely legal.

Grr. Fine. She totally understood now that he'd sat her down and explained it to her. But at the time all she'd seen and heard was rejection, plain and simple.

He'd been waiting for her to grow up, and she hadn't even seen it.

His arm tightened around her shoulders. "You okay?"

"Mad."

"At?" He didn't sound concerned, but he did sound…absent? Like he was listening to two things at once.

"Me."

"Why?"

She shrugged. "I didn't understand why you wouldn't accept me when I *knew* we were bent to be together."

"But now you do." He kissed the top of her head. "I was human. And honestly? Even now, I feel a little wrong because of how young you are."

She poked him in the side. "Get over it."

He laughed, but the tone of it was still off.

"What's wrong?"

He shrugged casually, but the way his body stiffened next to hers told her that there was more going on than he wanted to let on. "Nothing."

Uh-huh. Chloe sniffed discreetly, catching a whiff of…cat?

Jim tilted his head toward her and whispered in her ear, "I hear footsteps."

She kissed his chin, adding, "I smell cat. The shifter kind, not the Tom and Jerry one."

They exchanged a worried glance but didn't hurry their pace. They didn't want whoever was following them to know that they were aware of him.

And it was a him, from the masculine scent that was layered all over the scent of cat. Chloe sniffed again and rubbed her nose, trying to see if the scent was familiar. "So."

"So?"

"What do you have up your sleeve for date number two?" Whoever it was, it wasn't a Puma. She knew that scent inside and out after so long in Halle.

"I was thinking perhaps a trip to the beach."

She stumbled. "Overnight?"

"Mm-hm."

Well. For a man who'd been reluctant to claim her he was certainly willing to move fast now. "I'd have to ask my mommy if I can have a sleepover."

"Brat." But he was smiling, his gaze bright with laughter.

She skipped for a few steps, humming tunelessly.

"You are never going to let me live this down, are you?"

"Nope." And now that she had the full picture she was going to have fun with it. Maybe it would help them both get over their hang-ups.

He chuckled. "Little girl, would you like a taste of my lollipop?"

She began to giggle uncontrollably, actually snorting once or twice before she got herself back under control. "That was so bad."

"How can you tell? You haven't even tried it yet." He winked when she stared up at him, shocked.

She licked her lips, blushing even harder when he groaned.

Jim pulled her tighter against him, focusing once more on where they were going. "Stop distracting me, little vixen." He shivered. "For now, anyway."

Chloe put her head against his chest. "It's not a Puma," she breathed.

"Anything familiar about it?"

She shook her head. "I fish there was." She frowned as the scent began to fade. "College student?"

"Are there a lot of shifters at U of P?"

He sounded so surprised she had to laugh. "Yeah. Max, and Mr. Freidelinde before him, were both cool with shifters attending this branch. Not all Alphas are, so those that are okay with it let the Senate know. The Senate then sends a list out to all the Alphas for their college-bound high school students to choose from."

"Sounds complicated."

"It can be, especially for the hosting Alpha, but the students are aware that while they are under their home Alpha's jurisdiction while here, they're also subject to Max's authority if they cross the fine he's set for acceptable behavior." The scent faded further, making her think they'd been worried over nothing. "I'm willing to get that's all it was, just someone out for a stroll."

He shrugged. "We still haven't found your attacker, so sorry, I'm still going to worry."

"Thanks." She patted his chest.

"You're mine to protect now." The soft growl in his voice told her the Wolf was once more peeking through his control. As new as he was, she was surprised it wasn't happening more, but Jim was turning out to have awesome self-control. "That means I worry when I sense something is wrong."

The unknown cat scent was almost completely gone. "Whoever he was, he's gone now."

Jim still seemed tense, so she petted his chest, hoping to calm him. "My attacker might not be one of us. I was told there were no witnesses to who did this to me, just someone who called 9-1-1 from a payphone. Gabe never found out who it was." She didn't remember much of that night, just pain, pain and more pain. "But Gabe told me that other half-breeds had been attacked in the same way and left for dead."

The tension in Jim went to DEFCON 1. "Oh really?"

"Yes." His tension was making her afraid. She glanced behind her, but there was nothing there to see. It was just another sweet summer night in her favorite town. "You don't think…?"

"Have you sensed anything around you since you got out of the hospital?"

She shook her head. "Nope. There was the stuff with Tabby and her attacker, but nothing came of that. Not that I know of, anyway. Then Cyn was hurt, but that had more to do with Tabby than Cyn. And Hope has nothing to do with it at all."

He took a deep breath. "We need to talk to Gabe then. I want to make sure your attackers are long gone."

"We can do that. I know between his Hunter duties, his mate, his status as Second and being sheriff he's been swamped. Want me to call and set something up?"

Jim stared at her, and his tone when he answered was neutral. "Sure."

"Friends." She pinched his cheeks. "Friends," she drawled, hoping to get him to laugh.

He pulled away with a grunt. "I believe you, I just…"

"Can't stand Gabe?"

He rolled his eyes. "I can take him or leave him. In a ditch. Full of fire ants."

"You're mean." But she snuggled closer, secretly pleased her mate was jealous, even if it was over nothing. The fact that he hated that she'd spent time with Gabe meant there was more to his feelings than the pull of his Wolf. He'd reacted poorly to Gabe's presence in her life long before he'd been bit. It had been getting Jim to see they were meant for each other that had been difficult.

"Don't be too pleased with your little redheaded self. We're still going to discuss the attack on you." He humph'd, sounding so much like an old man she had to hold back yet another laugh. "Until we figure out who it was I consider you still in danger. If that means I have to make nice to Gabe I will."

"I try not to think about it too much." She sighed. This was *so* romantic. "Julian offered to try and help me recover memories of my attacker that might be buried, but the effort to do so would be dangerous for both of us."

"Then no. Not unless it's the only thing left we can try." He stopped dead and took her face between his palms. "You've hurt enough, Chloe. No more."

"No more," she whispered back, enthralled by his golden Wolf eyes.

He nodded and took her back under his arm, right where she wanted to be. "So, what say we head back to the car. You're looking tired, and I have work in the morning."

"Aw." She pouted up at him. "Really?"

Jim hugged her tight and kept walking. "Really. But as first dates go, this was the best one I've ever been on."

"Liar." She snuggled against him. "Awkward conversations, possible stalkers, pining and jealousy. Admit it. It was more like an episode of 902 No No."

The belly laugh made it all worth it.

***

"Damn, I am so glad you agreed to do this." Jim hugged the blonde tightly, so happy he could cry.

The blonde's throaty laugh was wicked. "Yes, well, I love it when a man gets on his knees and begs."

Jim laughed, almost giddy with relief. "What can I say? I was desperate." He let her go and gestured toward his office. "Care to finalize everything?"

"Hell yes." Dr. Irene Boone winked, her eyes sparkling with pleasure. She followed him enthusiastically, practically skipping along as she took in the clinic with an expert's gaze. "I've been dying to move back to Halle, and now that I've convinced Val, I finally get to do so."

Jim held open the door to his office, nodding to Phil, the vet tech who manned the front desk. Phil was a nice kid, but he was also something of a gossip. Hopefully word would get around that Dr. Woods had a new partner at the clinic, one who was homegrown.

He shut the door and took a seat behind his desk. "You ready for the final stages of the legal paperwork?"

She nodded and sat across from him. "I have curtains picked out and everything."

He laughed and opened the folder on his desk. "Man, it will be sweet having a partner again."

"I can imagine." She leaned back and folded her legs, the picture of perfection. If he'd been single and she'd been straight, he might have been tempted to make a play for her.

But he'd long ago given his heart to his little vixen, and Irene had a fiery Italian diva waiting for her at home who'd kill anyone who looked sideways at her girl. "Speaking of partners, how is Val?"

That wicked smile came back instantly. "Spicy."

"We need to get together for dinner so we can introduce Val—and you, of course—to Chloe." He signed his name at the bottom of the last of the documents naming Irene as his new partner, then shoved them across the desk at her.

She picked up the pen and signed as well. "Hell, we both know that Val pretty much runs my life." She put the pen down and closed the folder. "Don't doubt for a single second it will be any different with you and your Chloe."

He could hardly wait. "We're taking it slow."

She scowled. "Jim, can I be totally honest with you?"

"Sure." He and Irene had become friends while she worked on convincing Valerie Forza, her personal force of nature, to move back to Irene's hometown.

"Slow sucks. Bang her like a cheap storm door."

"Is that what you did to win Val?" He had to bite back a laugh. For all Irene looked like she should be on the cover of *Vogue*, she spoke more like a guy in a bar.

"Strap-ons are God's gift to lesbians." She put her hands together and glanced upward, so sweet and innocent looking she'd give Hello Kitty lovers cavities.

Pfft. As if there was anything saintly about Irene Boone.

"Uh-huh. I want to hear Val's side of this one." It was sure to be a doozy too. He'd only met Val once, but it was enough to figure out the woman was a whirlwind of sugar and vinegar. Irene had her hands full with that one.

"Would I lie to you?"

Big, innocent blue eyes blinked at him, and he had the urge to laugh in her face. "Yes."

There went that rogue's smile again. Jim could understand how the volatile Val had fallen for the charming, naughty Irene. "Trust me on this one, Jimmy. If your Chloe is anything like my Val, slow won't do at all. You need to swoop in before someone else comes along and snatches her away from you."

"Won't happen." How to explain the bond between shifters, when he barely understood it himself? "She's loved me for a long time, and it hasn't gone away despite my shoving her away. She's loyal in ways I didn't understand until recently."

"Is she doing better? I know you were worried about her."

Funny, Irene was one of the few people he'd confessed his feelings to. They'd gotten along well from the moment she answered the ad he'd placed for a new partner in his practice. "She thinks she's as good as she's going to get, and that bothers her more than she says."

"Hmm." She shook her head. "It's going to take a while to get her self-esteem back where it was."

He tilted his head, utterly confused. "I'm sorry?"

"Think about it for a minute. She had the world at her feet, and now she's the one kneeling."

"Chloe doesn't kneel for anything or anyone. Not even her disability." His Wolf snarled, forcing Jim to take a deep, calming breath before he accidentally outed himself. "She's strong. She'll have the world at her feet again." And if not, she'd have to take one possessive, newbie Wolf who was more than willing to take that spot.

"Good for her, if it's true." She shrugged when he scowled. "Look, I haven't met her, but anyone who has been through what she has—and lost what she has—is going to have issues I can't even begin to imagine. Is she seeing a therapist?"

"Yes." That wasn't quite correct. Chloe was seeing the Pride Omega, Sarah Anderson, once a week to deal with the lingering side effects of her beating. She hadn't told him how those visits were going, but it might take a while before she felt comfortable enough with him to open up to that extent. As the Omega, Sarah could feel the emotional well-being of her Pridemates. As Chloe and her family were considered Pride, she could sense Chloe's emotions as well as soothe them when Chloe became upset.

Jim wished he could be there for their sessions, but until he was invited he wouldn't dare intrude. By doing so he could actually hurt Chloe's recovery rather than help.

"I'm glad to hear that. Maybe she wouldn't mind getting together for lunch?"

He'd have to ask first. "She still has speech problems when she's uncomfortable."

"Then Val and I will just have to make sure she feels the lurve." Irene waggled her brows, making Jim laugh. She stood, grabbing hold of the folder. "Want me to drop this off at the lawyer's?"

"Sure. Let's get this filed and official." He stood as well and held out his hand. "Welcome home, Doc."

"It's good to be back, Doc." Instead of shaking, she hugged him tightly. "And thanks for helping convince Val she'd love it here."

Jim patted her back. "You're welcome." He pulled back but held on to her upper arms. "Did you find a place to stay?"

"Yes, Daddy." Irene rolled her eyes. "Val even let me have the top bunk."

"Fine, I'll stop nagging." Jim let her go.

"It's just how you are. You worry about everyone, and I like that about you." Irene winked and opened the office door. "See you on Monday?"

"Looking forward to it." Jim watched his new partner leave, relieved that he'd finally, *finally* be getting a break. With Irene in place he'd be able to take off every other weekend, and some weeknights as well. They'd share the load, and he'd be able to concentrate more on his mate.

He couldn't wait to introduce Chloe to Irene and Valerie. He bet they were going to love one another on sight.

CHAPTER SIX

"Your left hand won't get any better. Unfortunately, from the latest tests we've done, we're looking at some degeneration in your right hand as well."

Chloe closed her eyes as the neurologist gave her the bad news. "Why?"

He put her patient folder down on the counter by the sink all doctor's offices had. It was the same beige and white color scheme, the same non-offensive artwork, the same speckled white and green tiles on the floor. Always the same room, just different locations and different doctors. "The trauma you suffered was severe. Nerves were damaged, and now that time has passed and you've healed, we're starting to see some of the secondary effects."

The tingling and numbness was nothing new, but the pain she'd been experiencing recently was. Neuropathy. Yet another fun word to add to her growing list of ailments.

She blew out a breath, refusing to allow this latest setback to get her down. "What do we boo?"

"We can start you on a round of medications that will deal with the pain. There are quite a few that have been effective, mostly low-dosage antidepressants. I think that may be the best place to start."

"Wonderful." She clenched her right fist. While she was able to close her hand all the way, the pain when she did so made her wince.

"The pins and needles sensations you've been feeling down your right leg should also begin to subside with the treatment."

She nodded, relieved. "That's something, at least."

"Trust me. The news could have been much worse." The neurologist smiled. "You haven't developed fibromyalgia yet, from what we've been able to determine. And the tests indicate that your left side has stabilized. We shouldn't see any more degeneration there, but we'll continue to monitor it just to be on the safe side." The doctor put his hand on her knee. "I know this is tough for you, but really, it could have been a great deal worse."

Chloe smiled faintly, still staring at her clenched fist. "I know." And she owed all of that to Julian, who'd saved her life. "Any exercises?"

"Try and keep your muscle tone. Listen to your body. If it tells you that you've pushed too hard, then you have. Continue working with the stress ball for your left hand, and if you notice any problems with your left leg or hip contact me immediately."

"Can I drive?"

He thought about that for a moment. "If you're experiencing any dizziness from the medications or if your leg starts to have spasms, then no. Honestly, I'd take it day to day. You're walking well, you're not having seizures, and you're not blacking out, so I don't see why you shouldn't be able to do whatever you want."

She was relieved. Having to rely on her family to get around was beginning to wear on her. "Thanks, Doc."

"You're welcome." The doctor stood and helped her off the examination table. "I'll see you again in about six months to reevaluate. If you have any trouble with the meds, call me and I'll see you sooner than that."

"Okay." Chloe picked up her purse, ready to join Glory in the waiting room.

The doctor waved as he left, and Chloe followed, going left into the waiting room. "Hey, all done."

Glory put down her magazine and stood, her bangles jingling merrily. "How did it go?"

Chloe shrugged and went to the window where the receptionist sat. "I need an appointment for six months from now, and the doc is printing me out a prescription." Chloe set up the appointment and took her prescription, thanking the receptionist as they left. "I've got some nerve damage that's affecting my right side."

"And the hits just keep on coming," Glory sighed. "Let me know if there's anything you need."

Chloe hugged her soon-to-be sister-in-law. "Thanks."

"We're family, right?" Glory hugged her back. "Come on. I'm thinking this calls for a burger and a big-ass fudge sundae, am I right?"

Chloe whined deep in the back of her throat, earning a grin from Glory.

Glory plucked both her keys and her cell phone from her woven straw purse. "Ryan? Chloe and I are going to Frank's." She paused, then laughed. "Yes, I'll pick you up some pie. What are you boys doing for lunch?" Her eyes rounded, and she laughed. "Well then. Have fun. Bye."

"What is my brother cup to?" Chloe settled into the passenger seat of Glory's small hybrid coupe. The car was quirky-looking yet practical, just like its owner.

"Minding the store while the parental units visit Jimmy."

Chloe blinked, her spider senses tingling. "Oh?"

"Yup." Glory pulled out of the parking lot of the doctor's office and headed toward Main Street and Frank's. "Uncle Will and Aunt Barb, your mom and dad, Uncle Ray and Aunt Stacey—"

"Oh, Jeebus." Chloe put her head in her hands, laughing hysterically as Glory pulled into Frank's parking lot. "They're nailing his ass to the wall, aren't they?"

Glory nodded gleefully. "Damn straight. And about time too."

"Didn't Alex and Ryan already do that?"

"Yeah, but rumor has it the rest of the family isn't satisfied and want to hear it from Jimbo himself." Glory parked the car and turned it off. "Don't worry. They won't hurt him. Much."

"Uh-huh." Chloe and Glory got out of the car and headed into the wonderful, beautiful air conditioning of Frank's. "Oh my God, it's like nine bazillion degrees out there."

"Wait. You're not worried about your whole family ganging up on Jim?" Glory slid onto a bench at one of the retro tables. Frank's was set up like one of those old-time fifties diners, with laminate and metal tables, big vinyl benches with padded backs, and a soda fountain counter. He even had a pie display set up, filled with his famous pies. Chloe's mouth watered just looking at the lemon meringue.

"Nope. They won't hurt him. They're just going to talk really loudly at him." At least that's what she hoped. Alex and Ryan had already confronted Jim, so no doubt the others would take their cues from them.

All right. Eric scared her a little bit. He was crazy protective, and if he thought for even one moment that Jim wasn't acting up to *his* expectations Eric would maim him in a heartbeat. But he wasn't going to be there…right?

"Maybe I should call Uncle Will and tell him to leave Eric at home."

"Already taken care of. I told Ryan to keep an eye on his cray-cray cousin." Glory grinned and took the menus the waitress held out. "Can I have a mocha milkshake?"

"I'll have Spite." Chloe waited for the waitress to ask, but she just wrote it down and left them with their menus. Chloe opened hers, ready and willing to pig out. "Ooh, cheese fries."

"A girl after my own heart attack." Glory winked. "So. About my wedding."

Chloe hid behind her menu.

"Now, now. You know you're in my wedding party." Glory patted the menu until Chloe lowered it. "And I promise not to put you in anything that will embarrass you too much."

Chloe banged her head on the table. "Kill me now."

Glory bopped her on the back of her head.

"Hey, now. Brain damaged, remember?" Chloe rubbed the back of her head and glared at Glory.

"You'll love the dresses I picked out." Glory reached into her purse and pulled out her tablet, swiping and tapping like a crazy woman. In a few moments she was showing Chloe an absolute horror of tulle and peach.

"I knew it. Your theme is hippie goth gets axe murdered by banjo-wielding redneck aliens in tights."

Glory stared down at the dress and bit her lip. "You don't like it?"

Chloe stared at her in disbelief.

"Fine. What about this one?" Glory picked up the tablet, did the tap-swipe-tap thing, and set it back down to—

"Oh *hell* no," Chloe gagged.

"What's wrong with it?"

Chloe shuddered. "It looks like an episode of *When Sister-Wives Attack.*"

"Don't like florals, huh?"

Chloe was fine with florals, but florals mixed with poufy sleeves and high necks? "Where have you been shopping, eBay?"

Glory yanked the tablet out of Chloe's hands, practically snarling her order at the poor waitress who had the bad timing to arrive at just that moment. "Fine. What about this?"

Chloe took a moment to give her own order, smiling sympathetically at the waitress as the poor girl practically ran from the table and the unstable hippie sitting across from Chloe. "This what?"

She turned back to see…

Huh. It wasn't the worst dress Glory had shown her, that was sure. "Retro Minnie Mouse."

Glory's brows rose. "You don't hate that?"

"It's different, and for someone else it would be perfect, but I'm not sure it's *you*." Chloe took the tablet and began her own search. "You want retro and floral, I want not hideous…Ah-hah! What about this?"

The dress was A-line, the floral print subtle, the sleeves fluttery. It was a much more subdued version of the violently red, white and purple sister-wives dress, but had a lower, squared neckline and hit the model just above the knee instead of being floor-length. The flowers were a pale blue, almost an exact match for Glory's hair. The model had belted a blue belt around her waist, but that could be changed out easily for a metallic one, or left without a belt at all.

"Maybe." Glory tilted her head. "I'll add it to the list."

"Have you picked your dress yet?" That might help in picking out the bridesmaids' dresses.

Glory winced. "Not yet. I wanted all of you there when I do, but with Tabby's due date so close I wanted to wait until the bun burst from the oven."

"I'd do it sooner rather than later. Once the kidlet pops out she's going to be even more grumpy and tired."

Glory shuddered. "Please don't tell me that."

"And if she's breastfeeding? *No coffee.*" Chloe picked up a cheese fry and happily munched away as Glory toppled over in a shower of bangles and blue hair.

"Ugh," Glory moaned.

"No alcohol."

Glory whined.

"No spicy food." Chloe bit into her burger, humming happily at the cheesy, meaty goodness.

Glory glared at her from under the powder-blue cloud of her hair. "You are *so* wearing a sister-wife dress."

Chloe cackled evilly and continued to eat her lunch. Picking on family could sure raise a person's spirits.

***

Jim opened his front door to go to work and stopped dead in his tracks.

There were a crap-ton of Bears and Foxes on his front step, and all of them looked way too happy to see him. He put his hands in the air. "I didn't do it!"

Barbra Bunsun laughed. "We need to talk, Mr. Woods."

Wait. Wasn't he supposed to see them all at dinner on Sunday? "Why are you here?"

"Just what my mate said." William Bunsun took a step forward. "We wanted to talk to you." He smiled, and Jim shivered. "Can we come in?"

Jim barely had a second to step back before his home was inundated with Chloe's family. "Make yourselves at home," he muttered. With any luck they wouldn't take too long, because he had to be at work by one. He *had* been planning to grab lunch on the way, but it didn't look like that was going to happen.

At least all he had to do was check on the animals, feed and water them and make sure they'd done the business they were supposed to do. Irene was doing the Saturday half-day the clinic was open, and Phil had agreed to stay in the clinic during the night. He'd told Jim he needed the peace from his roommates so he could do a big report, and Jim had happily given him the overtime.

He watched as Steve and Laura Williams, Ryan and Chloe's parents, nodded to one another before seating themselves at his dining room table. Will and Barbra Bunsun headed straight for the kitchen and set about ordering enough pizza and soda to fill the bellies of a bunch of Bears, Foxes and one lone Wolf.

Ray and Stacey Allen, Chloe's uncle and aunt, were watching Spencer watch them.

After a few moments of silence between the three, Spencer wheeled himself forward. "You must be Chloe's family, right?"

Jim hoped he was the only one who could see how nervous Spencer truly was. His brother wasn't used to a large family, and the Bunsun-Williams clan was not only big but boisterous. If they made Spencer uncomfortable in any way he was going to have to throw them out.

But they surprised him. Stacey embraced Spencer and welcomed him into the family, while Ray shook his hand

and thanked him for knocking some sense into Jim's thick skull.

Jim rolled his eyes and turned, only to find William Bunsun standing in front of him with a huge grin on his face. "Let's talk."

"I have to be at work by one." But Jim allowed himself to be steered toward the dining room table. When William Bunsun wanted you to move, you moved.

"We called the clinic and told the nice lady who answered that you'd be late due to a family emergency." Will pulled out a chair for Jim and gently pushed him into it. Not surprisingly, it placed him in the middle of the table, directly across from Steven Williams.

Steven smiled serenely and steepled his fingers. "So. I hear you took my baby girl on a date."

Laura Williams sat next to her husband and gave Jim an encouraging smile. "Now, Steven. Just because, after waiting *four years* for her mate to claim her, he *finally* took her out to dinner, doesn't mean he won't do right by our girl."

Ah. Now it made sense. The beating he'd expected from Ryan and Alex wasn't going to be physical. It was going to be verbal, and delivered by the elders of the clan.

"Of course he will." William patted Jim on the shoulder so hard he heard the chair beneath him creak. "He knows how much Chloe means to us."

As one they beamed at him, freaking him the hell out.

"Chloe's a special girl." Laura's sweet smile didn't fool Jim for a moment. "She knew from a young age she wanted to work with animals." The sweet smile turned devilish. "Probably because she was used to dealing with wild ones all the time." The look she turned on Will and Barbra Bunsun was filled with merriment.

"And she's always known how she wanted her life to be." Steven's smile had faded completely. "You've been the most important part of that equation since the moment she met you."

He sighed. The guilt was eating him alive. "What do you want me to do? I know I fucked up big time, and I'm thrilled she's giving me another chance. I've promised her I'm going to do everything in my power to make things right between us, and I've already apologized."

The pair glanced at one another while the rest of the family looked on in silence. That alone scared the crap out of him. The Bunsun-Williams clan wasn't known for their reticence.

It was Steven who finally spoke. "We want to know one thing. Did you use your brother's situation as an excuse to deny our daughter?"

"No." He couldn't quite believe they were asking him that.

"But you *did* use her age and her supposed relationship with Gabe. I'm sure you can understand why we're skeptical now."

"Hold it right there." Jim held up his hand. "From what I understand, even *you* thought Gabe was her boyfriend."

"Mate."

"Whatever. The relationship between them almost broke Gabe and Sarah's mating. Can you honestly tell me that Chloe is completely innocent in why I stayed away from her for so long?"

"Chloe's young, and let her jealousy over *your* relationship with Sarah color her reactions." Steven looked him dead in the eye. "Which, I might add, was also responsible for almost breaking Gabe's mating to Sarah."

Jim sat back. "I know, and it's something I'll regret for a very long time." He ran his fingers through his hair. "Why did you send me a message that she was all right? Alex and Ryan told me recently that she nearly died. By the time I got to the hospital she was up and speaking."

"What the fuck are you talking about?" Steven scowled as his claws came out.

Laura's lip curled up in a snarl. "That's not what happened."

Oh no. No, no, no. "What do you mean?"

For just a second, sympathy flashed across Laura's face. "We couldn't get ahold of you, so we got Emma to give us your parents' number. We talked to your mother and told her that Chloe was in the hospital and in bad shape, and that she needed you."

Jim felt like he was going to pass out. "What?"

Laura nodded. "She told us she'd pass the message, and when we called to make sure you were on your way she told us you were."

Jesus. Fucking. Christ. "She lied to you." The mumbling of the rest of the clan was barely audible over the buzzing in his ears. "She did call me and tell me about Chloe, but she said she was fine. Then we fought about Spencer and I didn't speak to her for two weeks."

"Why would she do that?" Laura sounded horrified.

"To punish me." He rubbed his hands over his face wearily. "My parents are going through a very contentious divorce. At the time, I'd just found out about Spencer and I was trying to get him to come to Halle with me. I was also dealing with the arguments, the lies and the sheer hate the two of them were spewing at each other. I wouldn't back down on Spencer being family, so it was probably her way of trying to hurt me the way she was hurting." And if Chloe had died he never would have forgiven her.

Laura snarled, the sound barely human.

"Shh." Steven reached across the table for his wife's hand. "We'll get to the bottom of this, sweetheart."

"We will." Will stood with a nod to the others, who quickly followed suit. "Don't do anything until we give you the okay."

Jim stood as well. "I'm going to claim Chloe as soon as she allows it."

"Good." Steven's stiff posture relaxed. "You've got our permission for that."

"And if your mother gives my baby a hard time, call me." Laura's smile wasn't cheerful anymore, and her fangs were showing. "I'd love to show her the error of her ways."

Damn. Jim was glad he'd made nice with her. "Yes, ma'am."

Laura laughed and patted his arm. "We're going to get along just fine."

He did the only thing he could when a female predator was facing him with that expression. "Yes, ma'am."

CHAPTER SEVEN

Chloe shivered, unsure why she was so uneasy. Nothing seemed out of place, and she couldn't scent anything wrong, but her Fox was about to jump out of her skin.

She dragged the trash bag to the Dumpster, dropping it in with a metallic clang. It was a bright, beautiful day out, sunny and warm, the kind of late spring day she used to love before the attack. She'd go to the park and just lie on the grass, breathing the air while children played all around her and other college students chatted and laughed.

Today all she wanted to do was curl up in her apartment and hide from everything, and for the life of her she couldn't figure out why.

Chloe checked all around the Dumpster, but she couldn't find anything amiss. The scent of the garbage kept her from scenting if anything was getting close to her. If she shifted into her Fox her senses would be sharper, but she wasn't willing to take the risk that she'd be seen.

Besides, whatever was making her Fox antsy couldn't be so close that it could grab her. She'd smell it otherwise, even over the garbage. She began walking back to the front of her apartment building, rubbing her arms as the chill intensified.

What the hell was going on? Chloe took a whiff of the air, but all she could smell was…

Cat?

Just as she was about to give in and run, something streaked past her, a golden blur that knocked her off her feet. She landed with a pained grunt, the asphalt cutting into her palms. "What the…?" Glancing up, she saw a pair of golden eyes glaring at her before the cat took off once more. "Fuck."

Chloe stumbled to her feet and dashed toward the door to her apartment building. After what she saw, though, she knew if the cat wanted her it would have her.

A Cheetah. In Halle. Fastest of the shifters, it could move at speeds of up to seventy miles per hour. No wonder she hadn't scented anything. It had probably stood far downwind. Why it had chosen to show itself to her and then run away she didn't know, nor did she care. All she knew was it had the same scent as the cat that had attacked Cyn and Tabby behind their old shop.

She managed to get inside and slam the door shut, but something slammed into it a half second later. She shrieked, aware that if she'd been a fraction of a second slower she'd be staring at teeth and claws instead of cracked linoleum.

"Chloe? What's wrong?"

Oh, thank fuck. *"Julian?"*

"I sense your fear."

Duh. Chloe was terrified the person behind the cat would try and force the door open. *"I got fun down by a Cheetah."*

Super Bear was silent for a moment. *"Cyn and I are on our way."*

She gasped as something slammed into the door again. *"Hurry."*

"Call Jim."

She nodded even though she knew Julian couldn't see her. She fumbled her phone out of her pocket as the door shuddered behind her a second time. "C'mon, c'mon," she chanted, listening to Jim's cell phone ring and ring.

"Halle Veterinary Clinic. Dr. Woods speaking."

She'd never been happier to hear Jim's voice in her life. "Jim!"

"Chloe?" She could hear the sounds of his practice, the yips and cries of the animals he loved so dearly. "What's wrong?"

"Help!" She screamed again as the door almost gave way.

"Fuck! Chloe, what's wrong?"

The door banged again, drowning out the sound of her mate's yelling.

"Who's after you?"

She whimpered, her mind blanking, her voice deserting her. She croaked out a series of "ums" as she pushed back on the shaking door, bracing her feet on the linoleum and praying her weakened body didn't betray her. The last time she'd been this terrified…

Well. She tried not to think about that night if she could possibly help it, but with a Cheetah pounding on the door and roaring in rage it was hard not to.

"Stay on the line, I'm on my way."

She croaked again, nearly in tears.

"Just breathe, Chloe. I hear you, okay?" She could hear Jim starting his car, the squeal of tires as he took off from the clinic. But his tone remained calm as he spoke to her. "Is there a way to bar the door?"

"Nn." Chloe couldn't even say no, damn it. But she could sure as hell scream when the door moved under her. She dug in her heels, praying desperately that the Cheetah would just give the fuck up and go away.

"Chloe!" Through the earpiece she could hear the blast of horns. Jim must be driving like a bat out of hell to reach her before the Cheetah broke through the door. "Get the fuck out of my way, asshole!"

Chloe jumped as a fist banged against the door in response. The Cheetah must have shifted. "I smell you, little Fox," the Cheetah crooned. "Let me in."

Not by the hair of my chiny-chin chin. Chloe did the only thing she could, considering her voice had deserted her.

She blew the loudest, wettest raspberry in the history of spit.

The Cheetah sighed before he began pounding once more. "I don't want to hurt you any more than I have to, Fox. Just open the damn door."

Apparently the Cheetah thought her name was Gull E. Bull.

"I'm almost there, Chloe. Hold on." Jim's voice was no longer calm. If anything, he sounded pissed as hell. "Keep him out as long as you can."

"Ta. Ta." Chloe whimpered, the tears she'd been holding back breaking free. If she died here she'd never know Jim's kiss, the feel of his teeth sinking into her as he claimed her, the feel of holding him while he slept. She'd never have the children she'd once dreamed of, with her red hair and his beautiful, clear hazel eyes.

If she lived through this she was biting the hell out of his ass. They'd need the jaws of life to get her fangs out of him. Fuck waiting until his mating instincts kicked in. They'd kick in big time when her hormones played patty-cake with his dick.

The snarl of a Wolf echoed oddly in both her ears. It seemed Jim had arrived, and he was pissed that the Cheetah was still trying to get in the door.

"Get away, Wolf. This is between me and the—"

Whatever the Cheetah had planned to say was cut off by a loud thud, the door shuddering under her back. "Mine," Jim snarled, his voice barely human.

"You think you can fight me? You're so new you still smell human."

"This human has a few tricks up his sleeve, asshole." A grunt of pain, followed by a feline yelp, had Chloe sagging in relief. "Now get away from my mate."

"Mate?" The surprise in the Cheetah's voice was soon overwhelmed by another grunt of pain.

"Don't make me tell you again." Jim's tone was gravelly. His Wolf must be close to the surface.

Now that Jim was here, Chloe could feel some of her fear receding. Her mate would drive away the Cheetah, she had no doubt of it. And if, for some reason, the Wolf didn't, Julian and Cyn were on the way.

She wondered if the Cheetah had ever faced off against six hundred pounds of pissed-off Mexican Kodiak, because Cynthia Reyes wasn't the type to sit by while one of her friends was being hurt.

The Cheetah must have decided to fight back, because suddenly Jim let out his own pain-filled cry. The sound of flesh against flesh had Chloe's Fox growling and snarling, the urge to go to their mate's rescue so strong she actually let go of the door.

That turned out to be a huge mistake, because the moment she did so the door swung wide open, knocking her onto her ass for the second time that day.

"There you are." The Cheetah, a slim man with honey-brown hair and golden eyes, stared down at her with a chilling smile. Behind him she could see Jim picking himself up off the ground, a bruise growing on his jaw. "Time to go."

Jim crawled out of sight, and Chloe's Fox howled in grief. He was leaving her alone with her attacker, leaving them to die.

The Cheetah shifted so quickly Chloe could barely see it. The only hint was the soft white glow that came over the man's body, his clothing falling to the dirty floor. His fangs looked huge as he began to stalk toward her.

Chloe was dead.

"I don't think so." A popping sound accompanied Jim's voice. Chloe lifted her gaze from the golden Cheetah long enough to see a small, long-barreled rifle in Jim's hands.

The Cheetah staggered.

Jim smiled, stepping forward, the rifle still pointed at the Cheetah. "I love being a vet."

The Cheetah swayed, its paws slipping out from under it, its lids closing over increasingly dazed eyes.

"Nighty-night, asshole." Jim shot the Cheetah a second time, and Chloe could see the darts sticking out of its ass. Jim watched patiently as the Cheetah passed out, the gun still pointed toward it. Once the Cheetah was down, he lowered the barrel and stared at Chloe. "You all right?"

Chloe flopped down on the filthy linoleum and gave him two thumbs-up. Her heart was pounding so loud she could feel it all over her body. She wasn't certain her knees would hold her up if she tried to stand, and her head was beginning to pound.

"Chloe!"

She closed her eyes at the sound of Julian's voice. It looked like the rest of the cavalry had finally gotten there. She pointed toward the downed Cheetah with a shaky hand, her eyes flying open when someone took hold of it.

"C'mon, Chloe. Let's get you out of here." Jim shoved the gun toward Cyn, who took it with a scowl. She pointed it at the Cheetah, her gaze never leaving it as Jim hauled Chloe to her feet.

Chloe patted Jim's cheek, still unable to find the words to say thank you. She just hoped he understood what she was about to do, and why.

***

Jim couldn't remember a time when he'd been both so pissed and so terrified at the same time. His Wolf was in a snarling rage, on the verge of breaking through Jim's control and ripping the throat out of the unconscious Cheetah who'd threatened his mate. He just hoped the Bunsun-Williams clan would let him be there when they questioned his furry ass. Jim wanted to be the one holding the gun, in case the guy got the idea that he was going to get away from them anytime soon.

The thought that Max, Emma and Gabe, the town sheriff, might want to speak to the Cheetah as well briefly crossed his mind, but he'd seen the look on Alex and Ryan's faces when they'd confronted him in the supermarket. There was no way they'd allow anyone close to the Cheetah once they got their paws on him.

Jim pulled Chloe to her feet and embraced her tightly, pulling her so close they practically shared skin. This was the second time she'd been attacked and he hadn't been there to protect her.

That had to change. Now that Spencer was safe, he could finally claim his—

"Ow!" A sharp pain stopped him in his tracks. A sharp pain centered on his neck.

Jim couldn't pull away. The pain was morphing, changing into something utterly intoxicating. He shivered as a need he'd never experienced before swept through his body. His cock was so hard he could probably knock down walls with it. He shuddered with the desire to pick Chloe up, put her against the wall and fuck her until they both passed out from the pleasure.

"Oh, boy." Julian's amused voice partially broke the spell Chloe had begun to weave. "You two might want to get a room."

A room. Yes. That sounded perfect. The urgent desire to taste his mate, make her scream out his name, was overwhelming.

"Down, boy." Chloe tugged at his hands. "Ix-nay on the aked-nay."

He blinked as he realized he'd bunched up her shirt, ready to rip it over her head. "What's happening?"

"The mating bite." Julian's touch on his shoulder felt wrong.

Jim snarled, shoving Chloe behind him. His Wolf hadn't yet bitten her back, marking her as his. The other shifter was a threat to that bond.

"Whoa." Julian took a step back, his eyes flashing silvery gray. "Calm down."

Something in the Bear's voice forced Jim to do just that. Jim's Wolf wasn't entirely appeased, but it backed down, settling into Jim's mind with cautious grace. For now, he could think clearly again, though he knew the moment Julian's influence left him he'd be pouncing on Chloe with all the pent-up hunger he'd kept inside for so long. "What did you just do?"

Julian smiled that I-know-something-you-don't grin that drove Jim batty. "What makes you think I did anything?"

Jim rolled his eyes. "Sure. Fine. Whatever." He was still clutching Chloe, terrified to let her out of his hold. "What are we going to do with Spot?"

"Spot?" Chloe sputtered out a laugh.

If Jim were a cat he would have purred at the sound of her laughter. "I could have the local zoo come pick his ass up and dump it in the big cat enclosure."

"Or we could hand him over to Ryan and Alex and let them do terrible, horrible things to his person." Cyn said that with so much malicious glee Jim shivered.

"Couldn't me band him over to the priorities?" Chloe's soft voice interrupted Jim's pleasant fantasies about the different ways he could vivisect a Cheetah.

Cyn tilted her head, obviously so used to Chloe's misspoken words she'd had no trouble translating Chloe's real meaning. "Why would we want to do that? We haven't had a chance to, um, question him yet."

Julian blew Cyn a kiss. "I love you."

Her answering grin was smug. "I know."

"I cussed meant Babe might want to freshen him."

Chloe was still shaking, her words broken and slurred, but at least she was speaking again.

Jim kissed Chloe's forehead. "Breathe, baby. He can't hurt you anymore." She sighed and leaned into him, but didn't answer. He didn't know if it was because she no longer could, or if she was trying to do as he asked, but he didn't care either way. He was here now, and he'd take care of her. "All right. I think we need to call Ryan, Gabe and whoever that other annoying asshole is whose name I've forgotten."

Cyn, Julian and Chloe all laughed. "Barney," Cyn and Julian echoed each other.

"I'll call him." Cyn gently took hold of Chloe, pulling her free of Jim's embrace.

Jim fully expected both he and his Wolf would be pissed by that, but Cyn's quiet nod reassured them both. The five-inch claws, and the evil look she shot the Cheetah, also helped. Cyn would protect Chloe as well as he would. The fact that Cyn was female seemed to be more than enough to keep his Wolf calm. Cyn was no threat to their newly formed bond.

"All right, Julian. Spill." He crossed his arms over his chest and glared at the Bear, well aware Cyn had pulled his mate away for more than the obvious reasons. "What the fuck is going on?"

"There was more to the attack on Chloe than we let you know." Julian didn't look the least bit apologetic. "Things we couldn't tell you because you had no idea shifters existed."

"You'll tell me now." Jim couldn't protect Chloe otherwise.

Julian nodded. "Did you know that Tabby was attacked by a rogue Wolf named Gary?"

Jim shook his head. He hadn't heard anything about this. "When did this happen?"

"Months ago, right before the attack on Chloe. We thought that he'd been the one to hurt her, but we were wrong. He was, however, sent here to watch her."

"Why?" Jim found he couldn't keep his eyes off his mate.

"We don't know. He refused to tell us, even from shifter jail. Gabe was trying to track down who he worked for, who his Alpha might be, but got sidetracked when first Cyn then Glory were also attacked."

Jim took a deep breath and tried to still the urge to pace. Chloe did not need to know how upset he was. "What did Gabe find out?"

"Hunters in other parts of the country have found bodies with similar wounds, all of them fatal. Worse, all of the victims were half-breeds like Chloe."

"Someone wants to preserve bloodlines?" To Jim that sounded both elitist and futile. Even he, so new he still squeaked when he walked, knew fate chose your mate, not desire. "That's fucking stupid."

"We're not sure why half-breeds are being targeted, but from what Alex told me they might even be going after kids and making it look like accidents."

Meaning Alex and Tabby's child would be targeted, as would any kids Chloe and Jim had. "What do you need me to do?"

"Finish mating Chloe, then find Gabe and Barney. Maybe they have more information than I do." Julian shrugged. "I'm not a Hunter, so I'm not caught up in the loop."

"Hunter?" Jim finally turned his attention away from Chloe. Something about the way Julian said that word had him thinking it meant more than guys sitting in a deer blind waiting for a buck to wander by.

"Think of Hunters as the Feds of the shifter world. Their main purpose is to ensure that rogues are taken out before they do damage to humans or other shifters. Ryan, Gabe and Barney are all Hunters."

"How do you become a Hunter?" Because he could totally see himself in a shifter blind waiting to shoot whoever was after his mate.

"You're born one, not made, sort of like I was born pretty." Julian flipped his long hair back over his shoulder and batted his lashes at Jim.

"Uh-huh." Somehow Jim didn't think it worked quite that way, but until he'd spoken to the Hunters he wouldn't know for sure. "So they're definitely going to want to have a little chat with Spot."

"Especially since he was the one who attacked Cyn." Julian's expression, usually so easygoing, turned briefly fierce. "Unfortunately, I can't rip his arms off until they question him."

The human half of Jim was horrified that Julian sounded so serious. They were talking about torturing and killing a sentient being, a person who probably had family and friends back wherever he came from.

His Wolf half wanted to call dibs on the guy's hindquarters.

"Do you think he had anything to do with the attack on Chloe?" Jim stared down at the Cheetah and tried not to picture him folded into a pretzel.

"There was no scent of shifter near where Chloe was found, but it's possible I missed it when I was healing her."

"I owe you for that." Jim scowled. "No one saw the attack?"

Julian shook his head. "There was an anonymous call made to 9-1-1. By the time I got on the scene the paramedics were already there, working on her."

Jim's mind was whirling with possibilities. "Is there any chance at all that she wasn't attacked there? That she was assaulted somewhere else, then dumped there?"

Julian's eyes went wide. "Mother fucker." He pulled out his cell phone and began to dial. "You're a smart man, Doc Woods."

"Would the Hunters keep that kind of information from you, though?"

"If Gabe thought he was protecting us? Fuck yes." Julian held up his hand. "Gabe? We've got a problem."

Jim's attention was drawn inevitably toward Chloe. The knowledge that she was a target of something larger than a random bashing, that she was still in danger from her attackers, filled him with rage. His fangs descended and fur began to sprout on his arms. He was going to shift, and nothing Jim could do would stop it.

"Sit. Stay. Good woof-woof." Julian patted his shoulder, and Jim's Wolf once more calmed under the Bear's touch. His fangs receded and the fur disappeared.

"Whoa." He was beginning to understand why so many people called Julian Super Bear.

"Stick around. For my next trick I'm going to make a Cheetah eat its own anus."

Jim had no doubt Julian would do just that.

CHAPTER EIGHT

Chloe glanced at Jim, surprised to find him so calm and cool. She could have sworn she'd heard his Wolf growling so deeply she'd been certain he was about to change. Either that or take her down and claim her like a wild man.

Instead, he was chatting with Julian as if nothing at all was wrong.

"He's close, but Super Bear got his ass to calm down." Cyn put her phone away. "Barney's on his way."

"So is Ryan." Chloe had called her brother the moment she and Cyn were apart from Jim and Julian. It wasn't that she doubted that the three of them could keep watch over one Cheetah. It was more her brother deserved to be there when they questioned him. "I wish I blew why this was happening to we." Chloe rubbed her arms, chilled to the bone. She couldn't seem to get warm now that the threat was gone.

Cyn took one look at her chattering teeth and bellowed for her mate. "Jules, get your furry ass over here!"

Jim moved so quickly he left Julian in the dust. "Shh." He took her into his arms, wrapping her up tight. "I've got you." Jim pointed his chin back toward where he'd been standing. "Cyn?"

"I've got it." Cyn sauntered back toward the entrance of the apartment building. "If he so much as twitches I'm gutting the *cabròn*."

"I'm glad she's on our side," Jim whispered.

"Me blue." Chloe was shivering so hard she could barely stand. "I'm sowwy, but I need to spit."

Jim didn't hesitate. He picked her up like she weighed less than air and took her straight back into the building. He settled on the stairs with her on his lap, her head tucked on his shoulder.

God, he was so warm, and smelled so good. She'd marked him, but the claiming wasn't complete until they made love and he marked her back. Even so, just his scent helped settle her shattered nerves and the soothing heat of his touch made her feel safe in a way not even her family could.

She'd needed this, far more than she'd wanted anyone to know.

They sat quietly, not speaking, just holding one another. She could hear Cyn and Julian talking softly to one another, but she had no desire to leave the comforting embrace of her mate to find out what the two were chatting about. The more Jim held her, the more her shivers disappeared until she felt toasty from head to toe.

"Tank you."

He kissed the top of her head. "You're welcome. Feel better?"

"Mm-hm." She snuggled closer, surprising herself with a wide-jawed yawn.

"It's normal. You're no longer running on adrenaline, and now your body wants to sleep." Jim stroked his hand down her back. "Do you want to try and nap while Cyn and Julian talk to the others?"

"Are day here?" She didn't glance toward the parking lot. She didn't want to move at all.

"Not yet. You've got time." He rubbed his chin against the top of her head. "I'll make sure of it."

She smiled. "You're scent-marking me."

He stilled. "I am?"

Chloe giggled. "I like it." She wanted to bathe in his scent, have every shifter who came across her know that Jim was hers.

"Will you scent-mark me as well?" Jim sounded…intrigued.

"All over."

"Oh?" His voice went husky. He squirmed a bit, making her laugh again. "Tell me more about this all-over-marking thing."

She bit her lip and glanced toward Cyn and Julian.

Oh hell. From the thumbs-up they both shot her, they'd heard every word of what she'd said to her mate. "Jeez. A skittle privacy, people."

Jim's silent laughter shook her, but in a good way. "We'll have to discuss this, *in length*, when we're alone."

Chloe swallowed as he caressed her hip. "Uh-huh."

"I think they're here." Jim stood, cradling Chloe in his arms. "Jules? I'm taking Chloe upstairs."

"Don't start anything you won't have time to finish." Julian waved them off, his arm around his mate.

Apparently Jim didn't need any further acknowledgment, because he started up the stairs at a rapid pace. "We need to pack."

"Pack?" She lifted her head from his shoulder, looking around in confusion. "Why?"

"You're moving in with me."

She opened her mouth, but only a squeak came out. Her words had deserted her again.

"I'm going to have you work with some of the animals in the clinic. You can't do surgery, and you can't work the front desk, but you can sure as hell do other things." He opened the door to her apartment and carried her straight to her bedroom. "Your scent is so strong in here."

His tone was growly again, Julian's influence not as strong now that they were no longer in the Kermode Bear's presence. Julian's powers were sometimes frightening, but his big heart made up for any fear Chloe might have felt around him.

When he slammed her bedroom door closed with his foot she understood that Julian's influence was gone entirely. Jim's eyes were golden brown as he lowered her to the bed. "I'm sorry. I have to."

She stroked his cheek, smiling as he leaned into her touch. "I know. I taunt you to."

He chuckled softly. "I promise I'll go as slow as I can."

Considering she could feel how hard he was trembling she doubted he'd be going all *that* slow. But her voice was gone again, lost in a swirl of soft touches and tiny, maddening kisses across her collarbone. Jim knelt above her, pushing up her shirt as he peppered each patch of bared skin with butterfly kisses. He didn't hesitate at her scars as she'd feared he would, instead pausing at each one to stroke and caress.

When he licked the scar over her belly button she moaned, the sensation intensely erotic. He carefully removed her shirt, exposing her "cleaning day comfy bra".

Hell, it wasn't like she'd expected her dream man to throw her onto her bed and finally claim her *today*. She'd been throwing out the trash, for God's sake.

Jim didn't seem to mind the ratty-ass bra, though. She grabbed hold of her comforter, clenching it in her fists as he worked his way up to it, gently lifting her up enough so that he could work the clasp in back. He coaxed her into letting go of the comforter long enough to remove the bra, then sat back on his heels and studied her. "Beautiful." He stroked the tip of her breast with a gentleness that startled her. "My little Fox."

She held up her hands, smiling when Jim immediately leaned into her. She tugged him close, the feel of his shirt against her bare breasts intoxicating. She tilted her head, baring her throat to him, took a deep breath and prayed her voice would cooperate. "Claim. Me."

"With pleasure."

***

Jim struck, sinking his fangs into Chloe's creamy skin. She screamed, but it wasn't a sound filled with pain, like he'd feared. Oh, no. This sound was all about pleasure. Chloe's hips rocked under him, brushing against his cock until he thought he'd cream his jeans like a fucking teenager during his first make-out session.

She'd come just from his bite.

My God. Why the fuck did I wait so long? The scent of her pleasure permeated the room. Her breath came in gasps, her eyes became dazed and her pupils dilated. Her lips were parted, her tongue darting out to lick the bottom one.

"Wow." She smiled, the expression almost loopy. She raised her arms in the air and waved them around, almost clocking him. "Let's fro again! Let's go again!"

Jim chuckled. She was adorable, all rumpled and half-naked, waving her arms in the air like Kermit the Frog on downers. "Let's get you naked first, hmm?"

She nodded eagerly, pushing at his hips until he got off of her. She wiggled out of her jeans, using her right hand far more than her left, but when he tried to help she scowled at him.

He let her be. Chloe had been dealing with her physical limitations long enough to know what she was capable of. He would watch, see if she needed his help, but otherwise she was strong enough to do things on her own.

Between Chloe and Spencer he was being fed some serious humble pie. He didn't think he'd handle their issues nearly as well as the two of them did. He'd be a basket case, sobbing in the corner about his lost dreams. Spencer simply asked for a room and a bed, and Chloe?

She asked for him.

He was a goddamn ass, and he'd spend the rest of his life making it up to her. "Thank you."

Her brows rose. "For getting naked?"

"For giving me another chance."

Her expression softened. "Of course." Chloe's expression was both hopeful and fearful. "Are we really going to do this?"

"Do you want to?" As afraid as he was that his dick would fall off if he didn't get inside her tight little body, he'd gladly pick it up off the floor and hand it to her if she wasn't ready for this.

She bared her fangs at him with the most adorable snarl.

"Okay then." Jim knew Chloe was very inexperienced, so he wasn't going to rush this. He wanted to remember this day not for the terror of the Cheetah attack, but as the day they mated. It wasn't ideal, but he could stand the thought of waiting one second longer.

Chloe began taking off his shirt and he helped her, wiggling until it landed beside the bed. Next his jeans were shucked, along with his underwear, tangling with the shoes he hadn't yet kicked off. She giggled when he began shimmying like a crazy person, kicking until the shoes fell off and he could finally get his pants and briefs off.

"Think that's funny?" He licked her chin, her giggles intensifying. He was more than willing to embarrass himself if it meant she was relaxed. "Oh, are we ticklish?" He feathered his fingers over her sides, delighted when she shivered and tried to get away.

"Don't!"

"Don't what?" He did it again, enjoying the sound of her laughter. "This?"

"Jim!" She tried to glare at him, but the sheer joy in her gaze made it more kittenish than villainous. "I will end you."

He chuckled, the urge to run his fingers over the mark on her neck impossible to ignore. He stroked the mark, startled when her laughter stopped dead and she shuddered beneath him. The scent of arousal once more filled the air.

"Chloe?"

"Hmm?" She leaned into his touch as he continued to caress the mark.

"You like that?" His voice dropped, becoming husky as his own arousal rose to match hers.

She tilted her head, baring her neck further, her eyes closing. Her expression was yearning, nearly begging him to touch her more.

Jim kissed the mark, raking his teeth over it. The moan he got in return had him biting down gently, eager to elicit more of those beautiful noises.

She reached up and clasped the back of his head, holding him in place as he bit down. It wasn't until he tasted the copper of her blood that he realized his fangs had come down.

Chloe bucked beneath him as she reacted to his bite, coming from that alone. His Wolf grunted in satisfaction as she gasped out her pleasure.

His dick throbbed in response, the mark on his own neck pulsing as his heart raced. He needed to be inside her, one with her, feeling her clench around him as she came again and again.

Jim slid down her body, pausing long enough to pay homage to her breasts. He licked and suckled each one until her quiet moans became demanding cries, her fists clenching painfully in his hair. Her voice was gone, the only sounds erupting from her throat guttural and barely human.

She was lost in the pleasure he was giving her, and he couldn't be happier about it.

He kissed his way down her taut stomach, making sure to hit each and every one of her scars as he did so. When he was done she would know that he wanted every part of her, flaws and all.

He began to tease her opening with his finger, gently coaxing her to accept his touch. She seemed startled at first, her eyes going wide, but when he licked her clit and sucked it into his mouth her eyes squeezed shut once more. She began moving against him, barely flinching when he eased his finger inside her.

God, she was tight. He was right, then, that she'd had little to no experience. And as asinine as it was, the thought that he might be her first made him want to beat his chest like Tarzan.

He finger fucked her, watching her reactions, gauging when he felt she could take a second finger. He wanted her stretched, wet and ready for him, because the last thing that should be in bed with them was pain. When she seemed ready he added a second finger, sucking her clit hard to distract her from any sting she might feel.

If her face was anything to go by, she was more than ready for what he was doing. Still, he needed to make sure. "Ready for more?"

"M-m-m-m…" Her eyes opened, some of the passion fading as she couldn't get the word out.

"I have you, little vixen." He planted a soft kiss on the ginger curls between her thighs, then carefully eased a third finger inside her.

She winced for the first time and he stilled, allowing her to get used to the width of his three fingers. As she relaxed, he began peppering her skin with kisses again, soothing her, gently taking her clit once more into his mouth and gently sucking.

Before long she was bucking against him, taking him to the third knuckle.

She was ready.

Jim sat up and prayed that the condom he had in his wallet was still good. As much as he'd love to make children with Chloe they had to wait. He fumbled for his pants, pulling his wallet from his pocket.

"Uh?"

"Condom."

She grinned and lay back down, watching him with a slumberous, pleasure-filled gaze that had him dropping the condom twice in his eagerness to see her come yet again. He ripped the package open and slid the condom on. The feel of his own hand on his length made him grit his teeth and pray like he never had before. If he came before he even had the condom on he'd have to move to Siberia and change his name to Ivan Jerkov.

That expression on her face didn't help either. He could come just from the lust she was showing him.

He took a deep breath, trying to control the tremors racing through him. This was it. The rest of his life was on this single moment, when she'd accept him into her body.

Before he could get himself under control she tugged him down and nodded. Her gaze was pinned to his, urging him on.

He didn't need to ask. She'd already told him without words that she was ready for him.

Jim slowly eased into her body, the faint tightening and loosening of her expressions giving him clues as to when to slow down and when it was all right to move again. So slowly he thought his dick might die of blood deprivation, he forged his way inside her, never once breaking the contact between their gazes.

They didn't need words. In this moment, they both knew what the other was saying.

Before he knew it he was fully seated inside her. He kissed her softly, both their eyes open, waiting for her nod that it was all right to move.

She gave it, so he began fucking her in slow, easy strokes that had them both on the breathless edge far quicker than Jim would have liked. He'd wanted to make this last, to bring her to ecstasy over and over again, but it was just too much. The sensations were too strong, too tight, too perfect…too Chloe.

He came, shivering as lightning rushed through him, his Wolf howling in joy. Chloe shuddered as she, too, came once again. Her gasping, wordless cry fused with his own as the pleasure raced down his spine.

God, it had never been this good before. He leaned his forehead against his mate's and smiled.

God willing, it would be again.

CHAPTER NINE

Chloe felt like she was doing the walk of shame into her own living room. Her brother Ryan was sitting on the sofa, Glory cuddled close in his lap and a huge scowl on his face. Cyn was pacing and snarling at the bound Cheetah, while Julian watched her warily, ready to stop her from attacking…or to help her. Chloe wasn't quite sure. Alex and Tabby had also shown up, Tabby so far along in her pregnancy she looked ready to blow. Chloe was pretty sure the turkey timer was about to pop any second and her couch would be toast. In fact, she was surprised that Alex had brought his mate, but from the stubborn look on Tabby's face she must have convinced Alex to bring her. Alex's hazel eyes were completely brown, his Grizzly close to the surface.

The Cheetah was bound hand and foot, naked as a jaybird. His dark skin was flawless, his thin, twisty dreads hanging past his shoulders. His eyes, the gold of his Cheetah, were startlingly beautiful. He looked pissed as hell, ready to claw anyone who was insane enough to get close to him.

And then there was Barney, who turned out to be that crazy. The Hunter sat calmly on the floor, petting the damn Cheetah on the head. "Who's a good kitty? You are, yes you are!"

The snarl was loud even behind the duct tape covering the Cheetah's mouth.

"Congratulations on your mating." Barney winked at her. "It's about fuckin' time."

"Tanks." Chloe could feel her face heating. Her cheeks were probably bright red.

"Honey, I wasn't talking to you." Barney nodded to Jim. "If you hadn't claimed her I'm pretty sure you would have found some pissed-off Bears on your doorstep."

"Are you kidding? They got ahold of me at the supermarket." Jim shuddered. "I thought for sure they were going to maul me in the dairy aisle."

"Nah. I wouldn't hurt you there. I wouldn't risk it." Ryan grinned. "Glory's lactose intolerant."

"Am not." Glory jabbed Ryan in the stomach hard enough to make him grunt.

"I'm sorry, who was it who had a cheese sandwich and two hours later the neighbors were looking for the source of the sewer leak?"

Glory rolled her eyes and refused to answer.

Barney just continued to pet the Cheetah, his gaze bright with laughter.

"What I want to know is who this is and why is he after Chloe?" Jim crossed his arms over his chest and glared at the Cheetah.

Barney picked at the tape on the Cheetah's cheek. "Oh, that's easy. His name is—" The Cheetah began to kick furiously, staring wide-eyed at Barney when the Hunter slapped him on the ass. "Bad kitty! His name is Francois Prejean, from New Orleans. He's a Hunter for the Senate."

If Chloe had been on the receiving end of that murderous glare she would have been running for the hills.

"Wait. Senate?" Jim was behind her, but his confusion was clear in his voice.

"We have a structure that deals with shifter laws called the Senate. Each species is represented by a Senator, and together they make and help enforce those laws." Tabby rubbed her stomach and winced. "I really wish this kid didn't like to put his toes in my ribs."

Alex shook his head but picked up where his mate left off. "Just like in a Pride or a Pack, the Leo is the Alpha over all the shifters. The Senate runs the day-to-day issues of the shifter world, but on a grand scale. On the local scale, those issues are dealt with by Alphas or the heads of the family groups."

"Sort of like Alex's father rules over the Bunsun-Williams clan." Julian grinned. "He's not an Alpha the way Max Cannon or Rick Lowell are, but *I* wouldn't want to tell him no."

"Packs and Prides have their own hierarchies, with Betas and Omegas and Marshalls, oh my." Chloe giggled at Barney's wink. "And then there's the low men on the totem pole, which would be the rest of us peons."

Ryan rolled his eyes. "Hunters, like Alphas, are born, not made. We work directly for the Senate, usually two to three Hunters per territory. Gabe has all of Pennsylvania, while his partners work New York and New Jersey. Gabe and I shouldn't even be living in the same town—" Glory gasped, and Ryan hugged her close. "But I have no intention of moving and neither does he."

"Hmm." Barney eyed Ryan. "It is odd, come to think of it. Not one of the Senators has mentioned removing you from Halle, at least not that I'm aware of. And you *should* be reassigned. They wouldn't be at all sympathetic to your mate's needs." He tilted his head. "Come to think of it, no Senator has mentioned you at all. I wouldn't have known you were a Hunter if I hadn't already been here, looking into…" His lips clamped shut.

Like Chloe cared about all of this. "Why would a Bunter be interested in me?" She hadn't done a damn thing except get her ass kicked to hell and gone.

"I have no idea." Barney snapped his fingers and sat straight up. "I know! Let's ask him!" He then ripped the tape off the Cheetah's mouth.

The howl sounded almost wolf-like. "Fucking asshole!" The man's Southern accent was different from Tabby's, the drawl longer and somewhat sharper.

"Aw, I wuv you too, cupcake." Barney patted the Cheetah's cheek. "Now, tell me why you've been harassing Miss Chloe here."

Prejean clamped his lips shut.

"You know, I have more duct tape." Barney picked up a silver roll of tape that had been hidden behind him, twirling it on his finger. "I could do this *all day*."

"I say we just rip his arms off one by one until he tells us what we want to know." Alex flexed his hands, his hazel eyes the deep brown of his Bear. His five-inch claws scraped against his jeans with a *schrick schrick* sound Chloe knew all too well. She'd grown up around Grizzlies, understood how they thought. Alex was about to go postal on the Cheetah. If that happened, there wouldn't be enough left of the cat to fit into a peanut butter jar, let alone answer questions.

Prejean swiveled his head until he could see Alex. His eyes went wide, and he gulped. "I was told to bring her in, dead or alive."

Every male in the room except for Barney growled at the Cheetah's answer. Barney simply tilted his head and asked in a childish voice, "Why?"

Prejean rolled his eyes. "Because she's rogue."

Chloe felt faint. "Who…what?" She gulped, swaying. If she'd been declared rogue by the Senate, then…

"Oh fog." She turned to Jim. "Go. Now."

He glared at her, his hazel eyes dotted with dark honey brown. "No."

She whimpered and turned her gaze to Ryan, who would surely understand. "Peas?"

He shook his head reluctantly. "You know he can't. He's your mate."

Chloe spoke slowly, determined to get the words to come out right. "He'll. Die."

"Sweetie, they'll go after him anyway just for being your mate. You know that." Barney flipped the duct tape into the air and caught it. "So. When was Miss Chloe declared rogue, hmm? Because *my* orders were to watch her, not harm her."

Prejean glared at Barney. "Seems like we got different orders."

"Sure does." Barney bopped the Cheetah lightly on the head. "Why did you attack Cyn?"

"She's also wanted."

Barney scowled. "She wasn't a Bear when you almost killed her. She was human."

"I wasn't trying to kill her, just bring her in, *as ordered*. But the Wolf interfered."

"Is Tabby on your list?" Alex's voice had become gravelly, fangs sprouting in his mouth. The possibility that his mate and unborn child were being threatened was driving his Bear even closer to the surface.

"She is now." Prejean smirked. "And so's her kid."

Alex roared, his back hunching as fur sprouted on his arms. If he changed now there would be no stopping him from killing the Cheetah.

"Down, sugar." Tabby put her hand on Alex's shoulder. Her Georgia drawl was thick with worry. "I need you to stay calm for the baby."

Prejean sighed. "If you think I'm the only one watching and waiting, you'd be wrong. We will bring in the Senate-declared rogues as ordered."

Ryan scowled. "I thought…" He glanced at Barney. "We can sense rogues, right?"

"Yes." Barney snapped his fingers under the Cheetah's nose. "So. Who in this room is rogue?"

"The Fox—"

Barney made a buzzing noise. "For the love of little green shifters, use the senses the spirits gave you, boy." He leaned forward until he and the Cheetah were nose to nose. "Who. Is. The. Rogue?"

The Cheetah opened his mouth to respond, then slowly began to frown. "I…"

Barney began to hum the *Jeopardy* theme song.

"You're an ass."

Barney finished his little song. "Well?"

The Cheetah lowered his head. "There are no rogues in the room."

"Ding ding ding! We have a winna! Give this kitty some nip!" Barney patted him on the head.

"Wait." Chloe held up her hands, confused as hell. "Why would bey declare me vogue if I'm rot?"

The Cheetah stared at her in confusion, but the others, used to her speech by now, figured out what she really meant.

"That's my question." Ryan exchanged a glance with Barney. "There might be more than one reason this area has so many Hunters in it."

"The Senate is up to something, but what?" Julian scowled, exchanging his own look with Cyn. "I mean, they have no reason to go after any of us."

"That's my question." Barney sat back, playing idly with the tape again. "None of you have done anything that would warrant arrest, let alone a dead or alive order." Barney stared at the Cheetah. "Who did your orders come from?"

Prejean went limp, his defiance completely swamped by confusion. "The usual source."

"Who is the usual course?" Chloe needed to know if the whole Senate was after her or just one Senator with a grudge.

But again, who would have a strong enough grudge against a college student that he ordered a beating so severe Chloe was handicapped for life?

Jim pulled Chloe back against his chest. His warmth seeped into her, calming her. She hadn't even realized how badly she was shaking until he took hold of her.

Barney and the Cheetah exchanged a glance. It was the Cheetah, surprisingly, who answered. "Vaughn Clark."

"Is Vaughn Clark one of the Senators?" Jim tightened his hold.

"No, he's the Hunter liaison. He gets the order and passes it on to us." Barney began unwrapping the Cheetah's wrists. "We need to find out who gave him those orders and why."

"Agreed." The Cheetah…no, Francois, sat up and rubbed his wrists. He shot Barney an absolutely evil grin. "And I know just the people to help us."

Barney actually paled. "You don't mean…"

"Yup." And Francois laughed, the sound so wicked Chloe shivered in fear.

The big, bad Barney looked like he'd rather swallow tacks than deal with them. She just hoped Halle was ready for whoever it was that made the brash Hunter so afraid.

***

"All right. I want some answers from you." Ryan, Chloe, Barney and Francois the Cat were busy in the living room, discussing whatever the hell they were planning. Jim had decided to take this opportunity to get some answers of his own, so he'd dragged Julian away from the rest of the group. "Tell me about this bond you and Chloe have."

Julian sighed. "You might want to sit down for this."

Jim settled at the small dinette set Chloe had squeezed into her postage-stamp kitchen and waited for Julian to sit across from him. Julian grabbed two bottles of juice from the fridge before sitting down, opening one and handing it to Jim. "Well?"

"Has anyone told you about Spirit Bears?"

Jim blinked. "I know they call you Super Bear, and that Bears can heal little things like headaches and paper cuts, but that's about it. I also know you did something that helped Chloe, but you weren't able to heal everything."

Julian winced, cradling the juice between his palms. "Spirit Bears are the level sixty versions of normal Bears."

"Excuse me?" Jim had no idea what the hell Julian was talking about.

"Guess you don't play video games." Julian chuckled.

If only Julian knew. Video games were one of Jim's guilty pleasures.

"Look. We're…amped up. We've got healing powers far beyond those of normal Bears. So when Chloe was hurt, I felt the pull of someone who was close to death and arrived to find the paramedics getting ready to code her."

Jim glanced into the living room. He couldn't help himself. Part of him needed to see her, whole and talking and laughing, to prove to himself that she was right there, safe and sound.

"I healed her enough to get her on the ambulance alive, and once in the hospital I did…more. But she was in a coma and they didn't think she'd wake up." Julian's expression turned apologetic. "The price a Spirit Bear pays for having our ability to heal is that we're *compelled* to heal. Being in a hospital is sheer hell for any of my kind, so trying to take care of Chloe was difficult."

"But you did it anyway." And for that, Jim owed him big time. "Spirit bear. I've heard that phrase before. You're a Kermode."

Julian grinned, looking tickled pink that Jim knew exactly what kind of Bear he was. "Yup."

"I thought they were all in Canada." The Kermode, or spirit bear, was a species of black bear whose fur was creamy to white instead of black. They were an endangered species that roamed from Princess Royal Island to Prince Rupert, British Columbia, on the coast, and inland toward Hazelton, British Columbia.

"The rest of them are. I'm currently the only one living in the US." Julian took a sip of juice. "Anyway, Chloe wasn't waking from her coma, and her family asked if there was anything more I could do." He shrugged sheepishly. "I would have done it anyway, but I had to warn them that she'd be a little bit different when she woke."

"The white fur?" Jim sat back, the juice bottle sweating cold water between his palms.

"That, I admit, was an unexpected side effect, and not one I've seen before."

"So you've never heard of a shifter's fur suddenly turning white?" Jim was confused. He'd thought it was a side effect of what Julian had done to save her.

"Nope. Not once has a Spirit Bear saved someone only to have them turn white."

"Huh." Jim rubbed his chin. "Are you sure about that?"

Julian opened his mouth, then closed it with a frown. "You know what? I'm not. It seems there's more going on here than any of us thought, so I can't say for sure. All I know is *I've* never heard of it."

"Yet something else we need to look into."

Julian nodded thoughtfully. "I agree. Add in the link Chloe and I share and you've got one hell of an unusual situation. Also, she can contact the spirit world in a way other shifters can't, enabling her to talk to Fox the way I talk to Bear."

"So I can't talk to, say, Wolf?" And didn't he feel odd even thinking about contacting some sort of shifter guardian spirit?

"Nope. Only Kermode can, or those who attempt to become Kermode through a changing or mating bite. Even then, the Bear doesn't get the ability to speak to the spirits forever."

"Wait." Jim held up his hand, confused. "So when you turned Cyn, she was able to talk to Bear, but she can't now."

"Correct."

"But Chloe can talk to Fox." He wasn't sure this made sense to him.

"Yes. One of the things she can do is spirit walk, so we've been working on making sure that she's safe when she does so."

"And that doesn't seem odd to you at all?"

"I thought it was our link that allows it. Now, I'm not so sure."

"What else does your link allow?"

"She can also talk to me in my head." Julian stared him right in the eye. "She saved my life when Cyn was hurt. If Chloe hadn't snapped me out of the healing spiral I would have died healing my mate."

"Then explain to me the white fur." Jim leaned his elbows on the table, his juice forgotten. "She was a red Fox before the accident. You healed her, and suddenly she's a white Fox with the ability to contact the spirits."

Julian blinked. "Yes," he drawled.

"And you have a mind link, why?"

"To wake her from her coma, I had to travel into the spirit world and pull her back from death."

Jim shivered. "Okay. So that's how she got her link to the spirit world, but…why did her fur change color?"

Julian shook his head, frowning. "I have no idea."

"Has this sort of thing happened before?" Because the mystery of Chloe's fur might be why the Senate was so interested in his mate.

"I'm not certain. I don't think it has. I know my leader, Tai Buchere, hasn't heard anything about it. If anyone would know it would be him, but when I asked about it he was as mystified as we are."

"Could the Senate know something we don't?" Jim found himself staring at Chloe again, surrounded by Hunters and family. "If they're after her because of the unusual fur change that at least gives us a half-assed reason they might want to study her."

Julian cursed softly. "That does make a twisted sort of sense. But Francois's orders were to bring her in dead or alive. How can they study her ability to access Fox if she's dead?"

"Good question." Jim picked up his juice and downed half of it in one gulp. "Maybe I'm on the wrong track, then. Maybe it has something to do with someone else in her family. Didn't Francois say that he has orders to bring in Tabby as well?"

"So why not Glory or Cyn? If they're after those two, why wouldn't they want them as well? What's different about both Tabby and Chloe?"

Julian eyed the people in the other room before leaning forward, speaking softly. "Gabe told Alex that there have been mysterious deaths among shifters who happen to be crossbreeds."

"Like Chloe?"

Julian nodded. "And Tabby's child."

"Then there has to be a reason why." Jim tapped his fingers on the bottle. "We need answers before one of the girls is seriously hurt."

"We'll need the help of the Hunters for that. Gabe, Ryan and Barney are on our side."

"Maybe we can get Francois as well. I'm not sure he liked being lied to."

Julian began to laugh.

"What's so funny?"

"Nothing. Maybe I should call some Coyotes for a visit, that's all."

Jim tilted his head. "What aren't you telling me?"

"Coyotes can sense lies."

Oh. "Like Bears heal, Wolves have their Pack strength and Foxes hide their scent? That would come in handy." If Francois was lying to them, a Coyote would be able to ferret that out in a heartbeat.

"The only way to trip up a Coyote is if the person they're speaking to believes what they're saying is the truth."

"So if Francois is agreeing with us simply to get close to Chloe…" Jim grinned. "I like it."

"I'll give my friend a call. Maybe he'll send his Omega for a little visit."

And Jim knew enough about shifters now to know that an Omega could sense emotions. While the majority of Omegas could only sense the emotional well-being of their Pack or Pride mates, some Omegas were strong enough that, with some effort, they were able to sense the emotions of those who did not belong.

"We'll need to let Max know a Coyote will be in his territory." Julian grimaced. "I can't wait to explain all of this to him."

"Tell Emma." Jim smirked. "Then *she* can tell Max."

Julian grinned. "You're evil. I like that about you."

CHAPTER TEN

"Car." The therapist pointed to her lips. "Ca-ca-ca-car."

Chloe watched the way the woman's lips moved and tried her best to imitate it, but her brain just couldn't make the connection. "Bar."

"Relax and try again. Ca-ca-ca-car. Car."

Chloe frowned and licked her lips. "Ca-ar."

"Good!" The therapist smiled. "Much better. Now, what do you put in the car?"

"Gas." It sounded like a very stupid question, but the therapist wasn't checking her intelligence. They both knew she could understand what was being said. She just didn't speak what she wanted to say. Even in her own mind the words she spoke *sounded* correct, but weren't. It was why she was still in speech therapy after almost a year.

"Excellent." The therapist smiled, letting her know she'd spoken correctly. "Now. I want you to tell me where you would go in a car."

"The breach."

"Beach."

Chloe made an exasperated face. So close, yet so far away. "B-each."

"Good! Now, make sentences for me. Tell me how you'd get to the beach."

"We get into the car and put on our treat belts."

"Seat belts. Ss-ss-seat." The therapist exaggerated her lip movements, hissing the *s* sounds out like a snake.

"Seat?" When the therapist nodded, Chloe grinned. "Seat belts and start the car."

"All right. What next?"

"We start the car and put it in clive."

The therapist blinked. "That would hurt."

Chloe rolled her eyes.

"Drive, sweetie, not Clive. Clive might sue you if you put your car up his bum."

Chloe giggled, the vision of some poor schlub named Clive having a VW Beetle-butt just too much for her.

"All right. Let's start again."

Chloe got her giggles under control and spoke slowly, focusing on the therapist's lips. "We start the car and put it in drive."

"And what directions do you use?"

Chloe described how to get to the beach, correcting herself when the therapist pointed out where she'd gone wrong. When she was done, she had a mild headache, but that was to be expected. She was attempting to retrain the language centers of her brain, but she hadn't seen much improvement in the last few months.

"You're doing well." The therapist went through her notes. "You've improved a great deal since I first saw you." She tapped the paperwork, lining it up together neatly before putting it in Chloe's folder. "I don't think you're going to get much better, however. We need to discuss how you wish to proceed."

Chloe grimaced. She'd been expecting this topic to come up sometime soon. "I know the insurance only covers one beer of—"

"Year. Y-y-year."

"Y-ear. Of therapy." She sat back, thinking. "Do you see my condition improving burger, or should I call this good?"

"I think, with continued therapy, you can improve slightly, but you're always going to have problems. At this point, it is truly up to you, but you'd have to pay out of pocket and there are no guarantees you will get any better than you are now." The therapist stared at her for a few moments before sighing. "Do you want my honest opinion?"

Chloe nodded.

"As much as I hate to say this, and as much as you've improved, I think you should take what you've got and run with it. The last two or three months I haven't seen anything that would make me think you'll get back to where you were pre-accident."

Chloe tried to clench her left hand and failed. "I see."

"I'm sorry. I can teach someone else some of the techniques we've been using, if you like. You can continue the lessons on your own with a partner. At this point it's more a matter of exercising your brain, making the paths we've established stronger."

"Tank you." Chloe stood and held out her hand. "For everything."

"You're welcome." The therapist's face was filled with sympathy. "I wish I had better news for you."

"It whiz what it is." Chloe shrugged. "What are you gonna do?"

The therapist laughed. "I wish you the best, Chloe."

"You too, Brenda." Chloe picked up her purse and followed the therapist out of the tiny office, waving good-bye as she made her way into the reception area.

Chloe still had physical therapy and her sessions with both Sarah, the Halle Pride Omega, and Julian to get through this week, but for today she was done. She decided to head to Jim's veterinary practice to say hello to everyone, but mostly to see her mate and let him know she'd been released from speech therapy.

Gods, her *mate*. Chloe shivered in delight. She'd finally claimed her man, and damn if she wasn't thrilled about it. She could hardly wait to see him again, despite the fact that he'd left her bed at o'dark hundred to get to work, kissing her sweetly before departing for the day. They'd promised to see each other later that week, mostly because of Jim's work hours and Spencer's doctor's appointments, but Chloe just couldn't wait that long.

But first, she had to check in. She hopped into her car and dialed, turning the air conditioner up. It was damn hot today, and even in her tank top and shorts she was sweating like crazy. "Hey, dig brother."

"Chloe, any trouble?"

She smiled. She knew what he was talking about. All of her relatives were on alert now, keeping an eye on her. The fact that she'd gone to the therapist alone was only because they all had to work, and she'd promised on pain of major guilting to call when she got there and when she left. "I'm done with speech therapy. She fez I'm as good as I'm going to get."

"Damn." Ryan sighed. "Are you on your way here?"

Here was Cynful Tattoos, where Ryan was watching over his mate, Glory, while doing his own work in the break room. "Nope. I thought I'd drive over and visit Jim at the vet's office, then head to the tattoo parlor. I want Tabby to work some more on my kitsune."

"Call me when you get there."

"And when I'm on my way. I promise, gig bro."

She hung up after a brief good-bye and drove the short distance to Woods Veterinary Clinic, making a brief call to let Ryan know she'd arrived. She made her way inside, waving cheerfully at the vet tech manning the front desk. "Hey, Phil!"

The vet tech at the front desk grinned. Phil held the position Chloe had hoped to hold while she got her degree. "Chloe!"

They hugged each other over the counter amidst the sounds of barking, meowing and chirping. "Cow's it going?"

"Good, you?" She crossed her eyes and blew a raspberry, making Phil laugh. "You here to see the doc?" She nodded, and he shot a guilty look toward the back offices. "I'm sorry, but I think he's back there with his girlfriend."

Chloe's blood ran cold.

Girlfriend.

"You could come back later, maybe?"

Girlfriend?

"How about I buy you some lunch." Phil stood, as if to come around the counter. "It's almost time for my break anyway."

Girlfriend?

Oh, hell to the no. Chloe snarled and darted past Phil toward the examination rooms, sniffing out her dog of a mate.

"Chloe!" She heard Phil coming after her, but there was no stopping her. She would find Jim, rip off his testicles and stuff them in a drawer for safekeeping. "Don't go back there, you'll get my ass fired!"

She could barely hear Phil over the rage boiling in her veins. How dare Jim tell Chloe he was too busy to see her, yet bring his freakin' *girlfriend* over for a visit?

Chloe finally found her mate. She threw open the examination room door to find Jim leaning over a labradoodle puppy that was whimpering in distress. Across the table from him was the woman Chloe had seen the night she'd gone to dinner with Ryan and Glory. The blonde's hair was pulled back in a no-nonsense ponytail, her startled gaze a brilliant blue. Her tight jeans and low-cut tank top displayed her ample assets.

The blonde scowled. "Who are you?"

Chloe was so pissed she could barely speak.

"That's my fiancée, Irene. You'll be seeing a lot of her." Jim grinned at Chloe as if nothing was wrong. "Chloe Williams, meet Dr. Irene Boone."

"Oh." The scowl immediately left Irene's face to be replaced with a friendly smile. "Hello, Chloe. It's nice to meet you." She held out her hand.

Chloe stared at it for a moment before taking it. While she still wanted to take a chunk out of the blonde, Jim introducing Chloe as his fiancée had gone a long way to soothing her Fox's possessive streak. "Nice to beat you too."

Behind her, poor Phil choked on a laugh. "Need anything, Doc?"

"Who's manning the front desk?" Jim tilted his head, looking confused.

"Oh crap." Phil took off, leaving Chloe alone with Dr. Irene Boone and Jim.

"This is the lady who's taking over for my retired partner." Jim smiled at Irene, and once more Chloe wanted to bite someone. She was still deciding which one of them when Jim continued. "What do you think of having her and her girlfriend over for dinner?"

Chloe blinked.

Girlfriend?

She opened her mouth, aware her face was once more turning beet red. "M'kay."

Jim was obviously trying not to laugh. He must have known what was going through her head, because he winked at her. "Good. I think you and Valerie would get along like a house on fire."

"My girl has a thing for redheads. She has a huge crush on *Dr. Who*'s Karen Gillan." Irene laughed. "I swear, if I have to sit through that dinosaurs on a spaceship episode one more time…" She shook her head. "Anyway, we were thinking maybe this weekend we could all get together."

Chloe nodded, embarrassed beyond belief. At least Jim didn't seem upset by her behavior, busting in on them like a jealous idiot. "Sounds good."

"Chloe? Could you come here for a moment?" Jim lifted one hand from the wiggly puppy and gestured toward Chloe. "Tell me what you feel."

He took her hand and pressed her fingers gently on the puppy's abdomen. The puppy reacted, trying to move away from the press of her hand.

Chloe frowned, concentrating as she palpated the puppy's tummy. "Shh, it's okay." She pushed again, feeling along the pup's stomach. "Too hold for roundworm. Diarrhea or vomiting?"

"Vomiting."

"X-rays?"

"Haven't done any yet. You're thinking he swallowed something."

Chloe nodded, ignoring the way Irene watched her work. "I can feel something."

Jim nodded. "And this is why I still want you working here." He glanced at Irene. "Let's get this pup in for some pictures, hmm?"

Chloe took her hand away from the puppy, but didn't let go of Jim just yet. "Rescue pup?"

"Sort of. He was found on the side of the road by Carla. She took him here, cleaned him up, and noticed he was having problems. We're fixing him up and seeing if we can place him for adoption."

"Me." She petted the pup, who licked her hand almost desperately. She smiled as the puppy began to wag its tail.

"You sure?" Jim's indulgent tone told her he wasn't going to fight her too hard on this. She was pretty sure the vet didn't currently have a dog or cat of his own. Most people who worked with animals had their own personal pets, and the clinic had one or two cats that lived onsite as well, but she hadn't scented any animals on her mate other than the ones in the clinic.

"Mm-hmm." She picked the pup up carefully, giggling as it licked her face.

"All right, Chloe. Take him back to X-ray."

Chloe nodded and carried her newfound fur baby out of the exam room, happy as could be. Her mate did *not* have a girlfriend, and Chloe had a new puppy.

Life couldn't get any better.

***

Irene watched Chloe go, humming softly under her breath. "Does she have her two-year degree?"

Jim was watching Chloe go as well. He hated to admit it, but he was probably watching for the same reason Irene was. "Yes, and stop looking at my woman's ass."

Irene laughed, the sound rich and low. "Valerie isn't the only one with a thing for redheads." She picked up the puppy's chart, flipping through it lazily. "Seriously, though. You say she worked here as a vet assistant for a couple of years, right?"

"Up until her assault, yes."

Irene followed him out of the exam room and down to his office, now their shared office. "And she's familiar with the routine here and all of the equipment, so that's a bonus."

"You think we should get her certified as a tech?" Jim settled in his chair with a sigh. "God, my back hurts."

"Perks of the job." Irene sat across from him, wincing as she stretched. "She knows what she's doing, and her communication skills aren't *that* bad. We can compensate for her hand by having someone else assist in surgeries and keep her running X-rays, ultrasounds and labs."

Jim loved the idea of having Chloe work with him now that they were mated. "It's up to her, but I don't see why it can't work."

"She'll never be a full vet, but she can be one hell of a tech." Irene winked. "Plus, she'll pretty the place up."

"I'm worried she won't be able to get board certified because of her speech issues." Jim sat back, trying to stretch the soreness from his shoulders. "And we'll have to make sure the courses she's taken will get her the degree she'll need or see if she needs to take more classes."

"Something we can talk about later. Maybe over dinner." Irene stood. "So, you take your fiancée to lunch, I'll deal with the puppy."

"You sure?" But Jim was already standing, taking off his lab coat.

Irene laughed again. "Get outta here." She wagged her finger at him. "But I expect you to do the same when Val pops in."

"Deal." Jim hurried toward the X-ray room, where Chloe was finishing up with the puppy. "Hey, you."

She smiled. "Hey back." She picked up the puppy, who continued to lavish Chloe with love and kisses. "Good boy."

"Have you thought of a name?" Jim took the pup, smiling as it turned its affections on to him. It really was the sweetest little pup. No wonder his mate had fallen for it already.

"George."

Jim laughed, totally getting why she'd picked the name. It seemed his mate was as big a Bugs Bunny fan as he was. "And I will hug him, and pet him—"

"And squeeze him and love him."

He approved. Anyone who liked *Looney Tunes* was on Jim's happy list. "Okay, George. Irene is going to get the bad thing out of your tummy, so be a good boy for her, okay?" He popped into the exam room he'd just seen Irene going into. "You ready for Georgie-boy?"

"George? You named him already?" Irene chuckled when Chloe nodded enthusiastically. "Have Carla sedate him, I'll be in when I'm done with this little guy." Irene petted the older tabby cat.

"Hi, Mrs. H!" Chloe waved cheerfully at the owner of the building Cynful Tattoos rested in. "How's Butch?"

"He's good. He's just in for his yearly checkup and booster shots." Mrs. H, a tattooed older woman who adored the girls of Cynful and their mates, gave Chloe a huge hug. "It's so good to see you back here."

From the way Mrs. H eyed Jim, she expected to see Chloe here a lot more often.

"It's nice to visit." The sad little smile as Chloe looked around the exam room damn near broke his heart. "Anyway, I have to get going. I need to brag some lunch before I pass out." She put her hand to her forehead dramatically. "I might swoon from hunger."

Irene took one hand off Butch to wave them away. "Go. Feed her."

"Will do." Jim took hold of Chloe's hand and, ignoring the delighted look on Mrs. H's face, dragged her from the exam room. "Later!"

"Wait, where are you going?" Chloe didn't try and stop him, but she didn't lead the way either.

"I'm taking you to lunch." He grinned. "It's a fringe benefit of having a partner." He ignored the puzzled way Phil stared at them. The guy was something of a gossip, but he was good at his job and the clients loved him. Soon enough he'd be informing everyone that Jim was off the market.

Even better, he'd tell everyone Chloe was too.

"As long as there aren't any other fringe benefits," she muttered.

Jim pretended he hadn't heard her. They both had to work on their jealousy issues. He still had trouble seeing Gabriel Anderson as anything other than Chloe's would-be boyfriend. Never mind the man was devoted to his wife, Sarah, or that he'd made it clear on more than one occasion that he and Chloe were nothing more than friends. Chloe hadn't helped at all. She'd been jealous of his friendship with Sarah, making comments about how she'd spoken with Gabe, spent time with the man when Sarah hadn't seen him in months.

Little had she known that he'd been hung up on a redheaded kid with the prettiest eyes he'd ever seen and a smile that brightened his day, not the sweet, hurting Sarah who'd been pining for her mate.

Jim knew now that Gabe had gone away to train as a Hunter, but at the time he'd thought his friend had been abandoned by her new boyfriend. He'd stood by Sarah's side, trying to keep her spirits up, but in doing so, he'd gotten *Chloe* jealous. Chloe's reaction led to misunderstandings galore, because he'd been too afraid to make his interest in her known. Chloe, in turn, had nearly destroyed Sarah and Gabe's relationship with her jealousy over Jim's platonic friendship with Sarah. It had been a cluster fuck of epic proportions on all sides.

It made his head hurt just thinking about it.

It had taken Gabe and Sarah a while to straighten out their relationship. He'd been relieved to see his friend get her man, but Chloe's antics had made Jim believe that she didn't want him. If he'd known then what he knew now, if he'd been a shifter instead of human, he would have acted completely differently. He would have claimed Chloe the moment he sensed her doubts.

But he hadn't been. He hadn't known he was Chloe's mate, and they were both still paying for their actions.

"Hey." Chloe tapped him on the shoulder. "Where'd you go?"

Jim smiled down at her. "Thinking about lost time." She tilted her head, confused. "Remember when Max and Emma got married?"

Chloe grimaced. "How can I forget? Loved Disney, hated Sarah."

He chuckled and held open the door of Frank's Diner. "Me too. Except I hated Gabe."

"Did someone mention my name?"

Jim rolled his eyes as the deep voice of the town sheriff rolled over him. He reluctantly waved hello, ignoring the smirk on Gabe's face. As much as they needed the Hunter's help right now, the last thing he wanted was to see him. "Hello, Gabe."

Chloe clutched Jim's hand and waved. "Hi, Gabe."

"Hey, little vixen." The tone Gabe used with Chloe was soft and sweet, as if he was aware she was far more fragile than she let on. "How are you?"

"I'm good." Chloe smiled easily at Gabe. Jim held back the growl that threatened to escape, aware Chloe had ignored Gabe's attempt to hug her hello. She was trying, and so was he. "How's Sarah?"

Immediately Gabe's stance softened, his expression changing from concern for Chloe to a happiness Jim could only envy. "She's good. She set off the fire alarm again yesterday."

Chloe giggled. "How was dinner?"

"Smokey." Gabe winked before giving Jim a far more serious look. "I'm going to talk to that new friend of ours, see what he knows about Chloe that we don't."

Jim nodded. He hadn't forgotten about the attack on Chloe. In fact, one of the reasons he wanted to have lunch with her was to discuss something he should have brought up the day before. He'd been so focused on keeping the threat away from her that he hadn't asked her the most important question of all. "Thanks, I appreciate it."

Gabe nodded. When he spoke, there was a tone in his voice that had his Wolf's ears perking up respectfully. "Look. Chloe's a good friend, like the little sister I never had. I'll protect her, I swear it."

Much to Jim's surprise his Wolf immediately settled down, causing much of Jim's tension to ease as well. Apparently the word of a Hunter was good enough for both beast and man. "That means a lot."

Gabe tipped his hat to them both. "I'll call once I've got some information. You two enjoy your lunch." He stepped past them, pausing for a moment. "Want to come to dinner Saturday?"

Chloe looked up at Jim, and he couldn't resist the pleading gaze any more than he could have kicked a puppy. "Sure." The sheer joy that crossed Chloe's face, the relief, was worth the pain of putting up with Gabe. "We'd love to."

Gabe nodded once and walked out of the diner with a single wave.

Jim led Chloe to a booth, seating her before settling across from her. "So. I have a question for you."

Chloe bit her lip. "Everything all bite?"

"Yes, everything is fine." He covered her hand with both his own, startled at how she was shaking. "Chloe, calm down. It's just, I've been thinking, and there's something that would make me feel a lot better about certain…things. And I know I said you were going to, but I never really *asked*, and you deserve that." He smiled, hoping she wouldn't see his own nervousness. "Move in with me?"

Her mouth opened, but the only thing that came out was a cute little yip.

"Oh, good." All his tension eased at the expression of sheer want on her face. She needed this as much as he did. Jim patted the top of her hand, beyond pleased. "I'm so glad you agree." He held his hand up in the air. "Waitress?"

Chloe closed her mouth.

CHAPTER ELEVEN

"I never said I'd do it, you know." Chloe winced as Tabby worked on the kitsune tattoo she'd had done not too long ago. The pretty, feminine, three-tailed fox sat primly on Chloe's shoulder, the tip of one tail covering its mouth to represent Chloe's speech problems, and how she was overcoming her handicap. She wasn't hiding who she was anymore, or what was done to her, and her kitsune tattoo hopefully showed that.

The other two tails were wrapped demurely around the Fox's front legs, the left paw lifted and slightly twisted, but still delicate and dainty. The claws were barely visible through the fur, but there, a reminder that the fox, though damaged, could still fight with the best of them.

Chloe loved it.

Today Tabby was adding some green to the eyes to match Chloe's, and some white with subtle gray shading to the body of her Fox.

Chloe had decided to add a wolf to the scene, one with Jim's beautiful hazel eyes. She wouldn't have Jim's tattoo done until she saw him shift and could get a picture, though. She wanted to make sure she got his Wolf exactly right. The only thing she wasn't sure of was what pose the Wolf would take with the kitsune. Would he stand over her protectively, or would he lay himself at her feet? Neither seemed quite right to her, so until she saw Jim's Wolf she'd hold off on making the decision.

She knew he'd gone through his first shift already. Tabby had been kind enough to walk him through it, and Alex had been there as well. Tabby was so far along in her pregnancy that she could no longer shift herself, so while she'd talked, Alex had done the actual shift.

She should have asked Tabby to take a picture of Jim's Wolf for her, but at the time she hadn't even thought about it. It was too bad. She really wanted him inked into her skin along with her Fox, especially now that they were mated.

The buzz of the tattoo gun was almost soothing, unlike the current topic of conversation. "You bit him, and now he wants you safe in his den, especially since he and his Wolf know you're threatened. They won't be able to rest until you're there where they can keep an eye on you." Tabby's response was way too cheerful for Chloe's peace of mind. "All that's left is a little cub or two."

Chloe held still despite the fact that her heart was going a mile a minute. "Cubs?" Just the thought of tiny little Jimmys and Chloes running around sent her heart racing in fear.

"Or kits." Tabby's tone was far too innocent. "Want me to add one or two to your tattoo?"

"Gurk." Chloe banged her head on the headrest. She was so not ready to think about kits. She could barely think about living with her mate, let alone having children with him. They'd *just* mated, and while the pull to be near him was stronger than ever, he'd denied her for four years. Could she take that huge a step without making him grovel more?

"You know you're going to do it."

"Have kits?" Gods, Chloe was going to hyperventilate if Tabby didn't drop it. She could barely take care of herself right now. She had no business bringing a kid into this world until she was certain her issues wouldn't impact his or her tiny little life.

"Move in with him." The buzz paused as Tabby wiped away some of the blood and ink on Chloe's shoulder.

"Of source I am. I'm just…" Chloe blew out a breath. "Nervous."

"You think I wasn't scared when Alex mated me?" Tabby sighed. "My Bear might be cuddly, but I was terrified my problems would rub off on him and taint him."

"Bunny adores you." Chloe could see the love her cousin had for the green-haired tattoo artist. You only had to mention Tabby's name to see it. Everything about her big cousin went soft and sweet. Tabby was right too. Out of all her cousins, Alex was the most cuddly.

He was also the most deadly. He worked hard to keep his Bear's instincts under control, using yoga and tai chi, meditation techniques and humor. But if he got his hands on the person who'd ordered the attack on Chloe, nothing would stop him from ripping the guy to shreds.

"Speaking of cubs, when are you spawning again?" Chloe grimaced as Tabby ran the gun over bone. God *damn* that hurt like hell.

"Soon," Tabby growled. "And we're not changing the subject. When are you moving in with Dr. Delicious?"

"Spoon." Chloe blew out a breath as Tabby moved the gun away from the bone. While it still hurt, the thinner skin over the bone was particularly sensitive. "I'm blinking he's not going to wait."

"He's probably packing up your apartment right now."

She wouldn't put it past him. "He's at work, but he could have called in the cavalry."

Tabby lifted the gun as she laughed. "The cavalry being Alex, Julian and Eric?"

"Yup." It might be a Saturday, but vets didn't get Saturdays off automatically. Now that Jim had a partner he'd assured her he'd only have to work every other weekend. She hadn't realized how much he'd been doing without a partner; his time away from the practice, helping his brother Spencer, must have done some damage to his business, but he hadn't said a word about it.

"I bet Eric is bossing everyone else around." Tabby giggled. "How quick do you think Julian will put a stop to that?"

"Pretty damn quick." Ryan's voice cut through the buzz of the tattoo gun. Since Glory was working today he'd stayed at the shop, keeping an eye on his mate as always. It also meant that Jim had felt comfortable dropping Chloe off at the tattoo parlor. She'd assured him that between him and her family she was being watched twenty-four/seven. "I'm pretty sure he'll shut that shit down faster than you can say pig humper."

The gun stopped dead as both Chloe and Tabby looked over at Ryan. "Pig humper?"

Ryan shrugged. "Alex asked us not to curse in front of his kid, so we have to be creative, right?"

Chloe and Tabby exchanged a quick, amused glance before Chloe lay back down again, putting her face against the headrest. "That's one way to put it."

"The best you could come up with was pig humper?" Tabby shook her head and got back to working on Chloe's tattoo. "Did your mama drop you on your head when you were a baby?"

"She says no, but I have my suspicions."

Chloe bit her lip to keep from laughing, but that didn't last long as Tabby began going over bone once more. "Owie owie ow ow."

"I want to do some more work on this. What do you think about some color in the background? It would make the fox stand out more."

Chloe debated that for all of two seconds. So far she loved the work Tabby was doing. Seeing what Tabby could do with free reign would be interesting. "Go for it."

"Yes!" The cheery yell was accompanied by what Chloe assumed was supposed to be a dance of happiness. Instead, Tabby looked like a hippo wiggling on an uncomfortable rock. "You're gonna love this, sugar."

"I like it already."

Chloe gasped. She had the strangest urge to cover up Tabby's work, but her mate had already seen it. "Jim?"

"Hey, pretty girl." Jim's scent overwhelmed her, overcoming the smell of ink and blood. His lips brushed the top of her head gently.

"Why aren't you at twerk?" He'd dropped her off with orders to stay close to Ryan.

Ryan choked on a laugh. "Yeah, why *aren't* you at twerk?"

Ugh. Of all the words to get wrong, it would have to be that one. And in front of Ryan, no less.

Luckily Jim ignored her brother, focusing instead on Chloe's emerging tattoo. "I'm done for the day. I heard you back here, so I thought I'd see what was going on."

"You sure you like it? Tabby wants to approve it." She winced. "Im. Improve."

"I love it." He was quiet for a moment, but she couldn't move to see why. "Is that...my Wolf?"

"Wha?" Tabby had started Jim's Wolf already?

"Yup. Surprise, Chloe!" Tabby allowed Chloe to sit up long enough to look at Tabby's cell phone. On the screen was an image of a gray wolf. Jim's Wolf. "Did you think I wouldn't nab a pic for you?"

"Thank you." Chloe sniffled, hoping she wasn't about to start bawling like a baby. She put her forehead down on the headrest, trying to hide how red her cheeks had become.

Jim leaned over and whispered something to Tabby before kissing the top of Chloe's head once more. "I'm going to have a word with Ryan real fast before I have to head back to work. Stay here. Ryan will take you to my place before going home with Glory. All right?"

Chloe gave him a thumbs-up, but most of her attention was on the half-heard whispers between Tabby and Jim.

What had he meant by "play"?

***

"Any news yet?" Jim couldn't see Chloe from the back room, but he could hear the quiet chatter as she and Tabby spoke softly to one another. The scent of her blood was making his Wolf restless, but the knowledge that Tabby was inking his image on Chloe's skin made him shiver with a possessiveness he'd never known before.

She was his, body and soul. Now he just needed to make sure her heart was his as well.

Tabby was doing a marvelous job. The play-bow his wolf was doing in front of her blushing little kitsune made him smile.

"From Cheetah-boy? Not yet." Ryan scowled at something on his screen, muttering something about…manure overages? As a veterinarian Jim often found himself in shitty situations, but he'd never had to account for them on a spreadsheet before.

"So our buddy Francois hasn't managed to get ahold of whoever it was that almost made Barney shit petunias?"

"Language," Ryan muttered absently. "And no. Neither of them will tell me." Ryan sat back with a sigh. "Listen, Barney and Francois have both decided to keep my Hunter status hush-hush. They want me off the Senate books."

"Because of Chloe." Now it was Jim's turn to scowl. "They probably already know."

Ryan nodded. "I agree, but keeping me a non-sanctioned Hunter means that very few of them know."

"And that might flush out whoever's been watching Chloe?" Jim would have to do something about the security around his home. If both Spencer and Chloe were there, he wanted to make sure they were both safe from ravaging shifters.

"Exactly."

"Huh. It's stupid enough it might work." Jim tapped his finger on the tabletop. "I wanted to ask you or Julian something."

"Hmm?" Ryan stretched with a grunt.

"It's about my brother."

"I'm sorry." Ryan's expression became pained. "No, turning him into a shifter won't cure him."

Jim sighed. "I thought so."

"It's not like in books or movies. Whatever illnesses or injuries we have as humans carry over into our shifter selves. It's why the Poconos Pack Luna still has a limp, or Sheri is still legally blind. If you had, say, diabetes when you were changed, you'd be a diabetic Wolf."

Jim nodded. Ryan's remorse over his inability to help was far too obvious in his voice and face for Jim to disbelieve him. "I'm still thinking of asking someone to change him. Spencer and Chloe are the only family I have left, and I want to share this with him."

"Wait. First off, the moment you mated my sister you got the entire Bunsun-Williams clan as family."

Jim stared at Ryan, then shuddered dramatically. He'd seen the "clan" in the diner before, wreaking havoc. The poor waitress hadn't known whether or not to join in or run for the hills. "Oy."

Ryan laughed. "Let's talk to Max and Emma first, see how they would want to handle it." Ryan held up his hand when Jim started to protest. "It's how things work, Jim. This is Max and Emma's territory, not the Bunsun-Williams territory. They get final say."

"I don't think they'd say no." Glory stepped into the back room, making sure the curtain was shut behind her. "They're pretty easygoing about that sort of thing."

Jim nodded. He trusted Emma's judgment. "Emma's met Spencer. She seemed to like him."

"If Emma liked him I really don't think it will be an issue. In fact, she might offer to have him become a Puma." Glory pulled a couple of sandwiches from the fridge, handing one to her mate before sitting next to Ryan. "Some Packs or Prides would turn him away because of the wheelchair, but I don't think the Halle Pride would."

"Or the Poconos Pack?" Jim remembered Emma and Max's wedding, and the large, redheaded man who'd married Belinda Carlisle. Rick Lowell was a scary-ass man, but Jim doubted he'd have any trouble accepting Spencer into his Pack.

"Speaking of which, we need to have Rick formally induct you into his Pack. Tabby keeps poking Alex about that." Ryan sounded uninterested, but to a Bear, there was no such thing as a Pack or Pride. They, like Foxes, lived in family groups, where the head of the family was the unofficial "Alpha".

Jim, as a Wolf, should have felt that something was missing, something he desperately needed. Instead, he felt fine. There was no desperate need to belong, no howling desire for an Alpha. His Wolf was content just the way it was. "It's okay. I'm fine."

"Not your fault, Jim." Ryan took a humongous bite of his sandwich.

Before Jim could correct him Glory added her two cents. "Ryan's right. You got bit protecting us. No Pack would diss you for that." Glory patted his hand in a gesture that was probably meant to be reassuring. Unfortunately, she hadn't quite gotten used to the extra strength her Grizzly gave her.

Jim picked up his demolished hand and cradled it to his chest. "Ow."

Instead of apologizing, Glory grinned. "Told ya SG stood for Super Glory."

Ryan widened his eyes and shook his head no.

Jim waved his hand feebly in front of Glory. "I need this to fix kittens and puppies, you evil kitten-slaying woman!"

She started to stick her tongue out at him but let out a burp instead. Startled, Glory reared back, her eyes crossing as she glared suspiciously at her tongue.

Jim's brows rose. "That's attractive."

Ryan's head hit the table, his shoulders shaking as he laughed his ass off.

"Okay, so we need to talk to Max. Got it." Jim leaned in, keeping his voice down. Ryan was still busy laughing, so he'd have to rely on Glory to make sure Ryan understood what he was saying. "I need to figure out a way to up my security without making Chloe worry too much."

"Barney might have some ideas." Ryan lifted his head off the table and wiped a tear from his eye. "Ah, geez, I needed that laugh."

"You're welcome." Glory bit into her sandwich with a disgruntled look.

"You're going to have to explain to Spencer what's going on as well." Ryan finally got his laughter under control. "He'll need to understand why we're all worried about Chloe."

Glory nodded and swallowed. "There's also the chance that they'll go after him in order to get to her."

"Or you." Ryan pointed his finger at Jim. "So keep your ears perked for anything, and I mean *anything*, out of the ordinary."

"Alex and Tabby are busy getting ready for the birth, so you're going to have to rely more on Ryan and me, and probably Eric." Glory patted his hand, and this time she was careful of her strength. "Cyn and Julian will also be available whenever you want."

"We can watch your place the way we did Glory's." Ryan's sapphire eyes had specks of deep brown in them, the memory of the pain his mate had gone through bringing out his Bear. "We'll talk to Uncle Will and get a schedule set up amongst us, and the girls will work something out between them."

"We can keep Chloe here when she's not with doctors or therapists." Glory bit her lip. "In fact, why don't you bring Spencer here too? We can introduce him to the family and see what he thinks about shifters."

"He knows about shifters, it's just a matter of whether or not to change him."

Ryan froze, and Glory grimaced.

Jim glanced back and forth between them. "I'm going to go with I did something wrong."

"Not exactly." Ryan set his sandwich down. "But now it's not so much a matter of *will* he be changed as *what* he'll be changed into."

Glory was looking at Ryan with a pained expression. "We'll give him the choice, but now that he knows about us he'll have to be changed."

Ryan shot him a look full of sympathy. "And I hate to say this, but it will be painful. A non-claiming bite always is."

Damn it. The last thing Jim wanted to do was inflict the kind of pain Jim had gone through on Spencer. His brother had been through more than enough already. But if it was the only way, then Spencer would at least get a choice about what shifter he'd become. "I'll talk to him, then. He might have a preference."

"Bring him here first and let him meet the Bears and Foxes. He might not want to be part of a Pack or Pride, but since he's lost all his family except you—"

"And you're a Wolf," Ryan interjected.

"Exactly. He might crave that closer connection." Glory hitched her thumb toward the curtain. "Tabby knows more about that than even you."

"So bring him here tomorrow. Chloe might also have a few things to say."

"Hmm." Jim stared at the curtain as if he could see through it to his mate. "I need to talk to her about working for me again as well. My partner suggested she become a vet tech and work labs for us."

The excited, distinctly canine yip told him his mate could hear more than he'd thought of the conversation he was having with Ryan. A few moments later, Chloe barreled through the curtain and threw herself at him, nearly toppling them both over. "You mean it?"

He laughed and nodded. "Get certified and you've got a job."

The sloppy kiss she laid on him in thanks wasn't the most expert kiss he'd ever gotten, but it had to be the best one he'd ever been privileged to receive.

CHAPTER TWELVE

"One little, two little, three little koozies, four little, five little, six little koozies…"

Chloe giggled as Tabby tossed can koozies one after the other into a cardboard box. She hadn't realized how many of the foam can coolers she'd stuffed into that drawer until Tabby started emptying it.

"How many goddamn koozies does one person need?" Tabby shook her head. "Half of them are for different lawn products, and this one…" She shuddered. "This one has foam boobies on it."

"That one belongs to Ryan." Chloe wasn't going to take the fall for that one, no matter how hard Ryan shook his head *no*. "He hid it here when he mated Glory."

"Oh, really?" Glory glared at Ryan, who tried his best to look innocent.

He failed miserably. "It's for breast cancer?"

Glory put her hands on her hips. "Why was that phrased as a question?"

"Because he's in jeopardy!" Chloe crowed, ducking when Ryan took a swing at her.

"Traitor." Ryan stuck his tongue out at her before turning back to his mate. "Now, Glory, you know I only touch your koozies these days."

"Ass. Hole." Glory picked up the boobie koozie and threw it at Ryan.

Alex strode out of Chloe's bedroom, a huge box in his arms. "Where do you want this?"

"What's in bit?" Chloe tilted her head, trying to read Alex's chicken scrawl.

"Girl stuff." He shrugged as if the box weighed nothing.

"Ah. Put it by the door." It was more than likely stuff she'd need sooner rather than later. If Jim had his way she'd already be living under his roof, but she had years of living in this apartment to pack away. There was no way it was going to take less than a week to pack everything up.

Hell, if her family had their way she'd have been at Jim's before the end of last weekend. They wanted to know the Wolf was guarding her door night and day and that Jim was with her when they couldn't be. While that hadn't happened so far, even her parents were pushing her to move in with her mate.

"What do you think? Should we pack the boobie koozie or not?" Tabby waved it around, horrifying Ryan. "I mean, we wouldn't want Ryan to go without while he sleeps on the couch. Again."

"I hate you all." Ryan grabbed the koozie and threw it in the trash. "Thanks a lot, pal."

"Anytime, Ryan. Anytime." Tabby patted him on the arm. "Speaking of hate, how come y'all didn't beat the shit out of Jimmy-boy yet?"

Alex and Ryan exchanged a glance that set all of Chloe's senses on alert. "You didn't."

"We didn't." Alex grimaced. "We planned on it, but we didn't."

"Yeah. Although we did threaten his balls if he hurt you." Ryan grinned. "Good times."

"I still want to know why you have so many koozies." Tabby put her can of soda into one that Chloe had gotten at school.

"You threatened to beat up Jim?" Chloe crossed her arms over her chest and glared at Ryan and Alex.

"Are you having frat parties and not inviting me?" Tabby sipped her caffeine-free soda.

"Yes, Tabby. It's all orgies, boobie koozies and Dorito breath twenty-four/seven around here," Chloe deadpanned.

"Hah! I knew it." Tabby picked the boob koozie out of the trash and squished one of the boobs. "You know, I think these are fake."

Alex smiled at his mate, the expression so sappy Chloe gagged. "I—"

Whatever her cousin was going to say was interrupted by the doorbell. "I've got it." Chloe opened the door without looking through the peephole first, earning herself some growls from her relatives. It didn't matter, though, as Chloe knew who was on the other side. "Hey, Jim."

"Hello, sweetheart." Jim kissed her softly and entered her apartment. "How's the packing going?"

"Good. We're almond done."

Jim froze, his head tilted as he stared at Tabby. "Chloe?"

"Hmm?"

He had the most adorable look of confusion on his face as he asked, "Why is she squeezing a koozie boob?"

"Don't ask me, ask her." Chloe pushed past her mate. "Ryan, have you seen my elephant?"

Jim's gaze slowly panned to her. "Elephant?"

"It's not an elephant, it's Jabba the Hutt with the world's ugliest erection." Ryan shuddered. "And it's in the box over there."

Chloe snarled. "The one marked trash?"

Ryan nodded vigorously. "Don't let her take it, man. Don't let her take it."

Chloe lifted her elephant out of the trash bin and cooed. "Hello, little fella."

"Little fella?" Jim's eyes went wide. "Holy fuck, it does look like an erect Jabba." Jim tilted his head, his lips quirking into a small smile. "I never thought of Jabba getting a chubby before."

"It's not Jabba, it's an elephant." Chloe'd had this argument before. "See the ears?"

It was like she hadn't spoken at all, because Jim decided to give them an education on penile placement in the animal world. "Anatomically speaking there are a number of species here on earth that have a penis on their face, like the land snail. There's also a fish in Asia with a penis under its chin."

Ryan and Alex shared a horrified look. "So Jabba puts his face near your crotch?" Alex shivered. "No wonder he liked licking Leia so much."

"Was he licking her, or was he…?" Jim waggled his brows.

Alex gagged. "That is *so* wrong."

"Gives the term *giving head* a whole new meaning, doesn't it?"

Ryan widened his eyes. "Hell no. Jabba ain't licking *my* face."

"Or having sex with it?" Jim reached out and poked the elephant's trunk, ignoring Chloe's low growl.

"Face sex with Jabba the Hutt." Alex choked. "No. Way."

"He could like butt sex. That's how sea pigs do it." Jim stared at the elephant as his grin grew wider. "Think Hutt butt sex. With a love dart."

Ryan and Alex both covered their behinds, no doubt protecting their virginity from her ceramic elephant. "Love dart?" Alex looked ready to smash her elephant to bits, possibly looking for a "love dart."

Ryan backed up until his butt was against the wall. "I tell you, Jimmy, I'm protecting your ass here."

"Yeah. Don't allow that thing in your house." Alex put his rear against the wall right next to Ryan's. "It's evil."

"Evil in the I-want-to-make-with-the-Hutt-butt-sex way." Ryan gagged.

Glory came into the room and stopped dead at the sight of Chloe's elephant. "What is that? It looks like a mutated blob fish with a penis on its head."

"It does not." Chloe glared at Glory, cradling her elephant to her chest. "They don't mean it, you poor baby, you."

"Yes. Yes, we do." Ryan made the sign of the cross with his fingers. "Keep that thing away from me."

"It can't be that ba— Jesus Christ on a pogo stick!" Tabby, who'd waddled from behind Glory to get a better look at the statue, reared back in shock. "Someone stuck a penis on intestines."

The room erupted in laughter as Tabby stared in horror at Chloe's beloved elephant. "Jim."

He cleared his throat. "Your blob penis is lovely, Chloe. I know just where to put it in our new house."

"Under six feet of concrete?" Ryan muttered.

"Sprinkled with holy water?" Alex added.

"It's not *that* bad." Chloe stroked her elephant. "Shh. It's all right. No one will hurt you."

Tabby took a step back. "It's like watching a Stephen King novel come to life. Next thing you know it will be whispering to her in the darkness about it's the only thing in the world that loves her and she needs to move to Maine or something."

"I feel sorry for people who live in Maine." Glory plopped down on Chloe's sofa. "Killer clowns, aliens in the woods, ancient wizards…" Glory smiled. "You know, now that I think about it, it sounds kind of interesting."

Alex turned to Ryan. "When you and your goofy mate move to Maine can you take the creepy blob with you? It would fit right in."

Tabby waddled over and shoved the koozie over the elephant's trunk, then turned to the men. "Better?"

"I think I might be scarred for life," Ryan gagged.

"Guh." Alex stared in horror at the elephant. "For two whole seconds I didn't want to touch boobs."

Jim, his eyes shielded behind one hand, flailed at Chloe until he knocked the koozie off the elephant's trunk. "Is it gone yet? Tell me it's gone."

"And here I thought boobs made everything better." Ryan still looked repulsed. "I have now learned that they do not."

"My whole world is spinning," Alex muttered sadly. "I'm not sure I can survive this."

"If boobs no longer make things better, does that mean we're gay?" Jim joined Ryan and Alex against the wall. "Are we going to be looking at pictures of half-naked cowboys and getting boners?"

Just as the front door opened, Ryan yelled out, "I do not want to have Hutt face butt sex!"

Julian turned to Cyn. "See? I told you they were here."

Cyn strolled into the apartment ahead of her mate. "What the hell are you all yelling about?"

The three men pointed toward Chloe's elephant.

Cyn stared, her head tilted to the side. "Oh."

"What do you think it is?" Perhaps Chloe had one ally in her apartment. Chloe adored her elephant and wouldn't get rid of it no matter what anyone said, even Jim.

"A hairless proboscis monkey that died in a horrible limb-mangling accident? Maybe a naked mole rat with the world's ugliest dildo strapped to its face?"

"I give up." Chloe put her elephant into the box marked Living Room, ignoring Jim's muttered pleas to put it out of its misery.

Julian plucked it right back out. "Wow. It looks like an aye-aye and an elephant seal had babies. Really hideous ones."

She snatched her elephant back. "You all suck."

Julian put his hand on his chest. "Hey, now. I'm not the one toting around a ceramic ball sac with ears."

Chloe snarled and put the elephant in the charity box. "Happy now?"

The cheers were bad enough, but when they started dancing she decided they were all dicks. No pun intended.

***

When Jim's phone rang he stepped out of Chloe's apartment to answer it. The volume those Foxes and Bears could put out was simply overwhelming. There was no way he'd be able to hear his call, even with his enhanced hearing.

Without looking at the caller ID he answered, thinking it was Irene. She had the clinic today so Jim could assist in Chloe's apartment packing. While it meant he'd have the next two Saturdays it had been worth it just to see Chloe playing with her friends. "Hello?"

"Your father is trying to deny me alimony."

He sagged against the wall, cursing himself for not double-checking the caller ID. "Hello, Mother."

"How can he deny me alimony? I worked for that man, cleaned his home, made his meals, dealt with you, and now he doesn't want to pay me for that?"

Jim desperately wanted to hang up, but that would only bring a bigger rant down on his head than the one she was gearing up for. "Thanks, Mother."

"For?"

He sighed. She sounded genuinely confused, as if she couldn't understand why he'd be upset. "Nothing."

"Jim." The stern tone of her voice didn't bode well for the rest of the conversation. "You need to tell your father that he owes me."

He almost laughed. "I don't talk to him anymore, remember? I haven't spoken to him since—" Ugh. Damn it. The last thing he wanted to do was bring up Spencer, but it was too late.

"Since you decided to visit his spawn?"

Jim kept his mouth shut. Maybe he could put the phone on mute and rejoin his friends. She'd never know the difference, and he'd get a more peaceful afternoon.

"Jim? Answer me!"

Or not. "Yes, Mother."

"Don't 'yes, Mother' me in that tone, young man. Do you know how many hours of labor I was in?"

"Yes, Mother."

"I swear, you're worse than your father. You don't give a damn about anyone but yourself."

"Excuse me?" Jim practically launched himself from the wall he'd been leaning against. "I'm not the one who cheated, I'm not the one who calls their adult son to nag, and I'm not the one who's being an ass right now."

"James—"

"I'm also not the one who lied about the condition of her son's girlfriend." Jim was still pissed about that, but he hadn't had time to confront her over it. "How dare you tell me she was fine just to hurt me?"

"Oh, please. With as many women as you go through I'm surprised you remember her name."

He took the phone from his ear and stared at it for a moment before yelling into it, "That's Dad!" Jim was beyond done. If any more of his mother's vitriol spilled over onto Chloe, he'd be seriously pissed. "Listen to me, Mother. I'm done. I have listened to you rant and rave about my father, and I agreed that he shouldn't have cheated. He shouldn't have hidden Spencer from you." He ignored her snarl of rage and continued. "But I'm *not* Dad. I didn't cheat, I don't owe you alimony, and I'm sick and tired of being the one you hurt because he won't pick up his fucking phone."

"Jim?"

He turned mid-rant at the sound of his mate's voice. Just her scent calmed him. "It's okay, sweetheart. Go back inside."

"Are you sure?"

He ignored his mother yelling into the phone and focused instead on Chloe. "I'm sure."

"Okay. I'm here if you need me, beau."

"James! Is that another one of your girlfriends?"

Jim froze at the look on Chloe's face. She hid the pain quickly, but it was too late. She darted back into the apartment like her ass was on fire, shutting the door quietly behind her. "Mother?"

"What?"

"You just insulted the woman I plan on marrying. Don't call me for a while, all right? I really don't want to hear anything more from you." He didn't wait for the reply. For once, he hung up on her.

Dammit. Things were going well with Chloe, and now his mother had to go and ruin it. He'd have to do something to get Chloe to realize she was the only one for him, but what?

He entered the apartment to a frigid silence. Even Tabby was glaring at him, shaking her head and muttering under her breath. But the men were not glaring at him, they were talking quietly among themselves and watching their mates warily.

Only Chloe gave him a smile, and it was a wan, weak thing compared to the earlier laughter over her ugly ceramic ball sack.

Jim held up his phone. "My mother doesn't know anything about my life anymore. She's too caught up in the divorce from my dad, who cheated on her. Now she sees me either as an extension of him, or the go-between for them. She's…" It pained him, what he was about to say next, but it was the truth. "She's not my mom anymore. Not the one I remember, anyway."

"Told you." Alex shook his head at Tabby.

Chloe took hold of Jim's hand. "He told me some of this earlier. She's being a pain about Spencer too."

"Spencer?" Tabby's eyes went wide. "Oh. Spencer. Sorry, Jimmy."

And that easily, the women returned to their normal sunny (and slightly sweaty) dispositions.

"Anything we can do to help?" Cyn stood with her arms crossed over her chest, an Amazon ready to do battle.

"Nah." Jim waved her help away. "Other than making sure the B-A-L-L S-A-C never again sees the light of day."

Chloe smacked him on the arm before walking to the charity box. She sighed and shook her head. "Where is it?"

He'd never seen such bad acting in his life, as each one of them denied knowing what had happened to the horrible, misshapen sculpture. But it did the job, lightening the mood once more as they finished most of Chloe's packing.

"How many books do you own?" Jim grunted as he picked up one particularly heavy box.

"Textbooks." She grimaced. "Not sure I need them anymore."

"You do. I'd hold on to them until you know what courses you need to take for your vet tech certifications." He put the box down firmly by the front door. No way was she going to chicken out of going back to school.

She sighed happily. One of the things he admired most about his mate was her ability to bounce back quickly to her happy disposition after something had hurt her. It was a skill he wished he could master. "Good point."

"So." Alex clapped his hands together. "We move Chloe's stuff out tomorrow, after Jim is done working? Or move most of it today and get the rest of it tomorrow?"

"I vote all of it tomorrow." Tabby leaned against the small kitchen peninsula and rubbed her belly absently.

"I vote we get as much done today as we can since we're all here. Afterward, Chloe can treat us to pizza and root beer." Ryan rubbed his hands together. "I'll take double meat."

"I agree. Let's get the majority of the boxes over to Jim's place, eat there, then call it a day. The furniture can wait until tomorrow." Julian hefted another box of textbooks. "We should have enough cars to make it in one go."

And that was how it went, climbing up and down Chloe's stairs as they put her life into their backseats. At one point Jim decided to pull her aside. As rapidly as things were moving he wouldn't be at all surprised to find she was freaking out a little bit. "You all right with all of this?"

She stared at him like he'd grown a dick on his face. "I've been waiting for this, for *you*, for how long?" She grabbed his head and pulled him down for a quick, fierce kiss. "I'm *so* all right."

"Yes'm." He licked his lips, already pulling her closer for another kiss. "Okay."

She giggled, but the sound became muffled as Jim gave her a scorching kiss.

"Jim, can I talk to you for a sec?" Cyn gestured toward the bedroom, the last place to be packed.

"Sure." He was worried, because Cyn looked a little more serious than she had earlier. So he was surprised when she grabbed him by the ear and yanked his head down.

"I like you, you know," she whispered in his ear. "I think you're good for Chloe. But if you hurt her again I'll rip your *cojones* off, grill them with some garlic butter and serve them up with a side of salsa and guac. *¿Entendido?*"

Jim gulped. "Understood."

"Good." Cyn patted him on the shoulder and sauntered out of the bedroom. "Now, let's get you and your mate home."

Jim followed meekly, shaking his head when Chloe shot him a questioning look. The best way to save his balls from the sauté pan was to keep her happy, and he intended to do just that.

Chloe shook her head at Cyn, but she couldn't quite keep the smile off her face. She must have heard Cyn's fierce whisper. "Leave my mate alone, Cyn."

Cyn shrugged. "You're family."

"So is Jim."

Cyn grinned. "Which is why I won't kill him, just maim him a little." She held up her hand, her forefinger and thumb barely half an inch apart.

Chloe tsk'd. "Don't touch his man-bits. I need them."

Cyn's grin turned evil. "Super Bear could probably grow them back."

Jim shuddered. He had no desire to find out if that was true. From the way Ryan and Alex were clenching their legs together they didn't want to either.

CHAPTER THIRTEEN

"Welcome home."

Chloe glanced around, barely able to speak. She was in Jim's house, being welcomed as a mate.

She shuddered, holding back tears. She'd never thought they'd get to this point. She'd thought he'd never acknowledge her, that all her dreams were for nothing. Then he'd barreled back into her life and changed it forever.

No matter how much she wanted to cry with joy, she couldn't. The last thing she wanted to do was look like a weak little girl in front of the man who'd once claimed she was too young for him. She stiffened her spine instead and turned to him with a smile. "Thanks."

His brows furrowed as he stared at her. "Are you all right?"

Jim reached for her but she backed away, turning instead toward the stairs. "Just tired." She'd head to the bathroom and get herself back under control, then deal with the fact that she was moving into her mate's home. "Where's the bathroom?"

He pointed toward a door right off the front, beside the coat closet. She darted inside, waited a moment or two, and then flushed. She started running water in the sink, splashing it on her face. She took a deep breath and toweled her face dry before giving herself a stern look in

the mirror. "Okay, Chloe. You've bot this. You can do it."
She opened the door and squeaked.

Jim stood on the other side, his arms crossed over his
chest, his gaze filled with amusement. "Everything all
right?"

She nodded. "Yup."

"Mm-hm." He shook his head and took her hand.
"C'mon, Chloe. Let's get you settled for the night."

She let him tug her up the stairs, unable to look away
from him. His scent filled her, so strong here in his home
she felt wrapped in it.

"This is a spare bedroom I'm using for storage right
now. It wouldn't be hard to change it to a guest room."

She blinked, trying to focus as Jim gave her a tour of
the upstairs, but everything was a blur other than the feel
of his hand in hers.

"This is the guest bath, and this is the second
bedroom. I've got it set up for guests."

"It would make a great…" She gulped and shot him a
quick look.

"A nursery?"

She couldn't tell how he felt about that from his
neutral tone, but she wasn't going to lie to him and say she
didn't want kids. No matter how terrifying the prospect
was, today had reminded her that her family, and her mate,
had her back. "Yes."

He grinned back at her. "Good."

The relief made her light-headed.

"And this is the master bedroom." He opened a door
wide, showing a very masculine, very bachelor bedroom.
Dark cocoa walls, a king-sized bed with attached end
tables and the biggest television this side of a movie
theater were the only things in the room.

He seemed pleased by it. He waited for her reaction with a big grin on his face.

It was a good thing she was a shifter, because it was darker than the inside of a troll's asshole in here. "Where's the lights?"

He flipped a switch, and the ceiling fan she hadn't noticed before lit up.

"Oh." She bit her lip. "What about when you want to read in bed?"

His grin dimmed. "Kindle." He glanced around, as if suddenly realizing she was less than enthused. "You don't like it?"

It wasn't the eclectic, kind of crazy room she adored, but she could work with what was in here. "Can I bring my afghan?"

He seemed relieved. "Yup."

"Can I bring my pillows?" Because, God help her, this room needed color like a caffeine addict needed Starbucks.

"Sure."

"Can I—"

He put his hand over her mouth. "Whatever you want, put it in here."

She licked his palm until he removed his hand with a grimace. "Can we ditch the TV?"

"Fuck no."

"But—"

"No." He pointed to the wall-mounted entertainment center. "That's where I do some of my relaxing."

There was every game console she could think of on that wall, along with a ton of games. "Why not move it to the family room?"

"And let your brothers and cousins get at it?" He shuddered. "They'd delete all my saves."

She wanted to think up a compromise. He was taking her into his home, but it was going to be *their* home. "How about we make an 'us' cave?"

He stared at the television. "An us cave?"

She nodded. "Pick a room—"

"—and put the TV and game consoles in there?"

"If you make it off-limits to guests your games won't get messed up." The more she thought about it, the more she liked it.

He put his arm around her, his gaze still glued to the television. "But what would you do?"

She stared at the controllers. "Learn to pray."

"Huh?" He saw what she was looking at and laughed. "Oh."

She shrugged, unfazed by his amusement. She knew enough gamers to know cursing and praying went with the territory. "Might be good therapy."

"For your hands?"

She rolled her eyes at him. "Nope. I'm training for the perfect swamp ass."

He coughed, peering at her behind. "Two out of three ain't bad."

She blushed. "Shut up, you."

He swung her around and picked her up around her waist. "Wanna play with my joystick?"

"That depends."

"On?" He carefully put her down on the bed, then knelt and took off her sandals.

Chloe winked. "On whether or not you're going to mash my buttons." She wiggled as he pulled her pants down.

"I stroke keys. Caress them. I know which ones to press to get the achievement." He looked at her through his lashes, his T-shirt joining her jeans. "But if you try going offline I might have to unleash an AOE to wake you back up."

Okay, now he'd lost her. "What's an AOE?"

He laughed. "It means area of effect, like a fireball spell."

"Oh." She tugged her own T-shirt off. "I really don't want my tail singed."

"But I like it when you get all hot and bothered." He reached around and unhooked her bra. With a little wiggly help from her, he lifted it away and dropped it on the floor.

"There's a difference between tanned and burnt." Chloe unbuttoned his jeans, concentrating on that so hard she didn't realize he'd frozen. "What?"

"Little Miss Chloe." He nipped her neck. "Are we into kink?"

She snarled as her eyes changed color. "You are *not* turning my behind fifty shades of red."

"Don't worry," he snickered, his five o'clock shadow brushing against her sensitive skin. "I only spank bad pups." He flinched, rearing up as her hand smacked his ass. "Ow! What was that for?"

She wagged her finger at him. "Bad puppy."

He grumbled under his breath, but instead of making love to her, like she'd thought he was going to, he yawned so wide she could see the bumps at the back of his throat.

"Tired?"

"I'm fine." His lips clamped shut, but it wasn't like she couldn't see his chest expanding or his eyes squinting. He let the held-back yawn out in one long, slow breath. "See?"

"Bull pit." She tugged him until he lay down next to her, then reached for the covers. "Moving and mad moms make you tired."

He grimaced, his hand resting on her breast. "But, I want it."

She patted him on the head like the little kid he resembled. "You can have it later."

"Promise?" His voice was already fading.

She brushed his hair tenderly off his forehead, then kissed it. "Promise."

***

"I've always wanted a tattoo." Spencer glanced around Cynful with a gleeful expression and rubbed his hands together. "Can I have Grumpy Cat?"

Chloe laughed as Jim flicked the back of his brother's head. "Dork."

"What?" Spencer smacked Jim's hand away when Jim went to flick him again. "Asshole."

"At least get an animal that isn't a meme." Jim strode forward to shake hands with Ryan.

"Like what, a flamingo? Cause everything else is taken." Spencer rolled forward too. "Hi. You must be Chloe's brother, Ryan, right?"

Ryan blinked. "How'd you know?"

"You were snarling at Jim."

Chloe glared at her brother. "He didn't do anything bong, Ryan."

"Reflex. Sorry." Ryan held his hand out to Spencer. "You must be Jim's brother, right?"

"What gave it away?" Spencer grinned.

"You smell similar."

"That's because I stole his body wash." Spencer winked at Cyn, who stood behind the counter. "So, you're a shifter?"

Ryan eyed Chloe then nodded. "A Grizzly."

I've been dying to ask this." Spencer's eyes widened. "Can I be a wereskunk? That would be *awesome.*"

Ryan groaned and pinched the bridge of his nose. "There are no weremoles, wererats, wereskunks, werechipmunks, werebunnies other than Alex…"

Chloe giggled at that, then tuned them out. She'd heard a similar spiel before, when she'd questioned her parents about what kinds of shifters existed. Shifters were all mammals, omnivorous or carnivorous, no larger than a Grizzly and no smaller than a Fox. Those kinds of questions were common from those who were just learning about them, or from shifter children who either didn't know any better or just wanted to see that vein pop on their parents' foreheads.

"…and *no*, repeat, *no* werecapybaras."

Cappy what? Chloe shook her head as Spencer wheeled himself over to Cyn, talking quietly with her. From the expression on Cyn's face the two of them were going to get along like peanut butter and chocolate. "What do you think he'll choose?"

"I don't know, but I'm kind of hoping Wolf." Jim shrugged. "Still, I'll be happy with whatever he wants."

"You want my opinion?"

Jim nodded. "Always."

Chloe smiled, pleased with his instant response. "I think he's either going to choose the Pumas or the Bears."

"Why?" Jim was staring at her curiously.

"The way he interacts with people. He'd fit in beautifully with either my family or the Pumas. He's got the same sense of humor as Emma, but the tenacity of Ryan." She watched as Cyn shook her head and gestured for Spencer to follow her into her work area. "Five clucks says he comes back with a pissed-off cat tattoo."

"No bets." Jim kissed the top of her head. "I know my brother better than anyone, and he's in there right now getting a famous snowshoe Siamese inked somewhere on his body."

"You think Cyn will explain Bears to him?" Chloe bit her lip and eyed the closed curtain. "She's so new herself she might not be cable to answer all his questions."

"We can go in there, make sure he gets all the information he needs." Jim grimaced. "Or you can. It's not like I know much more than she does."

"I can get Ryan to talk to him after he drops me off tonight too." Chloe was beginning to think bringing Spencer into the shop to talk about shifters might not have been the brightest idea. Anyone getting inked or pierced in one of the other rooms could overhear, and if they weren't a shifter, it could be bad.

"Then let's go see how Spence is doing before I head off to work." He'd had last Saturday off, so today was his day to go in.

"Sure thing." She followed him into Cyn's workspace, grinning when she saw the beginnings of… "Is that a wheelchair?"

"Yup." Cyn shook her head, smiling slightly. "Got him to change his mind. We're putting something better on his leg."

"Like?"

Spencer winced as Cyn inked a thick, rounded line. "Professor X, the most bad-ass wheelchair-bound superhero known to man."

"Good call." Jim patted Spencer's shoulder, careful not to shake him and ruin the lines of Cyn's work.

"I want the cat on his shoulder, though." Spencer winked as Cyn rolled her eyes.

Cyn bit her lip and tilted her head, studying her design. "How about Nightcrawler perched on the back?"

"And have the Professor looking annoyed, while Nightcrawler looks smug?"

"I like the way you think." Cyn began free-handing the professor, something Chloe hadn't seen done before. Usually the design was done on transfer paper, placed on the skin, then the lines traced before color was added. Free-handing meant that Cyn was working without a template on the skin. It was something, watching Cyn work the ink into Spencer's skin, the design taking shape before them.

"How's your tattoo coming, little vixen?" Jim whispered in her ear, the brush of his lips sending shivers down her spine. "I haven't seen it yet."

That was because they hadn't been naked together again since he'd claimed her in her apartment. She'd gotten up before him that morning, so he hadn't had a chance to see it. "It's coming."

Jim coughed. "Really?"

The way he drawled that had her poking him with her elbow, hard. "Perv."

He chuckled. "I want to see it."

Since it was hidden under her T-shirt she'd have to practically remove it for him to see it. "Later."

"I'll hold you to that." Jim slipped his arm around her waist and tilted his head. "What say we leave Spence in Cyn's hands and go get some coffee?"

The gagging sound from Tabby's work area had Cyn shaking her head no at them with wide eyes.

Jim smirked. "Or, we could continue the family tradition of having sex in the break room."

This time it was Ryan who gagged.

"I don't think anyone here wants to see the Wolf moon today." Spencer shuddered, earning a glare from Cyn. "The beaver moon, on the other hand…"

Both women stared at Spencer, then reached out and smacked him.

"Ow." Spencer rubbed his head. "You two are no fun."

"Ugh." Chloe rolled her eyes and looked at Jim. "Maybe we should force Spencer to become a Wolf, because your brother is a dog."

"Hey, now. Just because I have specific reasons for wanting to go to the beach this summer does not mean I'm a dog."

Jim's face became suspiciously blank.

Chloe glared up at him, but asked Spencer, "Why?"

"Butt cheeks and boobs." He waved his hand slowly in the air, like Vanna White showing off a panoramic view of T&A. "Butt cheeks and boobs everywhere."

"Oh yeah. His ass needs to Wolf out." Cyn snorted and got back to work.

"Speaking of canines, George is well enough to come home tonight." Jim steered Chloe away from a comically leering Spencer and back toward the front door. "He's neutered, de-wormed, de-flea'd and out of the woods."

"Good." That was some of the best news Chloe had gotten all week. She couldn't wait to see George again.

"He's going to be huge, you know. Those paws of his are massive." Jim smiled fondly. "We should have named him Moose."

"Nah. We can still bug him and love him even if he is the size of the couch."

Jim cupped her cheek. "I have to go."

"I know." She missed working with him, but it wouldn't be long before she was back at the clinic, surrounded by the animals she adored and the mate she loved. "See you tonight?"

"With the puppy."

"Darn tootin', with my puppy." She lifted her lips to his, giving him a swift kiss.

"Is that all I get? That little peck?" He pouted adorably. "I'm bringing you a puppy, after all."

"Add some ice cream and we'll see what I can do when you get home."

The blue of his eyes was rapidly replaced by golden brown. "Deal."

Chloe smiled as he closed his eyes and inhaled, slowly letting the breath out. When he opened his eyes again, the brown had faded to a faint hint around the outer ring of blue. "See you at home, Jim."

He shuddered, his eyes once more brown. "Can't wait." With that, he cupped the back of her head and took her lips in the kiss she'd denied him. Slow and sweet, it was full of the promise she'd given him. When he pulled away, her own eyes had shifted to the reddish brown of her Fox. "Don't leave the shop without Ryan."

"Mm-hm." Chloe nodded dreamily, reaching for him once more.

Jim gave her what she silently asked for. This kiss was far more sensual, sending heat racing through her body. She gave some serious thought to dragging the man into the back room and fulfilling some fantasies, but damn it, just when she was about to give in he pulled away again. "I have to go."

She shook her head and whimpered. Dear gods, she *really* needed him to take her in the back for some nakey time.

"Be good, little vixen. I'll see you tonight." He brushed her hair back from her face with a wistful sigh. "And don't let my brother talk you into doing anything stupid."

"I heard that!" Spencer's laughing voice came from behind Cyn's curtain.

"I'll send someone to take him home when Cyn is done with him." He stepped away from her completely, backing toward the front door. His gaze never left her. "See you soon."

She nodded, still fantasizing about getting him undressed and spread-eagle. The chaise was soft and inviting looking. Cyn wouldn't mind too much, right?

Jim bumped into the door, jumping slightly, as if he'd forgotten where he was going. With a sheepish look he turned and opened it, heading out into the summer heat with a small sigh.

Damn. There went her afternoon delight, but at least the rear view was nice.

CHAPTER FOURTEEN

Ryan had dropped her off an hour ago, and she'd finally gotten over her nerves and decided to explore her new home. What she'd seen impressed her a great deal. It was nothing like his bedroom. He'd created a warm, inviting space in keeping with the style of the house.

Her mate never ceased to amaze her.

Jim lived just outside the main part of town, in one of the older brick homes. Built sometime in the 1920s or '30s, the home had a huge covered porch painted crisp white that wrapped most of the way around the house. He'd put a set of two rocking chairs out front with a table between, and for just a second she felt jealous over anyone who might have sat in that second chair, chatting with her Jim. But she could picture nights when the crickets were out and the fireflies were dancing in the bushes, just him and her, and she shivered with pleasure. She couldn't wait to just relax there with him and know that it was finally real.

Inside the main part of the house was a dream come true. Its original crown moldings were in place, as was the fireplace, but he'd remodeled it at some point. The original brick around the fireplace had been changed for a sleeker, more modern look of dark stacked slate. He'd also painted the built-ins that surrounded it, filling them with books and knickknacks. He'd painted all the trim white, brightening the space, and the walls were done in gold, like fresh honey. He'd filled the space with furniture done in simple lines and soft, buttery leather. The kitchen was small, but he'd brightened the space with crisp white Shaker cabinetry, oil-rubbed bronze fixtures and swirling gold granite countertops.

All the place really needed was some artwork and maybe some patterned fabric. Perhaps he'd let her change the plain drapes for something a little more fun? And she'd seen the prettiest chair on the Internet the other day, one that would go beautifully with his leather sofa.

"Jim wants to move. I want him to put in a stair lift for my chair. We're discussing it." Chloe turned to find Spencer watching her from the dining room doorway, his expression tense. At the moment, the formal dining room had been set up as a bedroom for Spencer, so she'd chosen not to go into that room without an invitation. "What do you think?"

She glanced around, her gaze lingering on the beautiful moldings and original hardwood floors. "What would be easier for two?"

Spencer shrugged. "Since I don't plan on living with my big brother for the rest of my life—" he gagged, and she laughed, "—I'm thinking he should stay."

"I agree." In her mind, she'd already started ticking off the minor changes she would like to make if Jim kept the house, like adding a backsplash in the kitchen or adding some pictures to the walls. He had spots where you could see pictures had once been, but for some reason he'd taken them down.

"His parents."

"Huh?"

"The pictures were family photos, pictures of him with his parents. He took them down when they both turned on him." Spencer shrugged. "Can't really blame him, but I feel bad about it."

"Don't. Not your fault."

"I still want to kick their asses for how they've treated Jim. They hurt him badly, and he's been mourning them like they're dead. It's why I'm glad you're finally here. Now he has someone besides me to stand by his side." Spencer shook his head. "C'mon, Jim should be home soon. Let's go sit in the living room and get comfy."

Chloe followed Spencer into the living room and settled on the sofa. There was a clear spot where Spencer could easily pull up his chair, making him part of anything going on. It was obvious that Jim adored his brother and was willing to do whatever it took to make him comfortable.

In a way, it was reassuring to her. If he could adjust his life so easily to accommodate Spencer, then maybe his easy acceptance of her disabilities was real as well. If only she could trust that he wasn't going to run away, or abandon her again. While she didn't have the panic issues Glory did about being left, she wasn't keen on the idea of her mate deciding once again that he might be too old, or too busy, or too anything for her.

"He really cares, you know. More than you think." Spencer's knowing gaze was full of sympathy. "He's just not very good at showing it."

She looked around the house and shrugged. "I'd say he's *berry* good at showing it when it matters."

"His parents have really fucked him up, you know." Spencer snickered. "Wait until the first time you answer the phone and it's Wanda. She'd give Gandhi indigestion."

"I heard." When he tilted his head in confusion she explained. "She called while we were packing my apartment."

Spencer grimaced. "Poor guy. She treats Jim as if he were the one who cheated rather than the sperm donor.

You'd think, since Jim is her only child, she'd do better by him."

"That might be why." Chloe sat back and tucked her legs under her. "If she feels abandoned—"

"But she wasn't. All Jim asked was that she accept that he wanted a relationship with me, and she couldn't do it. She put down this ultimatum, and every time he talks to her she screams her head off and tells him he's a backstabbing son of a bitch."

"At least she got part of it right," Chloe muttered.

Spencer leaned forward and patted her hand. "Anyway, I wanted you to know that you were all he talked about when I asked him about home."

She blinked, blushing furiously. "Really?" Jim had talked to Spencer about her?

"Really. He was worried about having our issues dumped on top of yours, that it might set your recovery back. He was worried that he was spending so much time with me and you wouldn't be willing to give him a chance because of it."

"I wish he'd balked to me." Chloe sighed. "I would have understood."

"I tried to get him to, but…" Spencer shrugged. "He's stubborn."

Chloe's eyes went comically wide. "No, really?"

"Like a dog with a bone." Spencer's smile turned sweet. "I'm glad you're here. He needs you more than he lets on."

"How?" Chloe could understand her need for Jim, but Jim was so strong, so self-contained, she couldn't see him needing anything or anyone.

"He…lives inside his own head too much. He needs someone who can force him out, who can get him to see the bigger picture. He's one of the most caring people I've ever met, but he tends to forget about himself. It's part of what makes him such a good veterinarian, but he's running himself into the ground trying to help everyone at once. Hell, he's still trying to get his mother to acknowledge me as his brother, and if anything's a lost cause, that is."

The front door opened and Chloe swiveled in her seat, draping her arm along the back of the sofa. "Hey."

Jim smiled so wide she could almost see his back teeth. "Hi." He put the pet carrier down and walked over, giving her a soft kiss. "You and Spencer getting to know one another?"

She glanced over at Spencer and nodded. "I tink so."

"She's cute." Spencer tilted his head. "Do you have a sister?"

"Nope, but I have a cousin, Tiffany." She laughed. "Then again, I'm not sure I'd inflict her on you. She's fierce."

Jim shook his head. "What do you two want for dinner?"

Chloe smiled. "You cook?"

Out of the corner of her eye she saw Spencer shaking his head wildly.

"Knock it off, butthead." Jim stuck his tongue out at Spencer.

"Our sperm donor should have been Italian. Then he could have named him Sal Monella."

Jim popped Spencer on the back of the head as he walked by as Chloe cackled and clapped her hands.

Spencer bowed. "Thank you, thank you."

Chloe was practically bouncing in her seat as she stared at the pet carrier. "George?"

Jim nodded. "Let him out."

"Wait. You brought home a dog?"

Chloe ignored the squeak of Spencer's wheels as she swiftly let her new puppy out. George bounced out, knocking her on her ass and covering her in puppy kisses. It took a good ten minutes for her to finally get up off the floor and let the puppy explore.

Jim's fond smile as he gazed at George morphed into something a great deal warmer as he looked toward Chloe. "What say we order in pizza and watch a movie?"

"Works for me." She winked at Spencer as Jim helped her up off the floor. "Chick flick?"

Spencer blinked, pausing in his rapturous scratching of George's floppy ears. "Only if you rip my testicles off first."

Chloe laughed again as Jim began ordering their food. Spencer was a riot. How could anyone not like him? Maybe she would figure out some way to get Wanda Woods to accept him, because it was obvious Spencer wasn't the only one who needed his brother in his life. If anyone could "pull him out of his head", it would be Spence.

"All right." Jim settled on the sofa, a beer in one hand and his remote in the other. "Have I got something for you." He rubbed his hands together as the beginning credits began to roll.

"What the…?" Spencer tilted his head. "Cartoons?"

Chloe gasped. "Oh my God! It's *Princess Mononoke!*" She hugged Jim tight, almost knocking the beer can out of his hand. "This is perfect!"

For a moment he looked utterly shocked, then hugged her back fiercely. "I love a woman who's willing to let her geek flag fly."

"Can we do *Spirited Away* next?" Chloe was practically bouncing in her seat, forcing Jim to put his beer down.

"I don't see why not." Jim kissed the top of her head.

"If we're doing cartoons tonight, we do Monty Python Saturday night." Spencer slumped in his chair, pouting adorably.

Chloe stared at him, hoping she wouldn't laugh. "Cartoons? *Cartoons? Princess Mononoke* is one of the breast fantasy films ever made." She hmph'd. "Heathen."

Spencer held up his hands. "Hey, no one told me it was a breast fantasy. *That* I'm down for."

Chloe rolled her yes. "Pig."

"Oink." Spencer started paying attention to the television, only moving to answer the door and pay for the pizza while Jim held George back. For all his razzing about cartoons, he was quickly as engrossed as Chloe and Jim in the epic tale of Ashitaka and San.

Jim's scent wrapped around her, warming her from the inside out. His easy breathing, the way he adjusted his arm automatically when she moved, the soft little kisses he peppered on her head, told her more than words that he was beyond pleased she was there, in his home, sucking down his pepperoni pizza like sausage was going out of style.

***

Jim was having one of the best damn days of his life. He'd woken up that morning to an armful of snuggly redhead, his mate's scent on his sheets making his Wolf practically purr in satisfaction. His brother had made blueberry pancakes for breakfast, proving once again that Jim had gotten his cooking skills from his mother. When he'd left for work, Chloe had been looking up ways to get certified as a vet tech so she could begin working at his clinic as soon as possible while fending off an overenthusiastic armful of puppy love.

Best of all, Chloe's things were in his bathroom, her clothing taking up space in his closets and drawers. The thrill he'd felt when he'd seen her feminine hygiene products snuggled next to his shaving kit should have given him the heebie-jeebies, but instead he'd pumped his fist.

You knew a woman meant to stay when her tampons were nestled up against your aftershave balm.

To top it all off, one of his clients had brought in a pregnant stray who'd just birthed some of the most adorable kittens he'd seen in a long time. She'd told him that she couldn't bring any of them home, so Jim was going to find places for the stray and her babies once he was sure they were all healthy.

He already knew where two of the kittens would go. Chloe would adore the little white one with the single black spot on its nose, while the only little tiger-striped baby would go straight to Emma. The other three he'd have to put up for adoption.

"We're keeping one." Irene smiled as she watched the little fur balls sleep. "The clinic needs another pet, and a cat is always a good one."

Jim shrugged. "We can do that, but you're cleaning the litter box."

She snorted out a laugh. "We'll see." She patted him on the back. "When will Chloe be starting work? We could really use the help."

"She's looking into her certs." Jim shrugged off his lab coat, eager to get home to his mate. "As soon as she has them she starts."

"Good. I wish we could have her come in earlier, do the work she used to do."

"Not with her hand the way it is." Chloe had done quite a lot around the clinic, helping with the animals, soothing the clients, and running the more delicate labs. She'd been a sparkling presence, and he missed her more and more each day he worked without her.

Damn it. He should have listened to Emma when she told him he was being unreasonable about Chloe's age, but he'd been blind to how much he truly cared about her until after she'd been hurt. He was going to spend the rest of his life making it up to her, loving her the way he should have right from the beginning.

"Earth to Jim, come in, Jim." Irene waved her hand in front of his face. "Where did you go to?"

Jim shrugged. "Chloe, who else?"

She laughed. "Ah, new love."

He didn't correct her. His love for Chloe had started when she still worked for him, way before she found herself in the hospital. But not only was she too young, it was unethical to date his employee, a rule he was happily tossing out the window now that he'd claimed her.

"You gonna put a ring on it before someone else snatches it up?"

Jim snarled, startling Irene.

"I'll take that as a yes."

"Sorry." Jim huffed out a breath and ran his fingers through his hair. "It feels like I've waited forever for her to grow up, and now that she has I'm all 'mine mine mine'."

"Well, I'm happy for you. I'm also glad I don't have to listen to you pining for her anymore." She shuddered dramatically. "I swear, you have more estrogen than I do."

He flipped her off, ignoring her laughter in favor of waving good-bye to the other vet tech, Clare. It was Saturday afternoon, his new partner had the evening shift, and Jim was off tomorrow.

Man, it was a *great* day.

He stepped outside into the sweltering heat of the parking lot, almost gasping at the sensation of stepping into a broiling oven. He was glad Chloe and Spence had chosen to remain home today rather than try and do the grocery shopping. While both were doing better healthwise, he'd worry far too much about them in the heat without being there himself.

A shadow moved up behind him, and he sniffed, automatically scenting the air.

The hair on the back of his neck stood up as he smelled the unfamiliar shifter.

When the shadow lifted what looked to be some sort of stick or bat into the air, Jim moved into action. He spun, his elbow tucked into his side to protect his ribs, his other hand raised to try and catch the arm of the shifter.

The shock on the shifter's face didn't stop him from taking a swing at Jim. Jim stepped in close, managing to grab hold of the shifter's arm at the biceps and elbow, blocking the baton from hitting him. He grunted a bit as he took a hit to his abdomen, but now that he had the man's arm locked, he pivoted, using his attacker's momentum to put the shifter on the ground. He kept hold of his attacker's wrist and twisted, managing to grab hold of the baton as his attacker moved under him.

The shifter was surprisingly fast, jumping to his feet with a canine growl. Without missing a beat, he threw a punch at Jim.

Jim expected something like that as soon as the shifter got up. He parried the punch, then moved his free hand up to grab his assailant's wrist. He then used his elbow to drive his opponent back, staggering him. As he stood back up, Jim got his first good look at the guy.

He was easily three to four inches taller than Jim, with massive shoulders, huge biceps and a thick jaw. The man was a tank with legs, and he was staring at Jim with sheer determination.

"Let me guess." Jim kept his voice low, his stance easy. He watched his opponent's eyes and body language, aware the guy was going to attack again. "Someone from the Senate sent you."

"You're rogue, and need to be brought in."

Jim shook his head. "Use your senses. What do they tell you, Hunter?"

The man grinned viciously. "I'm not a Hunter."

What?

Before Jim could process that, the man barreled toward him, looking to take Jim to the ground. If that happened, Jim would be damn near helpless against the larger man's body mass.

Instead of dodging, Jim took a step forward and did an overhand punch to the man's jaw, knocking the shifter sideways and disrupting his momentum. Jim pivoted and jabbed the shifter's stomach, then quickly followed it up with a roundhouse kick to the guy's groin.

The shifter somehow shook the jewel shot off and swung, but Jim was turning out to be faster than his opponent. He barely dodged out of the way, the man's beefy knuckles clipping his jaw.

Chloe was going to be pissed if he came home bruised.

"Thought I'd be easier to take down, you son of a bitch?" Jim smiled grimly. "Should have done more homework on your target, dick breath."

The shifter rubbed his jaw, not rising to the bait of Jim's insult. "I guess so." The shifter glanced behind Jim. "Looks like we're gathering an audience."

"Maybe you should give up, then. I'm sure James Barnwell will go easy on you."

The man grimaced at the sound of Barney's name. "Why the hell is he in town?"

"Ask him."

Instead of responding, the shifter threw a punch that nearly knocked Jim on his ass. He barely managed to block it, but his training kicked in, and he reverse punched the asshole right in the solar plexus. He then jabbed his palm toward his opponent's eye, forcing the shifter's head back.

It was time to take this asshole down.

He allowed his Wolf senses to come to the fore, his vision changing, losing the red-green spectrum. His sense of hearing became sharper, his nose twitching as he smelled his opponent's rising frustration.

That was good. If the other shifter was becoming sloppy Jim would be able to use that to his advantage. Jim went after his opponent, cursing to himself when the guy dipped and Jim's attack missed by barely an inch. The follow-up punch rocked Jim's head back, causing him to see stars. He barely had time to block the next attack.

It was a reminder not to get cocky or the other shifter would win.

The sound of sirens had his attacker backing off, his attention split between Jim and the street. "This isn't over."

"Not by a long shot," Jim answered. He stared as the shifter ran off, sliding into the copse of trees just behind the clinic.

Two police cars pulled up as Jim tried to pull his Wolf back. He needed his eyes to return to normal before he gave his report to the cops. Neither of the cops who got out of their cars were shifters, but Jim had seen them both around town. "Hey, Doc. Everything okay?"

He nodded. "Yeah. I think the guy wanted to rob me and I put up more of a fight than he expected." He couldn't exactly tell the two that he was a target of a shifter.

One of the cops loped into the woods after Jim's attacker. While he wanted to call the officer back, he couldn't, not without raising some suspicions he couldn't answer. So he prayed the shifter had gotten far enough away that the cop wouldn't find him.

"Any idea who it might have been?"

Jim was able to answer that one honestly, at least. "Never seen him before in my life."

"Anyone have a grudge against you?"

Jim shrugged. "Not that I'm aware of. It's not like snipping Rover's balls off is going to make me an enemy for life, right?"

The cop laughed. "I'd ask Rover about that if I were you."

Jim grinned, the adrenaline rush beginning to wear off. His hands were beginning to shake, and he was getting nauseous. If he hadn't seen the shifter's shadow, he was pretty sure he'd be, if not dead, then at least kidnapped. "I'm pretty sure Rover is pissed as hell. Want to question him?"

"I think I'll pass, Doc."

The other cop jogged up, panting. "He's gone."

Jim sighed in relief.

"Come down to the station and let's get a report, Doc." The cop patted him on the shoulder. "You've got one hell of a bruise coming up on your chin."

"Great." Neither Spencer nor Chloe was going to allow him out of the house by himself ever again.

CHAPTER FIFTEEN

When Jim walked in the door three hours late Chloe was ready to jump out of her skin. What the hell had happened to keep him from…?

"Jim?" She limped to his side, sore from unpacking. His face was bruised and he was clutching his stomach. "What happened?"

"We need to call Barney, Ryan and Gabe." He put his bag down with a pained grunt, greeting George with a few pats. "Seems we have a new player in the game."

She bit her lip as Jim walked past her. He was hurt, and there was little she could do about it. Unlike her brother or her cousin, she couldn't heal his wounds or ease his pain.

But she could dial the damn phone. She plucked her cell from her pocket and dialed Ryan first.

"Road Kill Café, you kill 'em, we grill 'em. Chef Billy Beau Bubba speaking."

She didn't even blink at her brother's weirdness. "Ryan, someone attacked Jim."

"Where is he?" All of the humor had left Ryan's voice. He was all Hunter now.

There was a pause as Ryan spoke softly to someone else, probably his mate. "I'm on my way. Bunny's coming too."

She sighed in relief. "Can you get hold of Gabe and Barney? Jim wants them here as well."

"Will do." He hung up, and Chloe turned to follow her mate.

She found him in the living room, talking to a worried Spencer. Poor Spencer looked bad, his face pale and his hands shaking. "So he just swung at you?"

"Yeah." Jim sat on the sofa with a wince. "I saw his shadow, so I was able to block the blow, but he got a few good ones in before the cops arrived."

Chloe ran to the kitchen and bagged some ice, wrapping it in a dish towel. She took it back to the living room and handed it to Jim to put on his jaw. "Did he say why he attacked?"

Jim nodded. "He called me a rogue, but he also told me he's not a Hunter."

"I don't understand." Why would a non-Hunter be after rogues? That didn't make any sense. Of course, the fact that Jim wasn't rogue, but was still being hunted as one, also didn't make much sense.

"Maybe Barney can shed a little light on it, but it sounded to me like the Senate sent this guy out to bring me back to them." Jim grabbed hold of her arm as she swayed, forcing her to sit in his lap. "Careful, Chloe. I won't let them take me anywhere, I swear."

Spencer, his expression grim, wheeled away without a word.

"Shit." Jim watched his brother leave but continued to stroke Chloe's arm. "He's lost so much. If he loses me too I don't know what will happen to him."

"Shh." She kissed Jim softly. "Neither of us will lose you."

He glanced at her, startled, his expression softening. She must look as scared as she felt, because suddenly he was hugging her so tight she could barely breathe. "Of course not."

She whimpered, aware the sound was far more canine than human. Her vision shifted, the warm tones of Jim's home cooling. She could almost feel her furry tail tucking between her legs and her ears lying flat against her head. She burrowed against her mate, sticking her nose in the crook of his neck. Not even his scent could calm her.

Her Fox was terrified that Jim would be taken from them.

"Do you need to change?" Jim's question was barely a whisper, as if he was afraid that if he spoke any louder she'd spook.

She nodded. Maybe if she let her Fox out she'd be calmer. The knowledge that she could more easily protect her mate and their den in her Fox form had her yipping.

"All right." Jim helped her stand. "Spence? Stay in the other room until I call for you, all right?"

"Okay, but if you're getting funky in there I want that sofa shampooed before I sit on it again."

Chloe, against all odds, giggled.

Within moments she was naked, the heat in Jim's gaze almost making her change her mind. What was a little sofa cleaning compared to having her mate buried deep inside her?

But her Fox wanted out. It wanted to sniff their den, mark it somehow as theirs. While males were more prone to scent-marking their dens, females were also known to do so. And Chloe was feeling not only territorial, but threatened, and her Fox was demanding that she do *something* to warn others away.

Chloe allowed the change to flow over her.

"Wow." Jim's gasp of awe had her wagging her tail. She'd watched her cousins change often enough to know exactly what he was seeing. It wasn't like the things you saw in the movies. No horrific crunchy bones and pain, but not sparkly jumping in the air and BAM! Foxy time.

Nope. It was more like watching water flow through the person, moving them, bending them, blending them with their animal in a liquid haze of a dream until the man was gone and only the animal remained. If Jim touched her during her shift all he would have felt was warmth flowing through his fingers, like holding out your hand to a comforting fire. The sensation was tingling and airy, and Chloe had been fascinated by it from the first moment she saw her father change into a Bear. It was both sensual and innocent in a way a non-shifter could never understand.

"You're beautiful." Jim knelt in front of her and rubbed behind her ears, laughing when her leg began to thump on the carpet. "And cute as hell."

She stuck her tongue out at him.

"Is that…?"

Chloe turned to find Spencer staring at her, fascinated. He wheeled closer at Jim's nod, holding out a shaking hand.

Chloe bounded forward, got up in his lap, licked his face twice then jumped down and went back to her mate.

Jim was growling, but Spencer was smiling like a little kid, wide-eyed and just as happy as could be. He looked over at Jim and sighed. "I want one."

Chloe began sniffing around the house, her senses on full alert. The strong odor of her mate and his brother filled her, soothing her. Even the scent of their puppy calmed her, because George now smelled like home. So far, no strangers had been in her den for the last week or two. While she caught the stray scent of Irene, Jim's partner, she also caught the scent of Val, mingled so strongly with Irene's that it was obvious the two were longtime lovers.

She checked upstairs, where Jim's scent dominated. Her Fox couldn't detect any scents other than hers, Jim's and Spencer's, and Jim's was strongest.

He'd been telling her the truth about not dating, then. Either that or he hadn't brought a woman into his home in a long time, long enough for the scents to fade completely.

With a happy yip she headed back downstairs and pawed at the back door. She needed to do a sweep of the outside of the house.

Oddly enough, it was Spencer, breathless with excitement, who answered. "Hold on a sec, I'll get it."

A sweep of fur against her flank, the scent of her Wolf, told her why Spencer was the one who was opening the door and muttering about dog gates. Jim had shifted, joining her in checking their den. Spencer held George back, and for that she was grateful. The puppy was far too young to fend off an attacker, especially a shifter.

She allowed Jim to lead the way. While the human in Chloe knew she now lived in Jim's home, her Fox was giving him the courtesy of having his Wolf show her around their den. Together, they sniffed the sniffs and smelled the smells, marking the edges of his tiny property side by side. Her slight limp from her damaged left paw was barely noticeable as she skipped happily at her Wolf's side.

Nothing seemed out of the ordinary. Chloe lifted her face to the wind, barking in excitement when she caught a whiff of her brother and cousin. She trotted back toward the house, Jim right by her side.

"That. Was. *Awesome!*" Spencer was sitting by the open door, a towel in his hands for wiping muddy paws. "When do I get to do that?"

Jim's ears perked up as the doorbell rang.

"I got it!" Spencer took off, followed swiftly by both Jim and Chloe. She wasn't about to let Jim's baby brother get hurt, even if she was pretty sure the people at the front door were Alex, Ryan and…

Was that Cyn?

What was Cyn doing here? And where was Julian?

She picked up her clothing, hoping her teeth didn't do any damage, and trotted up the stairs toward Jim's bedroom. Once there, she shifted back into her human skin, already missing her tail and ears. At least her Fox was content that there weren't any threats immediately around their den. She'd be able to sleep a little easier tonight.

"Is your Fox as content as my Wolf is?" Jim's arms slipped around her. The shift didn't heal the bruises, but Jim's tone was quietly happy, the weariness he'd displayed when he first got home completely absent. "It likes knowing you were out there with us."

"Mm." She closed her eyes and leaned back against her mate. "We were securing our den."

He froze for a split second before he laughed and began rocking her. "I guess that makes sense. Even though I shift, I still think of myself as me, not my Wolf."

"Your Wolf is a huge part of you now. You have instincts you didn't have before, senses that are sharper and more focused. Your needs and his will overlap, become one." Chloe was relieved she managed to get all of that out without tripping over her words. Jim was good for her, in more ways than one.

"Like my need to have my mate in my den?" He caressed her stomach, the gesture proprietary.

"Mm-hm." She lifted his hand and kissed the back of it. "Now we have to go see our family."

He shivered. "My Wolf and I like that too." He kissed the side of her neck. "*Our* family."

"It's like a Pack, but more…" The word she wanted eluded her, but she didn't care. She was far too happy to allow her disability to rile her up.

"In your business?"

"I was going with crazier than monkeys at a banana convention, but that works."

"As long as they continue to refrain from throwing poo at me, I think I'm okay with that." Jim slowly let her go, rubbing his nose against her shoulder before taking a step back. "Let's get dressed and tell them what happened."

She nodded, some of her calm evaporating at the reminder that her mate had been attacked. "I hope Barney knows bumping about who went after you."

"He might." Jim bent over, pulling his jeans on without underwear, distracting Chloe with the thought that he'd be walking around commando for the rest of the night. "The guy who came after me seemed to know who Barney was."

Uh-oh. That could be good or bad, depending. "You said he wasn't a Hunter?" Chloe dressed quickly, eager now to talk to Barney and Ryan.

"That's what he said, but I'd have no way to tell." Jim pulled on a T-shirt and waited for her to finish dressing. "C'mon, sweetheart. Let's go greet the monkeys."

***

Jim led Chloe down the steps, silently cursing the fact that he'd had to ruin the easy, happy mood they'd established during their quick run outside. He vowed he would take her out into the woods surrounding Halle at some point. He'd just have to ensure that they went with other shifters as well. He doubted Ryan would let Chloe run anywhere without him nearby, not at least until they discovered why the Senate suddenly had a hard-on for her cute little ass.

"Hey, guys. Thanks for coming." Jim shook hands with the three male shifters, taking in their grim expressions. Alex's hazel eyes were brown as he gazed at Chloe, his stance tense. Ryan seemed more relaxed, taking in his sister's calm demeanor with a small smile. And Barney seemed almost too relaxed. Jim wasn't fooled for a moment, though. He doubted Barney missed much, relaxed or not.

Jim held out his hand to Cyn, smiling when she took it. "Cyn, how's Super Bear?"

"He's good, thanks." Cyn hugged him tight. She patted him on the back and gave him a toothy grin. "Now, what the fuck is going on?"

Spencer tilted his head. "Super Bear?" He glanced between Jim and Cyn. "Do I want to meet this guy?"

"Oh, yeah." Cyn twisted one of the pink strands of her hair around her finger. She'd kept the tri-tones going, the blonde, black and pink suiting her personality. "He's going to want to take a look at you."

The hope in Spencer's gaze was heartbreaking.

"I don't think even he can cure you." Jim hated bursting his brother's bubble.

"I didn't even know that was on the table. I just thought it would be cool to turn into a bear with a huge-ass S on my chest."

Chloe rolled her eyes and focused on Ryan and Barney. "Jim was attacked outside his clinic by someone boo claimed the Senate sent him."

Jim took a step back and pulled his mate against him. "He also claimed he wasn't a Hunter, but he seemed familiar with Barney's name."

Barney's eyebrows shot up. "What did he look like?"

"Big. I mean, fire truck big. Dark hair and eyes, and he smelled canine."

Barney tilted his head. "Any accent?"

"Nope. He sounded like a news caster, his accent was so bland."

"Any other marks on him? Tattoos, scars, anything that comes to mind?"

Jim tried to remember if he'd seen anything of the sort. "Nothing that I can think of. Honestly, I was just trying to keep him from putting me on the ground."

Chloe shivered, tensing in his hold. "This sucks rocks."

"It also tells us the Senate is aware of Jim now." Ryan glanced at Barney. "We've got to figure out what the fuck is up with this shit before it escalates."

"I've got Francois trying to get a hold of Vaughn, but no one has heard from him in weeks." Barney sat on the couch, his ankle resting on his knee. His battered cowboy boots looked like they needed to be reshod. "I hate to say it, but I'm worried about him."

"We need to track him down." Jim sat in the chair next to the sofa and tugged Chloe into his lap. It was his favorite place now that his mate was in his home. Chloe seemed just as happy as he was with the arrangement, snuggling into him easily.

"What's this 'we' shit, newbie?" Barney cocked an eyebrow at Jim. "You're no Hunter."

"Neither is the man who went after him." Chloe's tone was low, filled with worry for Jim. "And if the Senate is sending out non-Hunters for so-called rogues? What does that mean?"

Barney's expression turned grim. "It means we've got a cluster fuck of epic proportions on our hands, and it's all centered around you, Chloe."

Ryan stood and began to pace. "All right. We know Jim and Chloe have been declared rogues, but they aren't. So someone in the Senate is either crazy, or they're up to something." Ryan waved his hand toward Jim and Chloe. "Why them, and why now?"

"It wasn't Francois that attacked you, I know that much." Cyn scowled.

"Francois's alibi checks out," Barney added. "He was hunting a legitimate rogue in Baton Rouge when Chloe was attacked."

"So we've got more than one would-be rogue hunter in the area." Jim cuddled Chloe closer in his arms, the danger to his mate once more riling his Wolf.

"How are they slipping in undetected?" Cyn put her hands on her hips and glared at Ryan and Barney. "I mean, shouldn't they be checking in with Max and Emma?"

The two looked at each other with similar *duh* expressions. Ryan shrugged. "If they haven't then they're in the territory without permission."

"At least the ones that aren't Hunters. Hunters have a great deal more leeway where that sort of thing is concerned, because the rogue could turn out to be the Alpha of the territory." Barney got up and went into the kitchen, helping himself to a soda out of the fridge. He came back carrying enough for everyone. It was pretty clear the man was used to being in charge wherever he was. It never seemed to occur to him to simply ask permission to do something. "However, even they could claim their presence is sanctioned due to the Senate."

"Do they have proof that they have that authority? Like cops have warrants?" Cyn had a good point.

"She's right." Jim stroked Chloe's back, the gesture soothing both of them. "There's no way to tell that someone is a Hunter. I mean, I can't feel anything different about either of you."

"You would if we were facing a real rogue." Ryan nodded toward Barney. "And I could tell pretty quickly what Barney was when I met him."

"Like calls to like." Barney grinned, and something about the way he moved altered. Jim's Wolf sat up and took notice, watching the man warily. "Too bad Jimbo here isn't one of us. Then we could tell the Senate to shove it up their collective poop-holes."

Chloe choked on her soda, some of it spraying out of her nose.

"Wait." Spencer held up his hand. "Jim was attacked because of Chloe?"

Chloe flinched, and Jim glared at his brother.

"That came out wrong." Spencer mouthed *Sorry* at Chloe, who nodded back even as she tried to wipe up the soda she'd snorted all over herself. "I meant that someone is after Chloe, not that this is Chloe's fault. And they're targeting Jim because of their connection, right?"

"Exactly." Barney stared at Chloe and Jim, his brows furrowing. "At least I think so."

"Nothing unusual happened to me before Chloe and I mated." Jim nodded his thanks to Ryan. He hadn't even seen the man leave the room, but he was handing Jim a dish towel to help wipe Chloe's mess up. "Other than that, the only time I've been on their radar was when the shifter that was after Glory changed me."

"And we all know he was loco." Cyn sighed and pinched the bridge of her nose. "I swear, this town sees more action than a porn star."

"So the guy who handed out the orders is missing, we have non-Hunters going after non-rogues, and the only tie they have is someone in the Senate is handing down conflicting orders." Ryan slumped down on the sofa and stared at his hands. "How high does this go?"

Barney stiffened. "You think the Leo is involved?"

Ryan shrugged, but refused to look at any of them. "As much as I hate to say it, it's a possibility."

"But, why? None of this takes pence!" Chloe grimaced as her nerves affected her speech.

"No, it doesn't. And that's beginning to piss me off big time." Barney tapped Ryan on the head. "And it's your job to ask questions and find answers, even if we don't want to think about it."

"What's a Leo?" Spencer tilted his head.

It was Chloe who answered. "He's the leader of all of the shifters, a white Lion who—"

"White, like you?" Spencer sat forward, his elbows on his knees. Jim was glad his brother was strapped in and had locked the brakes on his wheelchair. Spence had taken more than one tumble out of his puppy-like eagerness to learn all he could about Jim's "woof-ness".

"And like Super Bear." Cyn smiled, her gaze growing fondly distant. She had to be thinking about her mate.

"So white shifters are like the super-duper version of their plain old boring counterparts? Are there white Wolves too?" Spencer practically bounced in his seat. "What about—"

"Whoa there, Nellie," Barney laughed. "Nope. As far as we know, white shifters are rarer than rare. Chloe is…"

Barney's gaze slowly turned toward her, his gaze speculative. "Unique."

"There are more Spirit Bears like Julian, but only one white Lion like the Leo." Cyn frowned, her gaze, too, now glued to Chloe. "It *has* to be that."

"But she was attacked *before* she turned white." Alex stared at Chloe as if he could unravel the mystery with his gaze alone. "She only turned white after Julian healed her brain."

"Are you sure about that?" Jim frowned, thinking. "If she was in a coma, the trauma of the attack could have triggered something in her. Something that you would have noticed only after she woke and shifted for the first time."

"What's the interlocking factor here? What are we missing?" Barney grunted. "I need another beer."

"Gabe said shifters of mixed parentage were being targeted." Alex scowled. "What if white shifters only come from mixed parentage?"

"Then Chloe would have been born white, right?" Jim could barely follow any of this, but he did know that. "I hate to say it, but traumatic brain injuries don't change someone's hair color. There are rare cases of trauma causing it, but there's no evidence that trauma grants psychic abilities."

"But if the mutation is there, and Julian's power unlocked it?" Cyn shrugged. "Work with me here, Doc."

Jim nodded. "I…suppose that's possible." He had no scientific explanation for Julian's powers, let alone Chloe's. "It's extremely difficult to alter the DNA structure. It can be done with chemotherapy, but that destroys cells rather than alters them."

"And this isn't a simple melatonin change either," Chloe piped up. "I mean, we know the buildup of hydrogen peroxide in the system causes graying hair, but this goes seeper than that." She touched her red locks. "Only my Fox form is affected."

"Your eyes go gray, and so does your hair, when you access your powers in human form, just like Julian." Cyn sighed. "There may be more to Ryan's theory than I first thought. I'll need to talk it over with Super Bear, see if he knows of this happening with anyone else whose life was saved by a Kermode."

"I'll run by the clinic and see if I can catch a whiff of our non-Hunter." Barney stood, gesturing for Ryan to follow him. "C'mon, Boo-Boo. Let's see what we can sniff out."

"It won't be pick-a-nick baskets, I can tell you that." Ryan stood and gave his sister a quick hug. "I'll call you tomorrow, sis."

Chloe hugged her brother tightly before letting him go.

Jim held out his hand. "Thanks, Ryan."

"Hey, like Cyn said. You're family." Ryan smiled. "You poor sap."

Alex nodded. "I'm going to call the clan. It's time to circle the wagons."

"Shit." Chloe slumped against Jim and patted his chest. "All aboard the cuckoo train."

CHAPTER SIXTEEN

Fox tilted his head. "Two becomes one, one becomes three. Bear knows the way, but Fox holds the key."

Argh. "I know that, but what does it have to do with the Senate tracing my poor fuzzy ass down?" She crossed her arms over her chest. "And why am I always fucking naked in these dreams?"

"Calm down, little vixen." Chloe would swear Fox was smirking at her. "You don't have anything I haven't seen before."

She glared at the spirit. She'd long since gotten used to him. He seemed to visit once a month, sort of like her Aunt Flow, and could be just as annoying. "You're driving me crazy with this, you know."

Fox sighed. "It's no more fun for me." He shrugged, an odd look for an animal that wasn't in a cartoon. "My paws are tied here. I'm not allowed to tell you certain things. You have to either figure them out for yourself, or at least figure out who to warn."

Warn? That was a new one. "So it's not me who's the Fox."

Fox blinked, looking pleased. "Very good. Keep going."

"It's a relative?"

"It's *all* relative, when you think about it."

Chloe plopped down on the ground. "I hate you so much right now."

"Aw, don't be mad, cutie-pie." The Fox lay down beside her, its gigantic mass dwarfing her. It was easily the size of a Grizzly, but not nearly as snarly. "Those are the rules."

"What happens if you break them?" She leaned against Fox's side, breathing in his scent.

So she was very close to him when he shuddered. "Let's just say it's not pretty and leave it at that."

She began scratching behind Fox's ears, chuckling when he leaned into her. They had a different relationship than Julian had with Bear, more like friends than student and mentor. Still, she knew Fox could kick her ass without even moving. "So it has nothing to do with the Senate?"

Fox hummed, refusing to answer.

"Man. I suck at puzzles."

Fox licked her chin. "You'll do fine, little vixen. I wouldn't have chosen you otherwise." He rumbled out a laugh. "And that scary-ass family of yours will help."

She asked him a question she'd been dying to have answered. It was one that had been bugging her for some time, ever since this all started. "Why aren't there more white shifters?"

Fox stiffened. "That's…a good question."

She pulled gently on his ear. "And the answer is?"

"Who are you, Alex Trebek?"

Chloe began humming the *Jeopardy* theme song.

Fox turned his face away. "That's one of the things you're going to have to figure out. Change is coming. Whether it's for good or ill depends on whether or not you and your friends figure out the riddle in time or not."

"Can you at least tell me if I was always meant to be a white Fox?" Chloe was dying to know the answer to that one. Perhaps it would help her with all the confusion that surrounded her.

"Yes. You always had the potential, so when the time came I chose you because I knew you were strong enough to handle it." Fox rubbed his chin on the top of her head. "Leave it at that for now." He put his head back down on his paws. "There is one more white shifter in Halle, other than you and Julian, by the way."

"Yeah, come to think of it, Sheri is a white Puma." She sat up, excited beyond belief. "Maybe she knows something about all of this!"

Fox made a sound remarkably like a time-out buzzer. "Nope. Wrong answer."

"What do you mean? She's white, she's a shifter." Now she was confused.

"She was also made, not born." Fox tilted his head. "Although I will admit she was born white, she's albino. She's white no matter which form she's in. You aren't, and neither is Julian. Or… Never mind."

Chloe blinked. "What?" If it wasn't Sherri, then who the fuck was it?

Fox snickered. "And that's *all* I can tell you without some of the others getting their tails in a knot."

A loud, angry hiss sounded, followed by a snarl so deep it rattled her bones. Fox jumped to his feet, bowing his head as a gigantic white Lion padded toward them, larger even than Bear.

Chloe did the only thing she could do. She joined Fox, bowing deeply, tilting her head to the side as she'd seen the Pridemates do when Max Canon, the Puma Alpha, exercised his power over them.

A huge shadow blotted out the sky as a sandpaper tongue brushed over her cheek. "Rise, vixen."

Chloe stood, unwilling to disobey Lion, the spirit lord of all shifters and the Leo's personal avatar. "Lion."

He nodded, his snowy mane drifting around his head. Then he turned to Fox with a sigh. "Rise, Fox."

Fox, his legs trembling, did as told. "Man, I thought you were pissed at me."

Lion shook his head. "I'm angry over the situation we find ourselves in. We've lost more than your little vixen can understand."

"Then explain it." The words popped out before she could stop them, but damn if she'd take them back.

"There are laws even we must abide by, Chloe Williams-Woods." Lion's voice was deeper and far richer than Fox's, but she found she preferred the way Fox spoke to her over Lion's more formal speech. "Laws that were written as the stars were born. We may guide, but we may not interfere."

"In other words, we're allowed to show you the rope. It's up to you what you do with it." Fox leaned against Lion. Despite the fact that both spirits were roughly the same size, Fox was dwarfed by Lion's presence.

"Is the other white shifter in danger? Can you tell me pat much?"

Lion and Fox exchanged an enigmatic glance. It was Lion who responded. "Do not worry about that for now. What is coming will involve all of you."

"So all the white shifters are in danger?" She began to pace. "This all started when Julian moved to Halle, didn't it?"

Fox poked Lion with his snout. "Told you she was smart."

Lion snarled and knocked Fox on his ass. "Shush. You come dangerously close to breaking the rules."

"So it does have to do with Julian." Chloe bit her lip. "He's the one who healed me. In healing me, he unlocked something inside me." She began to pace, thoughts racing one after another in her mind. "Something the Senate is berry interested in."

The two watched her pace, neither one giving anything away.

"But the dead or alive order makes no sense." She paused, rubbing her hand over her head. "Unless…"

"Unless?" Fox drawled, his eyes sparkling with approval.

"They already knew." Chloe stared at Fox. "They *knew* about white shifters, knew there were more than the Kermode. The Polars are extinct, so are the Arctic Foxes. All the white shifters except the Kermode, who keep to themselves and have little to do with the outside world, and the Leo, who's special, are extinct. And it stayed that way until one Spirit Bear left his community because he had…" She stared at them, wondering how much of the rope they'd already shown her. "A dream."

Lion rumbled, but instead of anger she heard affection. It was almost a purr, but not quite, the sound a cat might make to its young to encourage it to keep trying.

"So, what happened? Where are all the other white shifters? And why are we so special that the Senate wants us dead or alive?"

The two spirits glanced at one another, then back at her.

"Oh. Yeah. I guess this—" she waved her hand around, indicating the spirit world, "—is pretty damn pretzel."

"It's twisted, that's for sure," Fox muttered, ducking away from Lion's raised paw with a laugh.

"So the Senate either wants to control access to you guys or to eliminate it altogether. But again, why?"

Fox shrugged. "That's one of the twists of the rope you need to figure out."

"You, or those who follow in your footsteps." Lion stood and shook his mane. "And now it is time for you to return to your world. The prey you hunt will not be found here, young vixen."

"Keep your ears, eyes and nose open at all times." Fox stood as well and rubbed his cheek along hers. "I believe in you. You're strong, stronger than your enemies think. You've overcome so much, fought so hard, and I see that." Fox touched his nose to hers. "I'm proud of you, little vixen. Keep up the good work."

"Stay safe, and guard what you hold dear." Lion also touched his nose to hers. "And know that we are watching over you."

That would mean a whole hell of a lot more if they could actually help her with any of this, but Chloe bowed anyway. "Thank you."

Lion chuckled as if he'd read her thoughts. And who knew? Perhaps he had. She had no idea what he could or could not do.

Lion padded away, his footfalls silent, fading into the mists.

"Look for allies in unusual places," Fox whispered as the world started to swirl around her. "And remember: it is *Fox* who holds the key…"

***

"Good morning, Chloe." Jim pressed a kiss to the top of his mate's head, noting with a frown the dark circles under her eyes and the way she barely acknowledged him. "Are you feeling all right?"

She waved her hand and yawned behind her fist. "Busy night."

That was odd. He could have sworn she never left his side the night before. He wasn't used to someone sleeping next to him, so he'd woken up several times just to make sure she was there, and safe. "What do you mean, busy night?"

The squeak of Spencer's wheels announced his arrival before his chair entered the room. "G'morning." Spencer wheeled himself over to the coffee pot and began fixing himself some caffeine.

"Good morning." Jim joined his brother at the coffee maker and had two mugs done up in no time flat. He handed one to Chloe, who took it eagerly. "What happened last night? I don't remember you getting out of bed." Had something happened in the middle of the night that had spooked his mate?

Chloe smiled. "That's because I didn't." She glanced at Spencer, then returned her gaze to Jim. "There's something special about being a white shifter that I haven't really explained to you jet."

"Do I need to be caffeinated for this?" Jim settled down, smiling as Spencer handed him a bagel and cream cheese. Jim had never been a huge breakfast eater, usually downing something on the fly as he raced out the door to the clinic. In recent months it had gotten worse. If it wasn't for Spencer handing him food he doubted he'd eat before noon at best.

Luckily, today he had the morning off and could find out just what the hell had happened to Chloe while she'd been tucked up against him in the night.

"I had a dream." Chloe sipped from her mug. "Well, not really a dream. More of a spirit balk."

"Huh?" Jim's Wolf was curiously silent, watching Chloe with sleepy intent. Whatever had happened last night, it hadn't been a threat to her.

"Did you know there's a reason Kermode are called Spirit Bears?" Chloe put her head on her arms, sagging against the table. "Bear is the guardian of the dream realm, Lion is the ruler of all, et cetera, et cetera?"

"You lost me." Jim was still learning about being a shifter. The things he knew about his inner woof would fill a thimble.

"Okay. This is the story most of us tell our kits, and the one we tell new shifters." She lifted her head and stared at him, confused. "No one told you the tale of how shifters came to be? Geez, Ryan loves telling bat story."

He shook his head. "I've been really busy up until recently, remember?"

She was adorable when she blushed. "Right. Sorry." She blew out a breath and straightened up, taking a long sip of coffee. "So, here's the 4-1-1. Long ago, the spirits, for whatever reason, possibly because they wanted to know what the big deal about dicks was—"

Spencer choked on his coffee. It took a couple of minutes for him to get himself back under control.

Chloe, her cheeks delightfully pink, continued. "For whatever reason, they decided they wanted a toehold in the material world. Instead of inhabiting animals, though, they joined with humans, granting them the ability to turn into their animal counterpart. What they got in return was an understanding of the world through human eyes. The humans, by agreeing to become the hosts of these spirits, created the first shifters, starting with the Lions. That's how the Leo became the ruler of us ball, because the first Leo was the very first shifter."

"Okay." So far he was following along fine. It made a certain amount of sense that the first shifter would be the ruler, the strongest of them all. A true leader always took the first steps in a new world, showing his people that there was nothing to fear. Jim could respect that.

"The Lion is the most powerful of our spirit animals. He's the one all the others bow to, so his chosen one was considered special. The first Leo formed the first Pride, his Lion instincts driving him to make a safe place for the other Lions who came after him."

"That makes sense." Spencer had finished making his own breakfast of cereal and fruit, and now joined them at the table. "I'd want my family safe too."

"Exactly." Chloe smiled sweetly at Spencer. "The Wolves and Coyotes also formed Packs, just like their animal counterparts, while the Bears and Foxes had their family groups. Most of the cat shifters are solitary creatures who prefer to live alone, or in groups of two or three, like the Tigers and the Cheetahs, except for the Lions and Pumas, who are just plain weird."

"Each shifter has a special ability, I know that." Jim stroked Chloe's hair away from her face, loving the way she leaned into his hand. Chloe seemed to be one of those people who thrived on touch, something he could definitely come to enjoy. "Like how Julian and the other Bears can heal people."

"Those were boons from the spirits. Each one was allowed to ask for a special gift to be granted to their species, one that would kelp them survive in a harsh, human-dominated world. The Wolf Alpha asked for the ability to talk to anyone in his Pack, making the Pack operate as a whole when they are in danger. The Leo can command anyone, and I mean *anyone*, because he is the shifter King. All Lion Alphas have that ability to some extent, but none stronger than the Leo. Foxes can hide better than anyone, Bears can heal, Coyotes got the gift of sensing lies, and Ocelots, who are pretty rare, can sense and manipulate the emotions of others, much like an Omega can. Unlike Omegas, though, they aren't bound to Packs or Prides and can use their gift on anyone within certain limits."

"What are those limits?"

"I think they need to touch the person they're trying to influence, but I'm not sure." Chloe shrugged. "I haven't met many Ocelots."

"What did Pumas get?"

"The ability to form Prides like the Lions did. They can't command others the way Lion Alphas can, but their connection grants them safety in numbers. It's why Pumas are still a pretty independent lot, despite their structure being Pack-like. A Pride gathering is more like a family barbecue, complete with screaming kids and your annoying Aunt Betty who keeps asking you when you're going to have kids."

No wonder the Bunsun-Williams clan fit in so well in Halle. A Pride structure sounded very similar to what they themselves lived by.

"And it worked too. Way back when, territory was at a premium thanks to the incursion of full humans into shifter territory. The need for secrecy kept the shifters on the move, and all sorts of tall tales were told about us when we could no longer stay hidden. When the more solitary shifters were hunted for rights to their land by other shifters, only the Pumas and the Lions were able to hold on to their territory. The Tigers were hunted to near extinction. Only the intervention of the Leo prevented them from dying bout completely."

"Just like what's happening now," Spencer whispered.

"Yeah, only the ones hunting the real tigers are humans." Chloe shivered. "Anyway, the spirits themselves rule over different aspects of the spirit realm, or the dream world, depending on who you ask. Bear is the healer, the guardian of dreams. It's said that he walks with the Kermode, guiding and guarding them, and that they are his chosen children."

"So Julian is special." And he was connected to Jim's mate.

Great.

"Yeah." Chloe's tone was filled with affection. "Kermode don't ever leave British Columbia. Julian's the first Spirit Bear to leave Canada in, like, forever."

"And you were attacked soon after?"

"Within a blue months, yeah." She sighed wearily. "And from what Fox told me, part of the reason the Senate is after me is because I became white and can now communicate with the spirit world."

Spencer grabbed the phone. "We need to talk to Julian then."

"Wait." Chloe held up her hand. "I don't want Julian to think any of this is his fault, because it's not."

"No, it's the fault of whoever thought it was a good idea to go after you." Jim got up and began to pace. "Promise me you won't go anywhere alone."

"You were attacked too. Do I get that promise as well?" She stared at him, determination igniting her gaze.

He clenched his jaw and nodded. "All right. I don't like it any more than you do, but I'm not stupid either."

She smiled, her shoulders slumping as relief overtook that fierce desire to protect him. "Thanks."

"I'll ask Max if he'll assign one of his Pumas to the clinic, all right? You get one of your family to stay by you." He'd thought of asking one of her family to watch him, but between Tabby's pregnancy and Glory's panic attacks, he didn't feel right asking them to do more than guard his mate. "I trust Max to do right by us."

"Me too." She grinned. "I'll chat with Emma too, make sure she helps select your guard."

Aw jeez. Emma was going to stick him with someone who would report his every fart, let alone move. But if it eased Chloe's mind, he'd put up with it.

CHAPTER SEVENTEEN

Chloe knocked on the front door of the Cannons' house, her hands sweating and shaking. Ryan had just dropped her off for her biweekly session with Sarah, the Pride Omega, but that wasn't what was making her so nervous. She was going to ask the Cannons for protection for Jim.

She knew Max and Emma would be more than willing to help her, but the Alpha pair had so much going on in Halle right now, she didn't know if they'd be able to do much. They were helping Hope, Glory's twin sister, acclimate to being free once more. They were also dealing with the aftermath of Marie Howard's murder and Jamie Howard's withdrawal from society. Add in their respective careers, a new child and running a Pride, they were swamped.

The front door opened. Max Cannon, blond, blue-eyed and looking like death warmed over, held a finger to his lips. "The baby's napping."

"Ah." Chloe nodded in sympathy. The poor guy probably had no clue what a newborn was like when his mate was pregnant, but Chloe remembered babysitting some of her younger cousins when she was around thirteen. The little boogers could scream loud enough to wake Godzilla. "How is Felix?"

Max smiled dreamily. "Sleeping."

Chloe covered her mouth to muffle her laugh. He sounded so damn happy that the little Puma prince was down for the count that she couldn't quite stop the chuckle that managed to escape. "Good for prim."

"Sarah's running a little late today. She's counseling Hope."

Oh. Chloe hadn't been expecting that, but perhaps she could kill two birds with one stone. If Hope was willing, Chloe didn't mind sharing her experience with the traumatized Wolf. "Think they'll let me talk to them?"

Max shrugged. "That's up to Sarah. Hope has a long way to go before she's able to trust again."

Poor Hope. And poor Jamie Howard. Hope was his second mate, a rare occurrence among Wolves and almost unheard of among Pumas. Jamie had lost his first mate to a sniper's bullet, and had almost lost his life with hers. Julian had saved him, but the cost had been horrendous. Jamie was now coldly furious and hurting so badly he couldn't be around other people. The only reason Chloe could see for Jamie not going rogue was Hope, who was too damaged to help him in any way.

"Come on in." Max took gentle hold of her arm and helped her inside, shutting the door behind her. "What's up, by the way?"

"Jim needs protection." And Chloe was going to ensure that he had it.

Max scowled, the Alpha's shoulders straightening. "I heard about the attack at the clinic. Adrian and Gabe are coordinating with volunteers to ensure that it's watched twenty-four/seven. We're also assigning someone directly to Jim, so he'll never be alone." The Alpha turned to her and patted her on the head. "We're also assigning someone to you, don't argue, it's done."

"Yes, sir." Chloe knew better than to argue with an Alpha. Once they came to a decision that was that. "And thanks. It's a load off my kind."

Max smiled. "You're welcome. And if you can, tell your uncle Will to call me. I'm not trying to step on his toes, but some of his family is Pride, and we protect our own."

Chloe grinned. "I'm so glad we're slaying in Halle."

"Me too." Max's smile turned predatory as his gaze darted toward the stairway. "Emma."

Emma's brows rose as she sauntered down the steps. She must have been in the baby's room, because she still had a burping rag over her shoulder. "What's going on, Lion-O?"

"Chloe asked for protection for Jim." Max walked toward Emma, holding out his hand for her. "I was just telling her what we decided to do."

She nodded. "Cool." She took off the burping rag and handed it to Max. "Here. Prince Felix puked all over me."

Max took the burping rag between two fingers, holding it like it was plague-ridden. "Thanks?"

"You're welcome." Emma ignored Max's gagging and dragged Chloe toward the living room. "I need you."

"I don't do puke." Chloe tried to tug herself free but Emma's grip was far too strong.

"Nah, no puking." Emma frowned. "Not yet, anyway. Hope needs someone who's been abused to talk to."

"Oh?" Chloe stumbled as Emma pushed her toward the sofa, where a shocked looking Hope sat. Sarah, the Pride Omega, was simply shaking her head at Emma's antics. "How can I kelp?"

Hope tilted her head, confusion written all over her. "Kelp?"

Chloe had gotten so used to the people around her automatically interpreting her occasional verbal mistakes that Hope's surprise was startling, and slightly embarrassing.

It was Sarah who answered, her voice calm and her expression serene. "Chloe has a traumatic brain injury from a beating she took. It affects her speech."

Hope stared at Chloe, her gaze still filled with surprise. "What happened to you?"

Chloe sat on the sofa. "I was walking Rome when some guys jumped me. They beat me so badly I almost died." Some days she wasn't certain she hadn't. "I'm not sure why they did it, but Alex, my cousin, thinks it has something to do with the pact that my dad is a Bear and my mom a Fox."

Hope's eyes went wide, her hands fisting together tightly. "S-Salazar spoke of something to do with shifters from mixed bloodlines. He said some people in the Senate were interested in them, but he thought it was a load of crap. Something about unlocking recessive genes, ghosts and mystical stuff that made no sense to me whatsoever."

Chloe and Sarah exchanged a quick glance. "That's…interesting."

"Mm-hm." Sarah sat back, her gaze returning to Hope. "But we can talk about that later. Hope, there was something you wanted to ask Chloe, wasn't there?"

Hope jumped, then chuckled nervously. "I will never get used to that."

"Used to what?" Chloe had no idea what Hope was talking about.

Hope pointed toward Sarah. "Her ability to read my feelings."

"Oh. All Omegas can do that. And if she's reading yours, it means you're considered a part of her Pride." Chloe smiled widely. "Congratulations."

"Thanks, I think." Hope shrugged. "I felt...*something* when Max and Emma accepted me, but I still don't understand it."

"Maybe you should talk to my mate, Jim. He was turned against his will boo, and he's still learning things about being a shifter."

"If he's all right with that." But the look on Hope's face wasn't reassuring. She looked frightened of speaking to Jim, and Chloe couldn't blame her.

"I'll be there while you talk to him." Chloe patted Hope's hand. "He's mated to me, so the last thing he'll ever do is touch you in any way."

Hope relaxed slightly. "Can I...?"

"Hmm?"

Hope blew out a breath. "How do you do it?"

Chloe tilted her head. "Do what?"

"Walk outside. Go places. Let Jim touch you." Hope's face filled with loneliness and fear. "I can barely stand to be in the same house as Max, and I've seen how he is with Emma. I can't even imagine going to a Pride gathering, or..." Hope stared out the window, searching for something.

Chloe sat back and thought about how she should answer. "It was hard at first, and I still get scared when I'm on my own. But my family helps a blot. I know they've got my back whenever I need it." She nodded toward Sarah. "She helped too. That's what Omegas do. They heal hurts of the heart."

Sarah smiled, but kept silent.

"It makes the trauma of what happened to me less immediate. I still have nightmares, and I probably always bill, but if I let them dictate how I live my life then that beans that the bad guys have won. I won't allow that. I can't." Chloe sighed. She had to calm down, because her speech was becoming worse. She did her best to slow down, but she always had trouble talking about that night. "It doesn't mean that it isn't hella hard to get over, because I never will. I'll always have problems with my hands, and I can't go to school and be a veterinarian, but I *can* live my life in such a way that the things that have been taken from me don't overwhelm the things that weren't."

"I had everything taken from me." Hope was staring at her, biting her lip. "I had nothing."

"You had more than you thought." Sarah placed her hand on top of Chloe's, joining the three women together. "Glory never gave up on you. She knew you were out there, she just couldn't find you."

Hope shrugged. "I guess so."

"I know so." Sarah squeezed their joined hands.

"Temp and Faith came to Halle as soon as she was old enough to legally set away from her father. They came here for *you*." Chloe hugged Hope, ignoring the way Hope flinched, because Hope quickly sagged against her. Even without Omega powers, Chloe could tell that Hope was starved for simple affection. The knowledge that she was safe might be lodged in her mind, but her heart was still terrified Salazar, though dead, would somehow come back for her. "You never really lost the important part of your family, because they never truly let you go."

"Exactly." Sarah smiled at Chloe. "You'll never completely get over what was done to you, but you have people who are willing to help you heal."

"Including Jamie Howard?" Hope shivered. "I know he's out there, watching. Waiting for me."

"He's your mate." Sarah's gaze became distant as she turned toward the front window. "He's already lost his other mate, so he guards you closely."

"Keeping me safe?" Hope's gaze followed Sarah's toward the window. "I can't decide if that freaks me out or makes me feel better."

"Go with option number two." Chloe stood. "Trust me, Jamie Howard would destroy anything that causes you a moment of pain."

"He killed Salazar." Hope's smile was grim. "For that alone, it makes me feel better. I'm just not sure I can be mated after…" The smile disappeared.

"Someday." Chloe held out her hand. "My mate didn't want me because he thought I was too young, and I gave up all cope of having him. After my attack, he disappeared and I thought that was the end, that I'd never be what he needed. But I realized that I had to become what *I* needed first. I had to heal, to come to terms with everything I had lost and what I'd gained. You concentrate on getting well. Jamie will still be there, waiting and watching over you."

"And doing his own healing." Sarah turned back to them, focusing once more on Hope. "When the time comes, when you're both ready, you'll know it."

"Maybe." At least Hope looked a little more relaxed and at ease. Chloe hoped she'd helped a little bit, but Hope had gone through so much that Chloe doubted she'd been able to.

"I have to get going. Jim's going to worry about me." Ryan was probably getting bored playing video games on his tablet. Despite her brother's presence Jim had fussed over her before she'd left. "Hope?"

"Hmm?" Hope gazed at Chloe, her expression filled with anxiety.

"Don't give up, okay?"

Whatever Hope saw in Chloe's face must have had an effect, because she nodded. "I won't. You're right. I can't let Tito win."

"Call me if you want to talk." And Chloe meant that. She'd do whatever it took to help heal Hope.

"Thanks." Hope glanced toward the window again, to where her mate watched over her from afar. "I just might."

***

"Jim?"

Jim froze, his hand on the exam room door.

"James, answer me."

He glanced over at his mother, ignoring her sullen scowl.

She looked like she always had. Her short silver hair was both stylish and efficient. The lemon-yellow capris, bright white polo shirt and tasteful jewelry screamed country club luncheon. Even her white sandals were perfect, without a single mark on them. They looked as good as the day his mother had bought them.

"I have a patient to see. You can wait in the waiting room, or better, make an appointment." He threw Irene under the bus without a second thought. "I'm certain my partner would be happy to deal with you."

Jim started to enter the exam room when his mother's vicious tone stopped him dead. "Your partner or your girlfriend?"

He almost laughed. "You've really been out of my life for a while now, haven't you?" He shook his head. "Listen. I'm marrying a girl named Chloe Williams as soon as she says yes." He heard a gasp behind him but ignored it. He'd already scented Chloe, heard the tap of her cane as she came down the hallway, and wanted her to know his intentions weren't just honorable but forever. Her leg had been bothering her that morning so he'd insisted she take the cane he'd bought for her a couple of days ago. "She's got red hair, the cutest freckles I've ever seen, and is the strongest woman it's ever been my privilege to meet." His mother's gaze darted to Chloe before settling once more on him. "Her family is incredible, and they've already welcomed me, *and Spencer*, with open arms, which is more than you've done."

"I will not welcome your father's bastard, Jim. I won't. Not now, not ever." She clutched the strap of her probably expensive bag and gave him a pleading look that might have worked on him six months ago. "How can you not understand that?"

"I do understand. All I've asked is you respect my decision to have Spence in my life." Jim crossed his arms over his chest.

"No. You're my son, James. Not him." Wanda Woods crossed her arms over her chest. "Never him."

"Fine."

She relaxed. "Have you spoken to your father about alimony?"

Jim rolled his eyes. "No. That's the place of your lawyer, not your son."

She huffed. "He wants me to get a job. Me! At my age!"

His brows rose. "You're healthy, smart, and barely over fifty, Mother."

"As if thirty years of marriage count for nothing." Her gaze darted once more to Chloe. "You'll understand when Jim leaves you for someone else."

Jim immediately stood between his mother and Chloe. "Don't. Do *not* drag her into your drama. She stays drama-free."

His mother scowled. "What is she, fifteen? You're more like your father than I thought."

"Get. Out." His teeth were clenched as he desperately tried not to howl at his parent.

"May I?" Chloe's sweet scent wrapped around him, calming him. "Mrs. Woods, I presume?"

"Not for much longer." Wanda relaxed her grip on her bag.

"Is all this really worth losing your son over?"

Wanda seemed perplexed. "What do you mean?"

"Look at your son." Chloe's hand landed on his biceps. "Really look at him. He's exhausted, he's angry, he's hurting. Is this what you wanted?"

"He's always been melodramatic." His mother's annoyed sigh was one Jim had heard many times before. "And it's not like you were around to get to know him, were you?" She tilted her head, and Jim wasn't quite fast enough to stop what his mother was about to say. "How is your ex-boyfriend, by the way?"

Chloe glanced up at Jim. "I don't—"

"Oh, don't play coy with me. I saw my son when you were dating what's-his-name. Were you even legal then? And he's in charge of the police." His mother looked delightedly scandalized. "Imagine the scandal if that got out."

She sounded positively gleeful. It wouldn't matter if it was all a lie. Gabriel Anderson would lose his job and any chance at a respectable one for the rest of his life. "Why are you doing this, Mother?"

She glanced at him with what seemed genuine regret. "I want alimony."

"Talk to your lawyer." Jim threw his hands in the air. "There's nothing I can do about it. Father no longer speaks to me, remember?"

She shrugged. "He would if you got rid of his bastard."

He growled, the sound no longer human. He turned away from his mother's stunned expression toward Chloe, lifting a hand to her cheek. "Go in and talk to the patient for me, pretty."

Chloe's eyes went wide. "What about——" She pointed to her lips.

He kissed her forehead. "It'll be fine, I promise."

She bit her lip, but straightened her shoulders. "Okay." She opened the door with a ready smile. "Hello, Mrs. Stanley. How is Van Gogh doing today?"

The door shut behind his mate, and Jim felt free to let loose on his mother. She'd just proven she was lying through her teeth. She knew *exactly* who Chloe was, and planned on using his mate to force him to do what she wanted.

Jim wasn't going to allow that. His mother would keep her poisonous claws away from Chloe, or else. "You're not welcome here."

"James—"

"No. We're done. Once and for all, done. I want a divorce."

She blinked in shock. "Excuse me?"

"I am not your lawyer or your husband. I'm your *son*, and you've done nothing but abuse that relationship since the moment you and Dad decided it was over. I'm sick of hearing you bitch, Mother. Get out of my business, get out of my practice and stay out of my life."

He turned on his heel and marched to his office, too upset to deal with any of the patients waiting to see him.

How dare she come in here and threaten his mate over something he had no control over?

He carefully shut the door, unwilling even in his anger to upset his patients. He leaned back against the door and blew out a cleansing breath, trying to get his rage under control.

The last thing he wanted was to hear a knock at his door, but Chloe's scent was on the other side. "Yes, Chloe?"

"Um, Van Gogh has a big boo-boo on his bum-bum."

Trust his mate to get him to laugh. He opened the door to find her holding a folder to her chest, her eyes wide and bright as she looked up at him anxiously. "A what now?"

Her shoulders shook. "A boo-boo on his bum-bum."

"Your words or his mommy's?"

"His mommy's." Chloe followed him to the exam room, glancing around anxiously. "Your mother?"

"Gone, I hope." He wasn't certain if forgiving her would even be worth it at this point. She'd been a good mother once, but his father's philandering had soured her. "I'm sorry. We'll need to warn Gabe about her threats."

"Mm-hm." She opened the door into the exam room with a cheery smile. "I brought Dr. Woods, Mrs. Manly." Chloe winced. "I mean, Mrs. Stanley."

Mrs. Stanley shot Jim an uncertain look. "Hello, Dr. Woods."

He smiled reassuringly at Mrs. Stanley. "Okay, Chloe, show me what you saw."

Chloe snapped on fresh gloves and showed him the wound, her hands shaking. Her left hand lay across the dog's back, holding Van Gogh steady. The big retriever merely panted, its eyes curious as Chloe probed the wound with her shaking right hand.

"It seems shallow enough. A few stitches and it should be fine." It was a clean cut, not a bite wound. "How did he get this cut, Mrs. Stanley?"

"Long story short, my boys were playing ninjas with my kitchen knives and the dog got excited."

Jim looked up at her. "Are they all right?"

She smiled sweetly. "Eventually they'll be able to sit down again, but otherwise they're fine." She sighed wearily. "I swear, it's like trying to raise wolf pups."

Jim coughed. "I can imagine."

"Foam swords?" Chloe's words were carefully measured as she put together the suture kit Jim needed.

"What?" Mrs. Stanley looked at Chloe in confusion.

"Buy them foam swords." Chloe began cleaning Van Gogh's wound in preparation for the stitches. "They can't hurt each other, or Van Gogh, with those."

Mrs. Stanley's brows rose. "Not a bad idea. If they're going to ninja each other, at least they won't get too damaged that way." She shook her head as Jim started stitching up her dog. "I'm just glad no one was badly injured."

"Who's watching them now?" Jim began carefully closing the cut, enjoying the way Chloe quietly crooned to Van Gogh the whole time.

"Their father. And man, is he good with guilt. By the time I had Van Gogh loaded in the car they were in tears and begging us to make sure Van Gogh lived." She shook her head again. "You think you've made your home safe, put things where the kids can't get to them, but it's amazing how resourceful they can be when they really want something."

"What did they do?"

"They pushed chairs over to the cabinet where I'd hidden the knives, grabbed what they wanted, and before I could stop them they'd already hurt Van Gogh." She shuddered. "I'm just glad it wasn't worse than it was."

"You'll need to make sure the knives are locked away." Jim finished up, cleaning up the suture tray before taking off his gloves.

"And the cheese graters." When Jim looked at her, Mrs. Stanley rolled her eyes. "Please don't ask. That was not a fun emergency room trip."

"What gave them the idea to be ninjas?" Jim patted Van Gogh on the head and helped him get down on the floor. The dog would be fine. It was his mommy who was having a meltdown.

"Something about teenage turtles who just happen to be ninjas." Mrs. Stanley took hold of Van Gogh's leash and snapped it onto the dog's collar. "Thanks, Dr. Woods. Thank you, Chloe."

"You're welcome." Chloe smiled at Mrs. Stanley. "And good luck with your mutant turtle wannabes."

"Ugh. Thanks. I'll need it." She shook both Jim and Chloe's hands and left the exam room.

"Wow." Chloe started cleaning the exam table. "Think she'll be all right?"

"Yeah. Her kids are a handful, but they're bright. She'll figure it out." He kissed the back of her head. "Just like ours will be."

"Scary thought."

"But true." Jim held open the exam room door for her. "How's your leg?"

"Weak, but it doesn't hurt." She kissed his chin. "Thank you for the cane, by the way."

"You're welcome, little vixen." He would do just about anything to make her life easier.

"Now get back to work, Doc."

"Yes, ma'am." He watched her limp away, smiling like a big old sap. Between Chloe and Spencer, he had all the family he needed.

CHAPTER EIGHTEEN

"So." Barney leaned back, tilting the dining room chair onto two legs. How it held the huge Grizzly Chloe would never know. His cowboy hat shadowed his eyes, and the corners of his mouth were turned down in a barely visible scowl. "Who the fuck is the other white shifter?"

They'd finally managed to arrange a time when all of the Hunters were free to discuss Chloe's dream walk. Chloe had gotten some chili and biscuits started, and they were just waiting for everything to finish cooking. In the meantime, they had already begun talking about the dream she'd had with Fox and Lion. Spencer had given up his makeshift bedroom for this meeting, keeping George occupied while Chloe and Jim moved the furniture around. They'd put Spencer's bedroom back together after everyone left for the evening.

Barney, surprisingly, seemed a bit grumpy, but she wasn't sure she had the balls to ask him what had crawled up his ass and died. Instead, she continued to quietly set the table, allowing the two Hunters to mull over what she'd seen and heard in the spirit world. They were still waiting for Gabe to arrive. He'd had to answer an emergency call just before his shift ended, so he was running a little bit late. Chloe was setting a place for Sarah as well, hoping Gabe's mate would come.

The men really needed to mend their fences with each other. Gabe and Jim were trying, but both of them were stubborn as hell. Her sessions with Sarah after her beating had helped her mend fences with the Omega, but there was still an underlying tension between them whenever Gabe or Jim was mentioned that Chloe wanted resolved. Gabe was a good friend of hers, who'd stood by her when she'd needed someone who wasn't a relative.

Spencer started doing wheelies, much to Chloe's amusement. "I dunno, but it ain't me."

Barney turned and stared at Spencer, the scowl lightening slightly.

"What?" Spencer, up on two wheels, started rolling backward, almost knocking Ryan over. "Sorry, dude."

Ryan shook his head and sat at the dining room table, a beer in hand. He took a swig and set the bottle on the table. "More importantly, what does Julian's presence have to do with all of it? If anything happens to him, Cyn will be upset. Then Glory will be upset." He grinned, his teeth turning into fangs. "Then I get pissy."

"Down, tiger." Barney edged his hat back. "Papa Bear has this one covered."

Ryan's brows shot up. "Oh? Do tell."

"I—" The doorbell interrupted Barney. "That must be Gabe."

"I'll get it." Jim headed for the front door, and Chloe, smelling that the biscuits were just about done, headed into the kitchen. She pulled the biscuits out of the oven and began putting everything together, the hot biscuits smelling like heaven next to the spiciness of the chili.

She ladled the chili into a serving bowl and carefully picked it up, aware her left hand could spasm and drop the damn thing all over the place. But she was determined to do this, to make her body work despite its handicaps. She was aware Ryan watched her every move as she took the bowl and placed it in the center of the dining room table with a relieved sigh. "Ryan, can you get the butter for the biscuits, please?"

Ryan followed her into the kitchen. "How are you, kiddo? The doc treating you all right?"

She shivered. "Hell yeah."

Ryan gagged as he opened the fridge. "Please don't make me picture anything that involves you naked."

She giggled and grabbed the basket full of hot biscuits. "At least I haven't had sex in a public place."

He rolled his eyes at her and followed her into the dining room, where Gabe and Sarah were greeting Barney.

Barney, on the other hand, looked like a cornered mouse. It only took one look at Gabe and Sarah to understand why.

Heather stood with them, smirking at the huge Grizzly, her hands on her hips. "What's wrong, Boo-Boo? Weren't expecting to see me?"

"Why are you here, Frodo? Don't you have a ring to destroy?"

"You're avoiding me." Heather took a step forward. Chloe hoped Barney didn't see the nerves riding her cousin. Heather was generally afraid of larger men, and the fact that her mate had turned out to be a Grizzly easily Alex's height, if not taller, had to make her apprehensive.

"Duh." Barney took another step back. "I don't have time to sit around eating elevensies no matter how cute a little Hobbit you are."

Heather glanced pointedly toward the steaming chili and biscuits. "Sure does look like dinner to me, Boo-Boo."

"Are you one of those people who buys a haunted house and plans their curtains around the ghost's tastes?" Barney shook his head. "What part of 'don't want a mate, go away' don't you get?"

Heather tilted her head. "The whole don't want a mate, go away part."

Barney snarled.

Chloe set a place for Heather right next to Barney's chair. If the big, bad-tempered Grizzly was what her cousin wanted, Chloe would help her get him. "Dinner's ready." Chloe settled down, smiling when Jim sat right next to her. "Hope you bike it."

"I love chili and biscuits." Jim grabbed the huge bowl, growling at Ryan. "Mine."

Ryan stared at Chloe. "Can't you put a muzzle on him or something?"

Jim turned to Chloe, still clutching the chili. "Next time he shifts, let's tranq his ass and sell him to a circus."

Chloe rolled her eyes and stole the ladle out of the chili, pouring some into her bowl. "I'm hungry."

Jim immediately put the bowl down, putting some biscuits on her plate. "You want butter?"

"You two are so sweet it's disgusting." Barney nabbed the basket of biscuits and took five. "You should make candy."

"You should shove a biscuit in your craw before Jimmy rips your throat out. In fact, I'll help." Heather did just that, shoving a biscuit in Barney's mouth, much to his obvious shock. "Now. I heard something about white shifters?"

"Hmph fd u fr ft?" Barney swallowed hard, barely chewing the biscuit. "I mean, how did you hear that?"

Heather hitched her thumb toward Ryan, who shrugged. "Family."

Barney grunted. "Right." He pointed toward Heather. "You're not a Hunter."

"But I'm just like Chloe. I'm half Fox, half Bear. If they went after her because of that, what are the odds they'll come after me?"

From the arrested expression on Barney's face, that hadn't even occurred to him.

"The rest of my family would be in danger as well. We have the right to know what's going on." Heather crossed her arms over her chest. "So they sent me."

"Why?" Chloe and Ryan were doing their best to keep everyone in the loop. Why had they sent Heather?

Heather shrugged. "Not sure, but here I am, on Uncle Will's orders."

Ryan and Chloe exchanged an amused glance as Heather once again focused on Barney. *Sure* she was here as a liaison. And Uncle Will was the most innocent man on the planet.

This was sheer matchmaking at its finest. Uncle Will had given Heather a job that set her with Barney in order to force him to acknowledge the bond, all with the appearance of legitimacy. It was brilliant, and there was nothing Barney could do about it.

Barney shot her a worried look before clearing his throat. "All right. This is what we've got so far. Francois is still working on tracking down our handler, but it's not looking good. His credit cards and bank accounts haven't been touched, and his landlord hasn't seen him in three weeks."

"You think he's dead?" Chloe shivered. "Why?"

"One of the many, many things we're working on." Barney managed to get the chili away from Ryan and gave some to Heather, much to her surprise. He then put some in his own bowl before passing it along to Gabe. "I'm beginning to wonder if we're dealing with more than one faction of Senators."

"A case of the left hand trying to jerk off while the right hand makes a peanut butter sandwich?"

Everyone stared at Sarah.

Sarah sank in her chair, her face red. "I'll shut up now."

Spencer grinned at her. "Do you have a sister?"

Sarah shook her head, smiling shyly. Gabe glared at Spencer and wrapped a possessive arm around Sarah.

"Damn. Too bad." Spencer grimaced. "All joking aside, as an outsider to all of this, I disagree with Sarah. I mean, what are the odds that you'd have some secret operation to eliminate a group of people simply because they're half-breeds and not have the whole shifter world aware of it? You'd think someone would get suspicious, right?"

Barney's brows rose. "We *are* suspicious."

"And the CIA doesn't necessarily know what Homeland Security is up to, and vice versa. It's possible." Gabe used a biscuit to sop up the last of his chili. "The real question would be, why?"

"And how does it tie in to the white shifters, or is that a different issue altogether?" Jim took hold of Chloe's hand.

She squeezed, trying to reassure him. "What about the person Francois was supposed to get ahold of? Has he found phlegm yet?"

"I got a call from Francois. He finally got a hold of Artemis Smith. He and his sister will be arriving in Halle shortly." Barney winced. "I *really* hate dealing with those two."

"Why?" Chloe couldn't understand the distaste on Barney's face.

"Because they… Well, they're sort of… They kind of like to…" He huffed out a breath like a two-year-old. "They're fucking annoying, okay?"

She stared, wide-eyed, and wondered just how bad the Smiths had to be to get this sort of reaction from Barney. "Okay."

"But they're damn good at their jobs," he added begrudgingly. "I just wish they'd grow the hell up."

Gabe choked out a laugh. "This from the man who broke into my house to play with my Wii?"

Heather was staring at Barney with unholy glee. "I can't wait to meet them."

"Over my dead body." Barney stood. "I'm outta here. Keep Frodo away from anything dangerous or I'll pull a Nazgul on your asses, got me?" Heather snarled, but Barney pointedly ignored her, turning instead to Gabe. "I'll let you know when the Smiths arrive."

Barney left without another word to anyone.

Heather slumped in her chair. "That was fun." She shoved a biscuit in her mouth and stared longingly at the door.

Chloe smiled, hoping to lighten the mood. "Pie?"

"With ice cream?" Spencer's puppy eyes were almost as cute as George's. George, who was currently being loved on by Ryan, had been a good boy while they ate, sitting quietly at Jim's feet until Chloe stood to get dessert.

"Sounds good to me. Need help getting it?" Jim also stood, tugging her into the kitchen without waiting for an answer. "What's up with Heather and Barney?"

"They're mates and Barney doesn't want to acknowledge it."

"Why?" Jim pulled out the ice cream while Chloe began slicing the apple pie.

"She's young, he's a Hunter, she's a Bunsun-Williams, who knows." She began plating the pie, smiling as he put ice cream on each slice. "But he won't be able to deny the mating bond for too long. The dreams will see to that."

"I hope so. I don't want to see your cousin suffer the way you did."

Jim sounded so remorseful she couldn't help but hug him. "We're over that, remember? No more beating yourself up, okay?"

He stared at her for a moment before hugging her back. "I really don't deserve you."

She laughed smugly. "I know, sweetie. I know."

He followed her back into the dining room, their arms loaded down with pie.

***

Three days. Jim stared out at his back yard, the desire to shift riding him hard. It had been three days since the Hunters left his house, reassuring him that they were working on Chloe's case.

Three. Fucking. Days.

He hadn't heard from anyone except Ryan in that time, and Ryan had mostly shrugged and asked how Chloe was doing.

It was driving him insane.

Chloe was sleeping upstairs, exhausted from her first few days on the job with him and Irene. She'd done well, but she still got flustered when dealing with their patients' owners, and her physical ailments made doing simple tasks more difficult. Her speech impediment was also a source of embarrassment for her, but so far he hadn't run across any complaints.

He expected that would change. Not everyone was as kind as the people he worked with. He would try to shield her from that, but Chloe was stronger than anyone he'd ever known. If anyone could survive a little rudeness intact, it would be his mate.

A sudden movement outside caught his eye. What was that? With the windows and doors closed, it was difficult to get a whiff, but Jim sniffed anyway. Was it an animal?

The hair on the back of his neck stood up. Whatever—no, *whoever*—was out there was a shifter. There was the faint scent Wolf, a familiar one.

The asshole who'd attacked him outside his clinic was back, and this time, he'd come to Jim's den.

Jim took off his clothes and opened the back door before allowing the shift to flow over him. His senses sharpened as his paws hit the dirt, scanning for the invader.

There. Golden eyes glared at him before the Wolf struck, snapping and snarling at Jim.

Jim barely managed to dodge, the Wolf's jaws snapping closed perilously close to his muzzle. The other Wolf was bigger than Jim. Odds were good he'd fought more often in this form, seeing as how Jim had never fought as a Wolf.

But Jim had beaten him to a standstill before and wasn't about to allow a little thing like experience stop him from defeating his enemy. This was Jim's den, and Jim's mate was inside.

No fucking way was this asshole getting past him.

Jim dodged another attack, analyzing the way the other Wolf moved, using his experience as a kick-boxer to figure out the best way to approach his larger target. He reared up on his hind legs when his adversary did, both of them scratching and biting, testing each other's resolve.

Speaking of getting past someone, where the hell were the guards Max had promised him? He doubted they were off getting a latte, which meant either the guy had slipped past them, or…

He hoped it wasn't *or*. Explaining to the Puma Alpha that his men were dead wasn't something Jim relished doing.

The Wolf grabbed hold of Jim's ear, yanking and pulling, drawing blood. Jim fought back, snapping at the Wolf's foreleg, forcing the other Wolf to let go.

This put Jim's muzzle near the Wolf's vulnerable neck, but before he could take advantage of that the other Wolf spun, forcing Jim's face toward the earth. He twisted free, managing briefly to get the upper hand as he in turn forced the other Wolf down.

The bigger Wolf easily shook off his hold. They both reared, paws on each other's shoulders, biting at each other's muzzles. Jim felt the Wolf's fangs rip his sensitive nose, but from the whine coming from the other Wolf he'd gotten his own back. They were both bleeding from the face, the pain almost overwhelming.

Jim forced them back up, his paws hitting the other Wolf's shoulders hard. He grabbed ahold of some of the Wolf's neck fur, pulling him back down and keeping the other Wolf's fangs away from his face.

The Wolf twisted again, putting a paw on Jim's back, raking his claws across his shoulder. Jim refused to let go, hanging on despite the pain, ignoring the way the other Wolf snapped and tried to break free.

The stronger Wolf broke Jim's hold, forcing Jim to rear back unless he wanted a lip piercing. Jim somehow managed to force the bigger Wolf down, using his speed to his advantage, practically climbing on top of him. He ripped and tore at the Wolf's shoulder, ignoring the yelps of pain. He knew just where to tear, to bite to make the shoulder useless. He ruthlessly used that knowledge, aware that what he was doing might be irreparable to the other Wolf.

Jim was hoping he didn't have to kill. All he wanted to do was incapacitate his enemy, but if the other Wolf threatened Chloe then Jim would do what he had to. He'd put animals down out of mercy before, but this time it would be to protect the most precious being in his life.

The other Wolf pulled free, limping on his wounded side and snarling viciously. He wasn't backing down. If anything, the wound seemed to merely piss him off more.

Great.

Jim snarled back, hoping the other Wolf would heed his warning. When the Wolf lowered his head, ready to attack again, Jim took the initiative. He latched onto the back of the Wolf's neck, shaking his head back and forth. The other Wolf lost his balance, falling to the ground with a yelp.

Jim managed to switch his grip, taking the Wolf's throat between his jaws and growling, forcing the other Wolf to acknowledge Jim's dominance or die.

The Wolf tried desperately to kick Jim off, but Jim held firm, dancing around the other Wolf's paws until he went limp beneath Jim. Jim's Wolf wanted to howl in triumph, but instead he backed up slowly, allowing the other Wolf to climb to his feet.

Defeated, the other man shifted. On his hands and knees, he glared at Jim. "You win. I surrender. If you're going to kill me, all I ask is you do it quick."

Jim shifted back. He ignored the sting in his wounded nose and ear, the scratches on his body that he only now felt. "Who are you?"

"Derrick Hines."

That didn't tell Jim anything, but he bet the Hunters would know who he was, especially Barney. "Why are you going after my mate?"

The wicked smile on the man's face made Jim want to punch him. "Because I was paid a shit-ton of money."

"You're a mercenary?"

"Yup." The Wolf sat back on his haunches, crossed his ankles together and then crossed his arms over his knees. His ease with his nudity startled Jim, who was still getting used to the whole thing. "And you surprised me, newbie."

"How so?" Jim crossed his arms over his chest, determined not to show how uncomfortable he was with his bits dangling in the wind.

"Most of those newly turned would quickly fall in front of me, or beg me not to hurt them. I rarely have to bring in a mark dead, especially the new ones." Reluctant respect lit the Wolf's eyes. "But you fought back. Twice."

"You came to my business and my home, asshole. Of course I fought back."

The man nodded. "If you were in a Pack you'd probably be a Marshall or a Second. I've seen others like you before. You've got that inner strength, that drive to protect."

Jim still wasn't clear on Pack hierarchy, but he knew a compliment when he heard one. "Thank you."

"You're welcome." Derrick was still watching him warily.

Jim had a few more questions he'd like to ask, but his ass was getting cold and he wanted to get back to Chloe. "Where's the man the Puma Alpha sent to watch us?"

The man smiled. "Don't worry. He's not my target. He's sleeping the sleep of the innocent right now. He'll wake with a slight headache, but that's it."

That was a relief. "So. You've obviously lost. What happens to you now?"

Derrick shrugged. "We don't get paid, and we move on to the next job. It's that simple."

Or the Senate went after the man for his failure. Jim wasn't forming a very high opinion of the shifters' politicians. They might actually be worse than the human ones. "And if I don't let you go?"

Derrick stared at him, his eyes becoming cold and hard. "You gonna kill me, Doc?"

"In my world, I don't put down an animal unless I have no other choice." Jim sighed.

The man shook his head, his expression softening. "Unreal," he muttered. "Look. You've won, and you're willing to let me go. I owe you one." His shoulders straightened and regret flashed across his face. "I didn't come here alone."

Jim froze. "What?"

"You pegged me right. I'm a merc. And I wasn't alone tonight. My partner's already inside."

Jim raced through the back door and into his house. He hadn't scented a damn thing other than the Wolf, so that had to mean…

That had to mean the man's partner was a Fox, just like Chloe. And like Chloe, he or she would be able to mask their scent.

He raced into the house, the sounds of crashing furniture alerting him to where Chloe probably was. And from the sound of it, she was in the dining room, where his brother's bedroom was set up.

Spencer and Chloe were both in danger, and if he knew his mate, she was defending him with every breath in her tiny, battered body.

Jim shifted and raced toward the sounds, praying he made it in time to save her.

CHAPTER NINETEEN

The sounds of snapping and snarling woke Chloe from a sound sleep. Something was wrong, desperately wrong. She checked for George, praying that he'd gotten hold of something and was simply playing.

George was hiding under the bed, shaking like a leaf.

Shit.

She reached over to the side of the bed where Jim usually slept, only to find the sheets cold.

She darted out of bed, ripping her pajamas off. Her Fox was growling, eager for the shift. Her mate was out there fighting, and it wanted to go to his aid. Jim had never had to fight in his Wolf form before. He'd be at a huge disadvantage against his opponent.

Chloe, on the other hand, had grown up sparring with both Foxes and Grizzlies and knew a few dirty tricks taught to her by her overprotective cousins. She wasn't above using each and every one of them to protect Jim.

She shifted, losing all sense of the color red. She darted out the bedroom door and down the stairs, determined to find where Jim was. His scent was strong, so following it was simple.

Of course, the Fox standing in the dining room, hovering over a terrified Spencer, had her freezing in her tracks.

Double shit. Jim might be brand new to shifting, but at least he could. Spencer was helpless against the Fox.

Hell, he couldn't even run away. If he tried to get to his chair the Fox could have his throat within seconds.

She knew what her mate would want, despite what her Fox demanded. Chloe had to save Spencer.

Chloe crouched, her ears back, her tail down. She snarled and hissed as she slunk toward the Fox who'd invaded her den, making her intentions clear.

She wanted him the fuck out of her home.

Before she could stop it she began gekkering, the stuttering cry of a Fox who was about to do battle, whether for real or for play. Chloe meant business, however, so she added in some warning barks, trying to get the outsider away from Spencer.

The Fox was frozen, staring at Chloe with an open jaw. Slowly, it lifted its paws off Spencer's bed, descending to the floor where Chloe waited.

She didn't want to give him a chance to use Spencer against her. She attacked, swiping at the Fox, hoping to knock him over so she could get her jaws on his neck. If she could get him to submit, the fight would be over.

But whatever had caused the other Fox to hesitate disappeared as Chloe attacked. It, too, crouched low and Chloe's swing went over his head. She leapt at him, kicking and scratching, forcing him to back farther away from Spencer's bed.

"Holy shit."

Out of the corner of her eye she saw Spencer edging toward his wheelchair. What he thought he was going to do she had no idea, and no time to deliberate. The other Fox came back at her, making its own gekkering sounds. They danced around each other, watching, taking turns darting in and out of each other's range. The high-pitched yipping echoed through the room as Chloe tried to get a hold of the other Fox.

The Fox lunged at Chloe, forcing her back into a chair. The chair toppled over, nearly trapping Chloe. She darted between the legs and came at the Fox's hindquarters, drawing first blood.

The Fox yipped and jumped at Chloe, forcing her onto her back. She kicked at his vulnerable stomach with her hind legs, digging deep and forcing him to arch his back to minimize the damage. She tucked her chin down and bit the Fox's bottom jaw, keeping him from getting hold of her throat and ending the fight.

She managed to kick him off. Hopping to her feet, she began circling the other Fox, looking for a weak point or an opening she could use to bring him down.

Instead, it was the Fox who found Chloe's weak point. He began attacking Chloe's left side, going for her weak paw. She tried to compensate, but the pain in her right paw when she tried to put more weight on it made her quickly rethink that strategy.

Instead, Chloe chose to go with a different tactic, one that she hoped would prove effective.

Super Bear had powers outside the norm for a Bear. With luck, the same thing would apply to a tiny, damaged white Fox.

Chloe dodged under Spencer's bed and used the ability of her species to cloak her scent.

Almost holding her breath, she peered from under the comforter to find the Fox had frozen in place. He lifted his muzzle, scenting the air, but was apparently unable to find her. He turned in place, whining slightly, obviously confused by her sudden disappearance.

Chloe sniffed discreetly, surprised to find that her scent was completely gone from the room. She wasn't entirely sure she was happy about that, but for now it was going to work to her advantage.

Slowly, stealthily, she made her way out from under the bed, using the furniture to cover her movements. She stalked the enemy Fox, keeping her eyes on it. She waited patiently as it sniffed Spencer's bed, smiling internally as Spencer quietly wheeled his way out of danger.

Good. With luck Spencer would get to a phone and call for help while she and Jim dealt with the shifters.

Her distraction almost cost her. The Fox was far closer to Chloe than she'd expected when she looked around for him again. While a Fox could mask their scent, sight would still reveal them. Chloe silently pulled back behind a piece of furniture, hiding herself from the Fox as it stalked across the floor. Once its back was to her she hopped up onto the back of the chair, prepared to fly at her enemy.

The Fox stared right back at her, and snarled.

Chloe leapt, tackling the Fox to the ground. She managed to get over him, clamping his throat between her teeth hard enough to draw blood but not hard enough to kill. She growled, forcing the other Fox to surrender. She *would* kill him if he gave her no other choice.

The Fox went limp beneath her just as Jim and a strange Wolf ran into the room. "Chloe?"

The Wolf stared at her, then at the fallen Fox. "Remind me you two shouldn't be messed with."

She backed up slowly, snarling at the Wolf in man form. He was far too close to her mate.

"Down, vixen. He surrendered." Jim watched as the other Fox shifted, turning into a blond man with a scar across one cheek and eyes so dark they should hold stars. If Chloe had seen him in his human form she would have been terrified. He looked like he ate babies for breakfast and nuns for lunch.

And he'd submitted to her dominance.

Yikes.

Chloe shifted, ignoring Jim's scowl. "Boo… too… sue… *who* are you?"

The man blinked and looked toward Jim before responding. "Casey Lee Coleman."

The man's thick Southern accent screamed Georgia to Chloe, who'd heard the same lilt in Tabby's voice. Oddly enough, the sound of it made Chloe relax. "Are you from Marietta?"

"Atlanta." The man—Casey Lee—stood, keeping his eyes respectfully down. He kept sniffing, as if trying to catch a specific scent. "May I ask how you did that?"

"Did what?"

"Disappear like that." He peered around, his brow furrowed. "Even now I…but it's different."

"Good," Jim grunted. He lifted one of Spencer's shirts from the pile next to his bed and tossed it to Chloe. "Here."

Okay. Apparently it was all right to wear his brother's clothes. Not all Wolves could handle their mate wrapped in another man's scent, even that of kin. She slipped the shirt on, holding it closed over her breasts. "I think I'm the Fox version of a Kermode."

The Wolf tilted his head in confusion, but Casey Lee seemed to know exactly what she was talking about. "The white Bears?"

"Julian DuCharme." The Wolf seemed to make the connection. "But instead of healing…" He shared a glance with Casey Lee. "You're a master at hiding."

She shrugged. "I guess so. It's the first time I've tried it since the beating."

The two men exchanged another glance. The Wolf, whose name she still didn't know, spoke up as the Fox leaned closer, sniffing her shoulder. "Your fur used to be red, right?"

She nodded.

He held out his hand, smirking when Jim tried to force him to put it down. "Derrick Hines."

"Chloe Williams." She took it, shaking firmly. She refused to be intimidated by the larger man. "Now tell me. Why the duck did you two invade my home?"

Casey Lee shook his head and turned toward the Wolf. "I can't fight her no more."

"Huh?"

Casey Lee sniffed her shoulder again. "She smells like family. Like kin. I can't fight family."

Chloe lifted her arm and took a deep whiff. She didn't smell any different, but for some reason Casey Lee felt comfortable enough to sit cross-legged on the floor. "I don't understand."

Casey Lee shrugged. "Neither do I, but Derrick and I need to return the Senate's deposit. No way, no how I fight family."

Derrick rolled his eyes. "Well, shit."

***

"Are you kidding me? He submitted because you smell like family?" Max Cannon shook his head. "I think I've heard everything."

"Not yet, but I'm working on it," Emma immediately responded, earning a grin from her mate. "Okay, Jimbo. We need to figure out what the hell is going on with those two."

Those two were the men who'd come to Jim's home with the intent of taking his mate. Jim was far less inclined to forgive them than Chloe was, but he was bowing to his mate's desire to make nice with them. The fact that she was cuddled up to him on Max's sofa, safe and sound, went a long way toward making that easier.

At the very least they were getting information from the mercs. They were currently sitting in Max's living room, talking to Adrian, Gabe, Barney and Ryan. They'd agreed to convene there once Jim called Barney to let him know what had happened. It was Chloe's idea to also call the Alpha pair, and they'd insisted on holding a council of war.

"*Who* told you to come after Chloe?" Barney sounded outraged.

Jim immediately turned his attention to the other men, ignoring Emma's comment. "What's going on?"

"They said it was the Bear Senator who sent them." Barney huffed. "I know the Bear Senator. He's a cousin of mine. Carl wouldn't send mercs after someone who'd supposedly been declared a rogue."

"Wait." Derrick pinched the bridge of his nose while Casey Lee looked sick. "Are you telling me we were lied to?"

"Aw, hell no." Casey Lee shot out of his seat. "Let me get the paperwork." He darted out of Max's house like his ass was on fire. He returned quickly with a manila envelope. "Here."

Barney took the envelope and began rifling through the documents it contained.

Jim stood at his side, reading over his shoulder. "Blah blah blah, Chloe Williams and James Woods, blah blah, preferably alive, blah blah. Who is Darien Shields?"

"My cousin's secretary." Barney scowled. "I don't get it. Carl doesn't handle Hunts. He shouldn't have called down mercs. He doesn't have the authority."

"As a Senator he does." Derrick shrugged. "It's not the first time a Senator has called on us to do what you guys can't."

Casey Lee coughed. "Are we sure about that?"

Jim didn't like where this was going. "I'm beginning to think Sarah was right when she said the right hand is spanking the monkey while the left makes lunch."

Derrick, who'd just taken a sip of soda, sprayed it everywhere as he laughed.

Casey Lee chuckled. "Damn, that's some good baloney."

"Speaking of baloney, what if your cousin doesn't know about this?" Jim picked up the letter. It had been printed on what looked like Senate letterhead. "Could someone else have written this, but used your cousin's secretary's name to cast suspicion on him?"

"Just in case we found anything out?" Barney stroked his chin. "It's possible. I don't know enough of the inner workings to tell you if it would be possible, but I'm betting it would. Who would think to double-check official correspondence was actually coming from the person it said it was coming from?"

"Damn." Chloe shivered. "This sounds like a conspiracy theorist's wet dream."

Max stood. "Adrian, Gabe, until further notice, treat all correspondence from the Senate as suspect." He turned toward Barney. "I want you here. You, Gabe and Ryan are the only Hunters I trust right now."

Barney nodded reluctantly. "I understand."

Jim wrapped his arm around Chloe. "The guards you guys assigned us weren't enough to stop Derrick and Casey Lee from getting into my home." Casey Lee had led them to where Derrick had knocked out the two men who were supposed to be watching Jim's place. The guards were pissed but all right. "What's to stop another group from attacking us?"

Max sighed. "Adrian?"

The Pride's Marshall stared at his Alpha, his expression grim. "I'm going to assign round-the-clock, in-house protection for Chloe and Jim. I'm going to do the same for Julian, just in case."

"I'll have some of my Puma deputies do daily drive-bys of their houses." Gabe grimaced. "Unfortunately, these two—" he hitched a thumb toward Derrick and Casey Lee, "—didn't ding my Hunter radar at all."

"Meaning the Senate could send more mercs and we won't know until we're attacked?" Jim growled and tightened his hold on Chloe. "You stay with me twenty-four/seven."

"Even when I pee?"

"Yup."

"That could get old fast."

He kissed the top of her head. "Nothing you do could get old."

She burped.

"Maybe some stuff you do."

The grim tension was broken as his mate giggled.

"We need to talk about Spencer as well." Max crossed his arms over his chest. "If he had a mate, I would stay back and allow nature to take its course. But since he hasn't found one and he knows about us, he needs to become one of us. If they attack him I'd feel better knowing he'd be able to defend himself long enough for one of us to get to him. He can't walk or run, but he can still bite and scratch." Max turned his attention to Jim. "Do you know which way your brother is leaning?"

Jim shrugged. "I'm not sure, but I think he's leaning in the kitty direction."

"Puma? Or there's a Lion living with the local Wolf pack as well. We can offer that option." Emma tilted her head. "Or we could just ask him."

"Yeah, you could just ask him." Spencer wheeled into the room from Max's kitchen. In his lap was a sandwich. "And I like the idea of being a Puma, if you'll have me."

"Done." Max grinned. "Welcome to the Pride."

"Who gets the honor of biting him?" Emma looked around the room, her glance landing briefly on the baby monitor. Felix was sleeping upstairs, undisturbed by the ruckus in his parents' house.

"I'll do it." Max gestured for Spencer to follow him. "It's a pleasure to welcome Jim's brother to the Pride."

Spencer grinned and blushed. "Thanks, man."

"And if you do find a mate, she'll be welcome as well."

The two disappeared into Max's office, and a few seconds later Jim could hear his brother cry out in pain.

He remembered that pain, but he hoped that Spencer's change was less traumatic than his own. Spencer knew what he was getting into and what to expect. Even better, he'd have the whole Pride behind him, helping him.

Jim still wasn't a member of a Pack. He hadn't had the chance to meet with the Wolf Alpha in the Poconos, had never felt that bond other Pack and Pride members seemed to crave. And for some reason, he was perfectly fine with that.

"You're a lone Wolf."

He turned to find Derrick staring at him. "What?"

"You're lone, like me. Strong enough that you don't need the Pack behind you, binding you to them. Not a lot of us out there." He grinned, and Jim saw something in the other man that seemed right somehow. "Either that, or we just haven't found the right Pack."

There was something about the way Derrick looked at him, the need he saw in the other man, that spoke to Jim. "Do you think…?"

Derrick shrugged. "If it's meant to be, it will happen. If not, we'll probably see what we need in the Poconos Alpha."

"Huh." He blinked, thinking things through. "Would it be odd to have Pack and Pride living in one town?"

"Any odder than Bears, Foxes and whatnot?" Emma laughed. "I'm pretty sure your Pack and Rick's would be far enough away from each other that there wouldn't be any issues."

"And if there are, we'll deal with them when it happens." Max and Spencer rejoined them, Spencer rubbing his shoulder and wincing. "But if a Pack develops here, then it's between me and the Pack Alpha, not Rick." Some of Max's power seeped into the room, causing the Pumas to wince. "I'm Alpha in Halle."

"Could you deal with a co-Alpha?" Jim was curious. Max said he was all right with a Pack in his territory, but when his authority was challenged by the possibility of Rick objecting he'd immediately let loose.

Max's power display disappeared. "I think so."

"Sure, Lion-O. If you say so." Emma patted her mate's arm. "We still need to figure out what's going on with the Senate."

"You think they'll send someone else after Chloe?"

Adrian stood straighter. "If they do, we'll deal with it. You're not alone in this."

"We've got your back, Jimbo." Emma smiled at Chloe. "And yours too."

"So does the family." Ryan, yawning, headed for the front door. "And on that note, I say we adjourn until we have more info."

"Agreed." Barney glanced around absently. "Guess I should start apartment hunting, damn it."

"Us too." Derrick crossed his arms over his chest. "Casey Lee and I are sticking around. I want to know what the fuck the Senate has gotten us in the middle of." His scowl was fierce. "I don't like being played."

"Yeah." Casey Lee ran his fingers through his hair. "I signed up to help uphold shifter law, not break it."

Derrick nodded. "Me too."

"You'll need jobs here." Gabe stared at them, his eyes narrowed. "Think you can handle police work?"

"Fuck yeah!" Casey Lee kept it to a dull roar.

"We both went to police academy." Derrick grinned. "It's where we met."

"But we both got recruited by the Senate." Casey Lee looked over at Chloe apologetically. "We were told we were going to be the shifter version of the CIA."

"So you *aren't* mercenaries?" Max whistled low. "Why did you lie about that?"

Derrick and Casey Lee exchanged a quick look. It was obvious the two had been partnered for a long time. Not surprisingly, it was Derrick who spoke. "We were told to stay on the down-low."

"We've taken in rogue Hunters before," Casey Lee added. "We thought it was just another assignment like that."

"But how do you know when a shifter is rogue? You can't sense it the way a Hunter can."

"No, and that part's bugged me for a while." Casey Lee rolled his eyes at Derrick's shushing motion. "Please. You know it's bothered you too."

"Fine. It has."

Gabe eyed them both for a moment. "I'll get you some applications, but consider yourselves hired." Gabe nodded respectfully to Adrian. "I'm heading home. I'll let Sarah know what happened tonight."

"Sure thing." Adrian followed Gabe toward the door, Derrick and Casey Lee on their heels. "Listen, Sheri wanted to get together for dinner with you and Sarah soon."

Jim tuned them out. "Spence? You okay?"

Spencer smiled weakly. "Peachy." He shifted in his seat, his foot twitching.

Jim stared, awed. "Spence?"

"Hmm?"

"Your foot moved."

Spencer smiled shyly. "Doc said with physical therapy and medicine I might regain some use of my legs. I didn't want to say anything in case it didn't happen." He grimaced. "I'll never walk without assistance, Jimmy, but if I can get out of the chair once in a while I'll count it as a win."

"So will I, bro." Jim's voice broke. "So will I."

CHAPTER TWENTY

"What a day," Chloe sighed as she slid past Jim into the house. It seemed like every time something good happened, something bad popped up just to keep them on their toes. At least Spencer's news was good. Jim was thrilled his brother had shown signs of regaining some of his mobility.

Spencer had chosen to stay at Max and Emma's for the night, learning more about the Pumas and their structure. One of the Pumas would lead him through his change. Already he seemed close to Max, and Max reciprocated. In fact, it was Max who suggested Spencer stay with them for a couple of days, and Emma had agreed without complaint.

It gave Jim and Chloe a little alone time, something they both desperately needed. Their guards were already in place outside and someone would be living with them in the next day or two, but for tonight…

Tonight, they were alone. And Chloe intended to take advantage of that fact the best she could.

"Tired?" Jim closed the front door and led the way into the kitchen, pulling two beers out of the fridge and handing her one.

"Eh." She took a sip, happy that he'd gotten her favorite brand. She didn't drink often, but tonight seemed like a good night to do so.

"I'm not entirely happy about having someone moving in with us." Jim leaned against the counter and stared at the bottle in his hand. "I just got you here. I don't want to share you."

She wasn't exactly thrilled either, but she'd take in-house protection over none any day. She'd do just about anything to make sure Jim was safe. "It won't be forever."

He lifted his head, and she saw his Wolf eyes. "No. It won't." The bottle of beer made a clicking sound as he placed it on the countertop. He sauntered toward her, his movements fluid, his intent clear as he began unbuttoning his shirt. "We're alone, Chloe."

All her intentions on seducing her mate flew out the window. Instead, she did what any Fox would do when hunted by a stronger predator.

She squeaked and ran like her bushy tail was on fire.

The low growl she heard was quickly followed by pounding footsteps as Jim chased her up the stairs. She laughed, darting into the first room she came to.

The storage room. She could hide in—

"Ack!" She giggled furiously as Jim carried her backward out of the room. "Help! I'm gonna get eaten!"

"Damn straight," he purred in her ear.

"Wuh-huh." She shivered. "Okay."

He chuckled. "I will huff, and puff and blow your mind."

She went limp in his arms and began to snore.

"Excuse me?" He plopped her facedown on the bed. "What's that for?"

"Lame joke put Chloe to sleep." She snored some more for emphasis.

"Guess I'll have to find some little piggies to nom on." Her shoes were pulled off. "This little piggie went to market…"

Jim sucked her little toe into his mouth.

"Ew!" She sat straight up and rubbed her foot on his shirt. "Get it off!"

His brows rose in confusion. "You have a problem with getting your toes sucked on?"

She gagged, scrubbing her foot with his comforter.

Jim shrugged. "At least you're awake now." He pounced, driving her backward until she lay under him. "Now, where was I?"

"About to brush your teeth, I cope," she muttered under her breath.

"Aw, baby, come on. Gimme kiss." He puckered up and made kissie faces until she was giggling again. When he lifted her shirt and began licking her stomach she fought back, trying to push him off of her, but she was laughing too hard to get a good grip on him.

It didn't take long for the struggling and laughing to turn into sighs and moans. Jim began touching her in all the *right* places, easing her clothes off of her as they played. Before too long she was naked beneath him as he repeatedly pressed kisses to her mating mark. She locked her ankles around his waist and brushed her mound against his jeans-covered cock, the fabric rough against her sensitive skin.

"Do that again," he muttered against her neck.

Like he had to ask twice, because damn, that felt good.

Jim sat up and wiggled out of his shirt, tossing it behind him, then unbuttoned his jeans. She'd never thought about the difference between button-fly and zippered pants. She was finding she liked her mate in button-fly, especially now. "You went commando."

"You like that?"

She cupped him, stroking his cock. "Yup."

"Nice to know." The tip leaked pre-come as he shuddered in her hands. Chloe firmed her grip, using her stronger right hand. He bucked his hips, thrusting into her hand with a groan. "God, baby, so nice."

She licked her lips, the desire to taste him nearly overwhelming her. She sat up and took him into her mouth.

He was salty, his skin warm, his scent so strong she was ready to hump the pillow for relief. Instead, she sucked him in, using her tongue to stroke the long vein on the underside of his cock. His moans urged her on, his touch gentle as he cupped the back of her head. His fingers tangled in her short hair, holding her steady as she sucked him down.

When his fingers began to tighten and his cock to twitch she eased back, looking up at him questioningly. She was willing to have him come in her mouth if that was what he wanted, but she'd want something in return.

He nodded desperately. "Please."

How could Chloe turn that down? Jim was begging her, his chest heaving, his cock leaking on her tongue, but if she pulled off all the way she knew he'd let go.

So she gave him what he asked for, concentrating on the head of his cock. He hissed, his cock pulsing as he spilled into her. His flavor exploded inside her and she swallowed, taking his essence inside her.

When he was done he gently eased her onto her back, kissing her so sweetly, so gratefully, she wasn't surprised when some of the urgency for her own pleasure faded. "Is there anything I can do for you, Miss Chloe?"

She sighed and pointed south. "Please?"

"My pleasure." He shucked his jeans off, then slithered down her body. When his tongue touched her clit she nearly screamed.

So much for the urgency fading. She was so primed she was surprised she hadn't gone off yet.

He ate her out, licking and sucking her into his mouth with slowly increasing intensity. She was fucking his face, desperate to come, eager to feel the heat only he could give her.

Chloe gasped as a finger or two entered her, Jim timing the thrusts to match the movement of her hips.

It was so good, so, so good, she wanted it to never end. She tugged on her nipples, bringing herself closer to the edge. The tingling of an oncoming orgasm blinded her, shoved her over the edge into gasping pleasure so intense her whole body locked. She threw her head back and screamed, her mind drowning in ecstasy.

When it was over he was petting her gently, rifling his fingers through her damp curls. "Good?"

She couldn't talk, so she nodded, hoping her sated grin would speak for her.

He nibbled gently on her mating mark, causing her pussy to give one final, lingering throb. "I'm glad."

"Uh-huh." She shivered and cuddled up against him, more than content to lie safe in his arms.

"Sleepy?"

She yawned, closing her eyes and nestling her head on his chest.

"You sure you don't want anything more?" He was still petting her, but she really was tired. His dick would have to wait until morning.

"Nighty-night."

He snorted in amusement as she yawned again. "All right, little vixen. But first thing in the morning your ass is mine."

"Mm-hmm." When she was awake they could play tail chaser all he wanted. But now it was sleepy-time, and Chloe was going to do just that.

"Mine," he sighed happily, kissing the top of her head.

"Mine," she replied, smiling. "Good night, Jim."

"Good night, love."

She blinked, too tired to ask if he really meant that or not, but it took her far longer to fall asleep than she'd thought it would.

***

A sharp knock on the front door startled Jim out of his doze. "Hmm?"

Chloe moaned next to him, distracting him. The sight of all that bare, creamy skin had him forgetting exactly what it was that had woken him up. He wanted to nuzzle and taste and tease all over again.

But whoever had knocked did so again, making Jim curse lightly as he got up and grabbed a pair of sweats. Sliding them on, he made his way down to the front door, ready to tell whoever it was to go the fuck away.

Two strangers stood on the front step. Both had bright blue eyes the color of the morning sky and short, dark, messy hair. One was male, one was female. They wore almost identical outfits of jeans, white T-shirts and sneakers. As one, they tilted their heads and spoke. "Is Barney here?"

Jim blinked. "No." He shut the door, ready to go back to bed. He was way too tired for anyone's shit.

The double-knock sounded again. Jim rolled his eyes and opened the door. "What?"

Barney stood there, blinking. "What what?"

Jim looked outside, but there was no sign of the Doublemint twins. "There were two people on my doorstep just a minute ago."

Barney's eyes widened fearfully. "Two *identical* people?"

"Yeah, why?"

"Aw, fuck." Barney pushed his way into the house, slamming the door shut after him. "Hide me."

"Why would you want to hide from us, Barnes?"

"Yeah, why?"

Jim slowly turned to find the two strangers seated on his sofa, going through his mail. "Who the fuck are you?"

"Allow me to introduce you to the most annoying people I've ever been forced to work with." Barney's disgruntled tone would have amused Jim if he didn't have two strangers on his couch he hadn't invited in. "Artemis and Apollonia Smith, meet Dr. James Woods."

"Hey," the male said, ripping open Jim's electric bill.

"Yo," the female replied, rubbing some magazine insert on her wrist and sniffing the result.

"How did you get in here?" Jim demanded.

Apollonia blinked at him innocently. "Through the door."

"How else?" Artemis waved the bill in the air. "Your electric company is ripping you off. You should go solar."

"Less environmental impact," Apollonia added.

"Save the tigers and all that shit." Artemis stood and stretched. "Anyway, we spoke to Carl, and he's hella confused."

"Like, totally," Apollonia added.

"Who are they again?" Jim stared at the two people making themselves at home in his living room. Hell, Artemis was scratching his balls while his sister stretched out on his sofa and yawned, apparently ready to take a nap.

"They're the Smiths. They're also the best at what they do. Unfortunately."

"Sleeping?"

"Hey, kitties sleep seventy percent…" Artemis blinked and looked at his sister. "That's right, right? Seventy percent?"

"I think so," Apollonia slurred. "Mm, I like this sofa."

"Yeah? Let me try it." Artemis shoved his sister off the sofa with one strong push, then flopped into her spot face first. "Oh, yeah, baby. Daddy likey."

Apollonia glared at her brother before turning to glare at Jim. "You need a fireplace. And a rug."

"A furry one," Artemis added.

"Fake furry one." Apollonia scowled harder at her brother, who seemingly ignored it.

"Can you two focus for two seconds?" Barney sounded frustrated as hell. "You said you spoke to Carl?"

Apollonia rolled her eyes and stood. "Yeah. And you're no fun, Mr. Barnwell."

"No fun," Artemis intoned, his voice muffled by the fact that his face still in the sofa cushions.

"And you're twenty-seven going on five." Barney gestured for the two to get up. "Can you please take your meds and tell me what I need to know?"

"We left them at home," Artemis sighed.

"Our meds, he means." Apollonia sat on her brother.

"Yeah, those." Artemis reached behind him and swatted his sister. "Get off me, heifer."

"Are you calling me fat?" Apollonia swatted him back.

"Yes."

"Children!" Barney walked over and grabbed each of them by an ear, yanking them off Jim's sofa. "I swear, if you don't start listening I'm going to ground you both."

"Oww," Apollonia whined.

Artemis rubbed his ear. "You're mean."

"Yeah, mean." Apollonia stuck her tongue out at Barney.

"Who the fuck are you?" Jim roared, his vision changing as his Wolf surged to the fore.

"Artemis." The male waved his hand, seemingly unconcerned that Jim had started to sprout fur from his arms.

"Apollonia." The female ran her fingers through her hair and looked him up and down. "You're cute."

"And mated. Happily, I might add." Barney smacked Apollonia upside the head, earning a halfhearted feline snarl. "This one is a Hunter, and her annoying brother is…annoying."

Artemis grinned cheekily. "Aw, shucks. I knew you liked us."

Barney shot a droll look at Artemis. "No. I don't."

"So…you two are here to help us with our problem?" Jim couldn't see how, unless they decided to sleep it into submission.

"Sure, let's go with that." Artemis yawned again. "I'm hungry."

"Me too." Apollonia draped herself across the back of the sofa. "Not it."

Artemis rolled his eyes. "Ugh. I hate cooking."

"You hate working." Barney shoved Apollonia off the back of the sofa. She landed on the floor with a rattling thump. "Tell me what Carl said."

Artemis tilted his head. "Oh God, not you two?"

"I can believe that." Jim shook his head. "Seriously, my mate is in danger and we don't know why. Can you help us?"

The brother and sister stared at one another before Apollonia shrugged. "Sure."

"It's not like I have anything better to do." Artemis stared at Jim. "Do you have donuts?"

"We're still hungry."

"And I *really* hate cooking."

"Jim?" Chloe's soft voice broke through the disbelief over the nonsense of the brother-sister pair. He glanced toward the stairway and saw Chloe descending, rubbing sleep from her eyes. She'd probably heard the voices of the others, because even though she hadn't brushed her hair she'd put on pajamas. "Who's here?"

The reaction of the brother and sister were immediate, and violent. Jim found himself shoved toward the door by the female, while the male, in a startling display of agility and speed, hurtled over the sofa and landed at the base of the stairway. He growled menacingly at Chloe for a second or two before he tilted his head. "You're a Fox."

Chloe, who'd stumbled at the sight of the strangers in her home, threatening her, slowly regained her feet. "Yes, I am."

"The *white* Fox." Artemis relaxed, going back to the sleepy man Jim had first met. "That's cool." He sauntered over to the sofa, climbed lazily over the back and slumped in his seat. "I think I want nachos."

Chloe blinked. "Jim?"

He held out his hand, and she darted to his side. She looked far more awake now. "Chloe, this is Artemis and Apollonia Smith." He gestured toward the female who was now sitting on the floor at his feet. "She's a Hunter, believe it or not."

"Yup." Apollonia tilted her head backward and gave Chloe a lazy smile. "I'm, like, totally bad-ass."

"She is," Artemis added, putting his feet up on Jim's coffee table.

"Nice digs, by the way." Apollonia stretched. "Where's my room?"

"Oh, good question," Artemis crooned admiringly.

"I thought so." Apollonia sounded smug.

"Oh *hell* no." Jim crossed his arms over his chest. "No fucking way are you two staying here."

"Aw, don't be a meanie-head, Jimmy." Apollonia pouted at him.

"Someone has to stay here and protect you two." Artemis looked smug. "That would be us."

"Like I said. Hell. No." Jim glared at the annoying duo before shooting Barney a dirty look. "You did this. Fix it."

"We've got someone moving in with them who can protect them. Your annoying asses are off to a motel." When they both began whining, Barney barked, the sound very much Grizzly rather than human.

"But we didn't get to the best part," Apollonia whined.

"Yeah," Artemis sighed.

Jim shook his head. "I'm almost afraid to ask."

CHAPTER TWENTY-ONE

Chloe stared at the two very strange people currently occupying her couch. "I don't understand."

Artemis sighed and stood. "Look. You're the white Fox, right?"

"Yes." She nodded, wondering what the hell he was getting at. There was something about him that kept drawing her eye, like she knew him from somewhere.

"And there's a white Bear in town?"

"Julian DuCharme. He's Kermode, so he's not unique." What were they trying to say?

"Don't count on it." Apollonia stood, still moving lazily.

Chloe could tell they were both cats, the scent one she hadn't smelled before. "What are you?"

The two exchanged confused glances. "I'm a boy," Artemis said slowly, like she was five or something.

"I'm a girl," Apollonia added. "Are you sure you're old enough to be mated?"

Chloe rolled her eyes. "What bind of shifter?"

"Bind?" Artemis smirked. "Kinky." He shot Jim a wicked look. "Lucky bastard."

Jim snarled. "Her brain has a problem with its autocorrect function. Now answer her question."

"They're Tiggers." Barney smirked back.

"Tigers. Ti-Gers." Apollonia shook her head sadly. "And they say you're the smart one."

"I'd say we should change our last name to Hobbes, but then my mom would kick my ass." Artemis shivered. "I make it a point not to piss off my momma."

Apollonia nodded, her expression fearful. "She scares me."

"You scare me." Chloe bit her lip, unsure of these strangers.

"Aw, sweetie. Don't be scared." Apollonia put her arm around Chloe's shoulders. "We'll protect you."

"From bagels."

"Donuts."

"Tuna."

"Mm, tuna."

Both brother and sister got faraway looks on their faces.

"Wait." Jim held up his hands, looking confused. She figured that happened a lot around those two. "You said *the* white Fox, like there aren't any others."

"Ding ding ding! We have a winner!" Artemis held his arms dramatically wide.

"And guess how we know that?" Apollonia held her hand to her ear. "C'mon, guess."

"You have phenomenal, cosmic powers?"

Chloe giggled at Jim's droll tone. "Bet me guess. One of you is a white kitty shifter?"

Artemis dropped his arms. "Yup."

"Him." Apollonia hitched her thumb toward her brother.

Well. That explained the sense of familiarity.

"So." He wagged his brows at Chloe. "What *does* the Fox say?"

"I swear if you make that annoying-as-fuck ring-a-ding-ding noise, mate or no mate I'll take you over my knee and spank you," Barney snarled.

She bit her lip, resisting the urge to do just that. Instead, she turned to Artemis. "Show me."

His eyes turned silver and a white streak appeared in his hair. His muscles bunched, taking the man from hunk to Hulk in seconds. Pale stripes appeared on his skin.

"Whoa." She tilted her head. "Does that hurt?"

"Nah." His tone was gravelly, more Tiger than human.

"Chloe?" Jim was staring at Artemis, and he looked both fascinated and horrified. "What is he doing?"

"Have you ever heard of a werewolf being half-man, half-wolf?"

Jim nodded.

"Tigers actually do that." Chloe remained calm. She instinctively knew Artemis would never hurt her. Her Fox was watching, curious and fascinated, the same as Chloe, but there was no urge to hide or fight the Tiger. "They have a third form, the man-beast. There was a time when they were the fiercest warriors of the shifter world."

"We still are." Apollonia walked over to her brother and poked him. "Shift back, show-off."

Artemis complied. "I've shown you mine." He winked. "Now show me yours."

Chloe dampened her scent, aware her eyes had gone silver and her hair now had a white streak just like Artemis's.

"Wow." Artemis stared at her in admiration. "Now *that's* a useful skill."

"I can't scent her at all." Apollonia sniffed the couch. "Not even on the furniture."

"It's like mega-Febreeze." Artemis snapped his fingers. "Oh! Can you do that in my car?"

"It smells like Cheetos and old farts," Apollonia added.

"And whose fault is that?" Artemis shot back.

"Not mine."

"You let your ex borrow my car, heifer." Artemis shuddered. "The guy was a slob."

Apollonia shrugged nonchalantly. "You were out of the country."

He glared at his sister. "Cheeto. Farts."

She glared back. "Betty Lou Hinton in the back of my seventy-six Monte Carlo."

"She was pretty and oh, so pink," Artemis sighed.

"Ew. No one should have to clean up their brother's—"

Barney screamed, startling all of them.

"Um." Heather stood at the front door, staring at Barney like he'd lost his mind. "Can I come in?"

Without a word Barney turned, flung Heather over his shoulder, and left. They could faintly hear Heather cursing him out before the roar of an engine cut her off.

"Who was that?" The gleam in Artemis's eye did not bode well for him if Barney caught him lusting after Heather.

"Barney's late."

Artemis blinked. "Late for what?"

Chloe sighed, frustrated.

"My mate was beaten and suffered a traumatic brain injury. As a result, she doesn't always say the word she means." Jim held her hand tight, letting her know she wasn't alone. "Her cousin, the redhead Barney just carried out of here? That's Heather, Barney's mate."

"Oh?" Artemis's gaze turned from hungry to filled with unholy glee. "Oh," he drawled.

Apollonia cackled. "Lo, the mighty hath fallen."

"Yes, well, he's ready to chew his own paw off if Heather so much as comes close to him, so it might be a while before he hits the ground."

"The bigger they are," Artemis snickered.

"Does that mean Barney's staying in Halle?" Apollonia looked delighted.

Artemis rubbed his hands together. "I'm gonna like this town."

"I think we should move here."

The two shared a look. "House hunting!"

"And these are the two who are going to guard us?" Jim muttered.

Chloe smiled weakly. They were in deep doo-doo.

***

Jim stepped out of the master bathroom to find Chloe staring out the window into the street below. She was dressed in sleep shorts and one of those thin-strapped tank tops he found he loved slipping off of her.

"I'm scared."

Her voice was so soft he barely heard her. "Because of the Senate?"

She nodded once. "Don't want you or Spencer hurt."

He wanted to dismiss her fears, but he couldn't. "I won't lie to you. I can't promise we won't be." He moved cautiously toward her, afraid he would make things worse rather than better. "I can promise we'll do our best to stay safe."

"Not a Hunter."

"No. I'm not." He was just a lone Wolf who barely knew what he was doing. "But we have good friends who are. We've got a Pride full of people who want to help us, and we've got your weird family to protect us."

She almost smiled as she turned toward him. "My family isn't *bat* weird."

Her words weren't coming out slurred, but she was speaking slowly, as if measuring each one on her tongue before doling them out in bits and pieces. "What's really going on?"

She bit her lip. "Is it worth it?"

"What?"

She gestured between the two of them. "This."

"Don't doubt that for a second." He pulled her close, snuggling with her in the darkness. "This is worth everything."

"You're a snap."

He waited, unsure for once if she really meant that or something else.

"But I like that about you."

He kissed the top of her head. "I'm glad." She was still speaking slowly, still obviously worried. "Promise me something?"

"Hmm?" She wiggled, lifting her nose to his neck. She sniffed his skin, relaxing against him bonelessly.

"If you get scared, you tell me. Even if you can't speak, I'll know."

Her arms tightened around him and he took her weight, holding her easily as she sagged. "Don't want to see you hurt."

He thought about that for a few moments. What was the best way to ease her fears? "What would you like to do? Do you want Glory and Ryan to move in with us?"

She poked him in the side hard enough that he flinched. "Serious."

"So am I." He'd do anything to ensure Chloe never again spent a sleepless night. "If that's what it takes to make sure you feel safe, I'll invite them in a heartbeat."

She stood silent, swaying slightly in his arms, a quiet midnight dance as she thought. "Air hole." She shook her head. "Egg roll." She made a fist, her frustration clear, but Jim couldn't do this for her. He knew what she was about to say, but she had to do it herself. "Petrol." She screamed in frustration. "Patrol!"

He nodded. "Your family is doing that already, but if it makes you feel better we can ask Francois and Barney to do it as well."

"Skate this," she sobbed.

"Shh." He rocked her again, stroking her hair. He'd been wondering when it would all become too much, when the pressure of her disorder and the people trying to hurt them would cause her to break down. And even though all he could do for her was hold her, a part of him was glad that she felt comfortable enough around him to allow herself to cry.

It killed him, how hard she broke when she finally did. She sobbed until her breath hitched and her knees gave out. He lifted her up, settling them in the bed, Chloe awkwardly draped across him. Her arms were so tightly wound around his neck he was afraid he'd have bruises, and his T-shirt was thoroughly soaked with her tears.

He lay there, his arms going slowly numb while his mate cried out her pain. When the sobs finally slowed down to hiccupping breaths, he eased her down until they weren't clinging to each other quite so tightly. "Things can only get better, Chloe."

"Pfft."

He chuckled. "It's a figure of speech, sweetheart."

She sat up, her eyes red-rimmed, her nose running and her cheeks blotchy. "One bray at a time?"

"Something like that." He carefully turned them until they were both on their sides. "Chloe?"

"Hmm?" She settled back down against his chest, tucking her knee between his legs.

"I'm glad."

"That I got snot on your T-shirt?"

"No." He blinked. "Wait. What?"

She shuddered through another sob. It seemed she was one of those people who didn't really stop crying when they were done. No wonder she hadn't let herself truly go before. It was the kind of hard crying that left you with a sore throat and eyes even after you slept.

If she'd cried like this in front of her family they would have never let her live alone, no matter what she or her doctors said.

So Jim did the only thing he could think of. He sighed deeply. "It's my favorite T-shirt too."

She wiped ineffectively at his chest.

Jim took hold of her wandering hand. "Stop." He kissed her knuckles. "You can smoosh around the goo on my chest later. Let me get this out, okay?"

She giggled and shuddered at the same time. Her breath caught on a whine and she almost began crying again.

"Hey. Do you need to let go some more?" She shook her head and put her fist to her mouth. "I don't mind, and I'm not going anywhere. No matter how much snot you sniffle on me."

She laughed again. "That's h-horrible!"

"No, what you're doing to my shirt is horrible." He stroked her hair, hoping she understood what it was he was trying to do. It might be the wrong thing to do, but he believed with all his heart that she'd had the emotional storm. Now she needed the sunshine to heal. "It's vintage."

"Just because you ran it through the wash with bleach does not make it vintage."

He hid his smile against the top of her head. Her speech was back to normal. It had worked. "Does so."

She sighed, and this time her breath only hitched a little bit.

They lay there quietly, Chloe occasionally shuddering out another breath as he held her. Right when he thought she'd fallen asleep, he heard her whisper his name. "Yes?"

"What were you going to say?"

He blinked, on the edge of sleep himself. "Oh. Love how strong you are, but love even more that you can let yourself grieve with me."

She'd stiffened when he said the *L* word. "You keen it?"

"Yup."

She relaxed once more. "I shove you too."

He laughed when she groaned. "It's all right, little fox."

"No, it's snot."

He laughed even harder, almost doubling over when she began smacking his chest.

"Bass hole."

"Even if you don't say it right, I get it, Chloe." He kissed her forehead. "It's just a figure of speech, after all."

"Hmph." She laid her head on his chest again. "Words are important."

"They are," he agreed, his laughter subsiding. "But actions are even more so. Trust me, I've learned that the hard way." He stroked her hair, the action soothing both of them. "Besides, I understand what you're saying, and what you're not."

"Yeah?"

The wistful need in her voice was killing him. "Yeah."

"You know I love you, right?"

"I do now," she grunted.

He couldn't help it. He laughed again. "And you love me."

She pinched his side. "Do not."

"Do too."

"Do not."

"Liar, liar, plants for hire," he sniffed.

Chloe giggled. "Don't mess up words. That's my bob."

"You'd better not have a bob." He blinked. "Wait. If by bob, you mean battery-operated boyfriend—" He yelped at one particularly hard pinch. "What?"

"Go to sleep, you dork."

He sighed happily. "We okay?"

"We okay," she echoed.

When George, their puppy, joined them on the bed and tried to wiggle between them, all thoughts of sleep disappeared in a haze of wet noses, wetter tongues, happy whining and lots and lots of kisses.

And most of it happened after they kicked George off the bed.

EPILOGUE

"Hey," Chloe whispered, opening the hospital door as quietly as she could. She glanced around, hoping she wasn't about to wake the newest member of the clan.

"Hey," Tabby replied wearily. "She's awake, it's okay."

Chloe's shoulders sagged in relief. "Cool." Chloe entered the hospital room, Jim right on her heels. "Can I see?"

Alex, sitting by his mate with the sappiest expression on his face, gestured them forward.

A tiny white bundle lay in Tabby's arms. Chloe wanted to hold her new cousin so badly she was shaking with it. "Oh. Please?"

Jim wrapped his arms around Chloe. "Shh, little vixen. Give them a moment to hand her over."

Tabby laughed. "Here, Chloe darlin'. Meet—" she darted a quick glance toward Alex, "—Wren Usagi Bunsun."

Jim choked. "You named your baby 'little bird'?"

"You two are *so* bad," Chloe giggled, snuggling her nose against the baby's forehead and taking in her scent. "Especially since she smells like Wolf."

"What?" Jim sniffed the baby too, causing the baby to wrinkle her nose and turn her head. "Man, she does!"

Alex grinned. "What did you expect from a Bear named Bunny and a Wolf named Tabby?"

Tabby blushed. "I like the name Wren. It's pretty."

Chloe giggled harder. "And Usagi means bunny. You named your daughter after Sailor Moon."

"And yourself," Jim chuckled.

"You knew he was going to slip some *Sailor Moon* in there somewhere." Tabby smiled when Chloe stroked the baby's whisper-fine hair.

Chloe glanced at her cousin. "What would you have named a boy?"

Alex grinned. "Lobo."

"No." Chloe shook her head. "You are not naming my baby cousin Lobo, you nut."

"Fenris?"

"No."

Alex pouted. "Suppose Canis is out then?"

"Ugh." Chloe rolled her eyes. "Can we muzzle him?"

Tabby just shook her head. "Can't. Someone's gotta help me feed the baby bird."

"Damn."

"Fine." Alex crossed his arms over his chest. "How about Connor?"

He looked far too smug for this to be anything but some sort of trick. "Okay, Bunny. I'll bite. What's wrong with Connor?"

Alex shrugged. "I don't know. You tell me?"

Chloe looked at Tabby, who shrugged. "I have no idea what he's up to this time, but I like Connor."

"So if we have a boy, Connor Shingo Bunsun it is!"

"Shingo?" Chloe groaned.

"Yeah, Usagi's brother is named Shingo." Alex sighed happily. "I'm so glad you guys agreed."

"Damn it, Alex," Tabby groaned. "Couldn't you use, I dunno, Darien? That's Tuxedo Mask, right?"

Alex stared at her, horrified. "That's just *wrong*. Sailor Moon and Tuxedo Mask get *married* and have *kids*. I don't want three-headed grandbabies, thank you."

Tabby sagged against her pillow as Chloe laughed. "Fine. You get Shingo, I get Connor."

"Done." Alex held out his hands. "Now give me my baby girl back."

"Need to tell her the evils of men in tuxedos?" Jim helped Chloe hand the baby over.

"Damn straight." Alex's whole face brightened as he stared lovingly down at his daughter. "No tuxedo-wearing, rose-wielding asshole is gonna get by Daddy. No he's not, baby girl. You and me forever, right?"

"Ahem." Tabby cleared her throat.

"What?" Alex barely looked up from the baby in his arms. He gasped. "Oh, you farted! That's so *cute!*"

"And on that note…" Jim grabbed hold of her arm and started edging toward the door.

"Why is your butt so warm?" Alex frowned. "Is something wrong?"

Chloe grabbed hold of her mate and darted into the hallway. "Three…two…one…"

"Holy shit! What the hell is that?"

Jim collapsed against the wall, dragging Chloe down with him. "Think he meant that literally?"

Chloe nodded, laughing too hard to answer.

With their shifter hearing they could still hear Alex's disgust. "Tabby, I think Wren's ass is possessed."

"Why's that, sugar?" Tabby sounded calm, but Chloe could hear rustling, like Tabby was playing with her sheets…or changing a newborn's diaper.

"Should it look like something from *The Exorcist* is living in there?"

"Alex, we were told about this." Tabby's tone was patient. "The black stuff, the…what did she call it? The poo cork? Is out now, and we're going to see the poop rainbow for a while."

"I'll never look at Skittles the same way again," Alex groaned.

Jim tugged on her hand and Chloe followed, silently laughing. "Sk-skittles."

He bit his lip, holding it in until they were in the elevator. Then he let it out again, collapsing against the elevator wall. "Oh, jeez, that was bad. Poo cork?"

They were holding each other up when the elevator finally hit the first floor. There stood Eric Bunsun, Alex's brother, a big-ass stuffed bear in his hands. "What's gotten into you two?"

"Not a poo cork, that's for sure," Chloe gasped.

"Or rainbow candy," Jim added.

"Okay," Eric drawled. He pushed his glasses up his nose. "Can I go see my niece now?"

"Sure thing." Chloe and Jim stepped off the elevator and headed for the hospital door.

"You still want one?"

"A Skittle?" Man, her mate must have gotten oxygen deprived if he thought she wanted rainbow candy after that.

"A baby."

"Eventually. I think we need to get carried first, though." She didn't dare look at him. He hadn't once mentioned the M-word, and she'd been living with him for a couple of weeks now.

"How does September sound?" He put his arm around her shoulders.

She began to tremble. Did he mean it?

"Yup, I mean it." He stopped her and turned her around. "With everything crazy that's going on, I'd like to keep it small. It's safer that way."

"Big party later?"

He nodded, the tension she hadn't noticed before falling away from him. "Sounds good to me. How about you?"

"Yes."

His eyes turned golden brown. "You mean it?"

She nodded.

"Thank fuck." He picked her up and twirled her around. Then he plunked her down, his eyes wide and worried. "Rings?"

"Rings?"

"Can we wear them? You know, when we…" He lifted his lip. "Fur out?"

"Nope. But we can hare them when we aren't."

"Oh. Good."

She poked his lip. "You can put that down now, big bad."

He chuckled and put his arm around her. "I love you, you know?"

"I blow, Jim." She patted his hand. "I blow."

He blinked, staring at her in confusion, but no way was she telling him whether or not she'd misspoken intentionally.

She blinked up at him, trying to appear as innocent as her newborn cousin. "Can we go get some Red Butt now?"

"Naughty little vixen." He nipped her earlobe. "I like the way you think."

"Wait."

He took off running toward the car.

"Damn it, I didn't mean that one!"

Chloe chased after her Wolf, but as she always would in the future, this time she caught him.

Look for these titles by Dana Marie Bell

The Gray Court
Dare to Believe
Noble Blood
Artistic Vision
The Hob
Siren's Song
Never More

Halle Pumas
The Wallflower
Sweet Dreams
Cat of a Different Color
Steel Beauty
Only In My Dreams

Halle Shifters
Bear Necessities
Cynful
Bear Naked
Figure of Speech
Indirect Lines

Heart's Desire
Shadow of the Wolf
Hecate's Own
The Wizard King
Warlock Unbound

*Maggie's Grove
Blood of the Maple
Throne of Oak
Of Shadows and Ash
Song of Midnight Embers

The Nephilim
*All for You
*The Fire Within
Speak Thy Name

Poconos Pack
Finding Forgiveness
Mr. Red Riding Hoode
Sorry, Charlie

True Destiny
Very Much Alive
Eye of the Beholder
Howl for Me
Morgan's Fate
Not Broken

*Published by Carina Press

Dana Marie Bell Books

www.danamariebell.com

Printed in Great
Britain
by Amazon

32224825R00168